HAIR OF THE SERPENTINE

TRILOGY

HAIR OF THE SERPENTINE

TRILOGY

JAMES MATTHEW

authorHOUSE®

AuthorHouse™
1663 Liberty Drive
Bloomington, IN 47403
www.authorhouse.com
Phone: 1 (800) 839-8640

Published by AuthorHouse   06/14/2018

ISBN: 978-1-4817-5464-4 (sc)
ISBN: 978-1-4817-5463-7 (hc)
ISBN: 978-1-4817-5462-0 (e)

Library of Congress Control Number: 2013909065

Print information available on the last page.

Any people depicted in stock imagery provided by Thinkstock are models, and such images are being used for illustrative purposes only.
Certain stock imagery © Thinkstock.

This book is printed on acid-free paper.

This is a work of fiction. Names, characters, businesses, places, events and incidents are either the products of the author's imagination or used in a fictitious manner. Any resemblance to actual persons, living or dead, or actual events is purely coincidental.

Front cover and back cover art by Yekaterina Komarovskaya.

Because of the dynamic nature of the Internet, any web addresses or links contained in this book may have changed since publication and may no longer be valid. The views expressed in this work are solely those of the author and do not necessarily reflect the views of the publisher, and the publisher hereby disclaims any responsibility for them.

DEDICATIONS

This book is dedicated to two different groups.

First and foremost, it is dedicated to my beautiful wife and three children, of whom the youngest is working on a much harder mystery than Jack and Sophie have ever tried to solve: the mystery of autism.

Secondly, this book is dedicated to all the brave spirits I met while pursuing my own dreams in the Fine Arts. From the ballet dancers, to the violin players, to the piano players, to the vocalists, to the clarinet players, to the trumpet players, to the composers, to the theater actors, and to the artists who make their art visually: on a canvass or on a screen. These people amazed me with their bravery, individuality, spirit, tenacity, and creativity. They followed their hearts, pawning possessions for extra cash, and starving themselves on Ramen Noodles, so that they could live cheaply in order to spend more time on their art instead of joining an assembly-line like career just to be "safe". I made it further than some did, and some made it further than I did. But I will never forget the people I met while playing fine music in the 1990s, and they will always have my utmost admiration.

PART I
Hair of the Serpentine

I

Jazz at Turtle's Bar

    In my earlier years, once I reached the age of twenty, I thought I knew just about everything. I thought that vulgar language exuded both a toughness and a sense of the profound. I now know that neither conclusion is accurate. I was not alone in my inaccurate assumptions. I was surrounded by others who both enabled me and were enabled by me. But do not assume I am looking down at either myself or my companions. I cherish that old self and the bohemian 1990's neo-hippies with whom I associated. Although we were wrong about many things, we were right about some of the most important things: loving life, expressing ourselves, and creating both an artistic and humanistic environment in the way we interacted with each other. I made many mistakes back then, and something inside me, inside many of us at that time, gave us that deep inner intuition down in the crypts of our souls to recognize that this decade would be the last decade in which young people would be allowed even the privacy and freedom to ever make such mistakes again. For the generation that came of age just a decade later, the horrors of 9/11, terrorism, and war led to street cameras, home cameras, body cameras, email tracking, phone tapping, and cell phones designed with homing devices to track a young person wherever he or she may go. It seems that today, young people are given such a short leash that they are reeled in at even the first thought or hint of an inappropriate idea. The leash for my companions and me sometimes seemed to stretch to lengths immeasurable, and as a result, we lived life to the fullest back in the 1990's. We knew something was going to change in the next millennium – and change it did.

But before it changed, I walked the streets of my then city carelessly and curiously. I listened to music and played music in bars, watched pretty girls and winked at them on the streets, and lived life like a 20th century Henry David Thoreau – minus the cabin on the lake part. On this particular evening, I had chosen to visit one of my favorite jazz bars. And as I begin my story back in time, I will also change my voice to my voice back then – the voice of a young, arrogant, know-it-all artistic musician who cursed with the worst of them and allowed his mind to wander and dwell on any bad thoughts that the devil made available to him.

*   *   *

When I walked into the bar, there were a few people sitting at the other end: a black girl, a white guy with the old long hair and goatee, and a black guy with one of those jazz-wanna-be berets.

The girl was hot. When it comes to attractive women, I bear absolutely no prejudices. I just don't quite care for the whole scene of trying to get somewhere with a woman who already has more than one desperate dipshit glued to her like wallpaper.

I walked over to the bar and there was Steve. Good ole' Steve. Steve kept his head well shaven and had one of the longest goatees you could find. He would often segment this work of art from top to bottom with a colorful array of rubber bands, a popular fashion trend for the still relatively new alternative wave peaking in that late spring and early summer of 1995.

"Give me a Düsseldorfer," I told him. I liked supporting the local beers and this brew tasted smooth on top of it.

The Jazz was soft on this particular night. There was a long-haired, bearded guy playing tenor saxophone and Charles was accompanying him on the piano. Charles is phenomenal. He is also in his late 40s or 50s and is too old to break through in the "cutting edge" of popular jazz recording artists. He doesn't spend 30 hours a week in the gym, and he doesn't romance the female record executives for professional gain.

The saxophone player struck my interest. He was more of your true lost soul than most of the types that tried to look odd or individual. This man did not have to try – he was a natural. You could tell he was poor as sin, too. He probably didn't have a home; maybe he hung at other musicians places or slept on the streets. You could get away with that in Indianapolis at the time. Crime there, especially back then, was more infrequent than in your bigger cities like New York, Baltimore, or Chicago. You didn't have to worry about being mugged constantly. I didn't think the city had much personality when I first moved there, but it grew on me.

I liked the way this guy played. It was earnest – like Miles. Technically he was a little rough around the edges from time to time, but I liked that. What he played seemed very spontaneous and from the heart. Music to me has slowly become more and more comprised of the slick and the organized types than of the spontaneous, inwardly searching and odd-ball losers. This fact disappointed me, but I had now accepted it and understood it, having tried to break into the professional music scene myself. The planners, organizers, and rehearsers seemed to be the ones who cut through – the anal organizers…I couldn't bear it. To me, it took the magic away, planning out your solos note for note, doing the same phrasing every time. You only have to get noticed once, and this guru that gets you your gig doesn't have the time (and knows that 99% of the population doesn't either) to listen long enough to hear whether a musician is monotonous or not, whether the phrasing is different the second, third, and fourth time the verse is played. People don't care about that shit anymore. They want to hear something generic. Play a samba and then play a fast 12/4 with a walking bass line and then all of the sudden the group is "diverse". *Listen to that, man! This song has a totally*

5

different feel to it! I would rather hear a guy that stuck with the same sound and rhythmic style, but at least had taken the time to develop his own style as an individual musician and not just reproduce a bunch of highly different sounding exotic noises. Oh well, *c'est la vie.*

Another girl had walked into the bar. She was short, thin and cute with short black hair. I had seen her here before and had admired her then as well.

She took out a cigarette and lit it. She looked over toward me and cracked a quick, polite smile acknowledging that yes, she knew I liked to hang out here too, but I was not on close enough terms with her to receive a hello. I decided to try and change that.

"You wouldn't have an extra cigarette on you would you?"

She looked at me and began to open her mouth, then paused for a second to give me a quick look over and said, "Sure". I walked over to her bar stool and she fixed me up with a cig and a light.

"Thanks," I said and sat down next to her. "What kind of cigarettes are these?"

"They're from Turkey. My boyfriend got them for me."

I quickly began to close out any romantic expectations with this girl.

"Well, I should say ex-boyfriend."

Maybe not.

"Wow," I said, "what was he doing in Turkey?"

"He is an international tobacco dealer. He'll buy large shipments of tobacco products from foreign countries and then sell them somewhere else for a much higher price."

"Hmm," I said, "sounds like a shrewd business man."

"What do you do?" she asked.

"I work in a claims office for an insurance company."

"I've seen you play from time to time around here. It's not quite paying the bills, I guess."

"Yeah," I said, "either that, or I spend too much money to be able to support myself through true musical endeavors."

"Do you mean that you spend too much money, or that the music that makes money isn't true music?" she inquired.

"Well, you are very insightful," I responded.

"Not really." She said, "I can just tell you're one of those people that think the world should be their way."

"Well," I said, "that's probably true, but it doesn't mean that my way wouldn't be better." I responded.

There was a pause.

"I'm Jack, by the way."

"Hi Jack, I'm Sandy."

"Do I really wear my unsatisfied-ness so obviously?" I asked.

"Yeah, you do," she said, "but I usually do too. It's probably why we are attracted to each other."

I paused again for a longer time after that one. I knew she might be testing me to see how I would respond. "I think we're attracted to each other because of the way we look," I said.

"No, that definitely isn't it," she stated.

I chuckled, "My ego is definitely on some kind of roller coaster ride here."

"Your ego?" she replied almost offended.

"We just met each other." I responded, "Should I attach my deepest intimate feelings and soul to this little social interaction we are having?"

I was sensing she was drifting away. "I know. I analyze situations too much. It ruins most of my social interactions.

"Conversations."

"Yeah, whatever."

"Do you usually associate your conversations with women as ego-motivated?"

"Well…"

"Well, that isn't a very good line to use with women."

"Well neither is telling me that I'm bad looking."

"You're not, you're good-looking, but that isn't why I was attracted to you."

"Well, I disagree." We looked at each other for a while and then turned to our drinks.

"So why has this tobacco guy become your ex-boyfriend?"

"He's on cocaine." I looked back towards her, "You are a very candid person. You know that?"

"Yeah," she replied, "I don't like to waste time."

"Waste time?" I asked.

"with small talk."

"Oh," I said. I paused very briefly. "Don't you think this is wonderful weather we're having?"

"Why am I talking with you?" she exhaled frustratingly to herself.

"Maybe because there isn't anybody else to talk to," I replied.

Again we looked at each other. "So how old are you?" I asked.

"27."

"I'm 24."

"I didn't ask."

"I know. I like volunteering information." That made her smile. "How long have you lived in Indianapolis?"

"About six years."

"You like it?"

"Yeah, it's OK."

"I like it. It has some of the culture and entertainment of a big city without as much of the slums and the crime."

She looked at me funny. "Cultural events maybe," she retorted, "but I don't know about actual culture. The city is at least 80% white, I think."

"I bet it's over 90%."

"Whatever, something like that."

"Well, artistic culture is what I was saying."

"Yeah, I can agree with you there," she replied, "but as far as the crime – Indianapolis doesn't report a lot of its crime to the press or the census."

"Oh, really?" I was genuinely surprised. There was some background music playing on the juke box. It was *Jeepers Creepers, Where'd You Get Those Peepers?* It had that low-quality fidelity to it that just made the mood for a place like this. Yeah, this was definitely my kind of place. "So are we still attracted to each other?" I asked.

"We may be getting into the non-exciting, friendly, familiar zone now," she said.

"Uh oh, I better start being much cooler."

"Your humor is strange," she looked at me puzzled.

"It may go with my tendency to overthink about things and wish everything could be my way."

"There you go again."

"No, I'm being serious."

II

Enter the Serpentine

Just then Sophie walked in with a couple that spoke with an accent. It sounded German. The man and woman were both tall and thin. I hadn't seen Sophie in almost two years. Before my last girlfriend, I had never thought I would ever desire someone like the way I desired Sophie.

She had long wavy, sometimes curly red hair. When the weather was humid, it would frizz. She was tall, close to six feet. I had remembered that she was the first woman I didn't have to bend down for when I kissed her – in those few moments when she did let me kiss her. She was gorgeous – at least to me she was. Her personality was very out-going which balanced out my passive intellectual side. I wished then that I had been able to love to her. I usually wished that when I saw her. She either hadn't noticed me or did notice me and decided not to say anything yet. I decided to stay with my current buddy and then pretend later to first notice her if the opportunity arose.

"Do you know those people?"

"I might know one of them, if it is who I think it is. She looks a little different than she used to."

"Why don't you go and say hi?"

"Nah, not yet. Maybe I will later. Besides, don't you want to enjoy my company as long as you can?" I smirked.

"Either your ego is way too elevated or your self-esteem is sub-zero or you like psychologically playing with people way too much in an attempt to feel them out."

"Maybe I should go say hi to her. This really is nothing new for me. I often don't hit it off well with women even when they happen to find me attractive or good-looking."

"Maybe you're just having a bad day," Sandy said.

"Well, I liked talking to you anyway."

"It was OK."

"Can I have your phone number?"

"Farley!" Sophie exclaimed and ran up to me with her usual caution-to-the-wind, long embrace.

"Sophie, how are you?" I concentrated to make sure I didn't fall over my bar stool.

"My God, I haven't seen you in soooo long. You look so good. God, I love what you've done with your hair!"

"Yeah, I decided to clean up that awful mess. Didn't you go away to Austria or something?"

"Oh, Farley, I had the most awesome time in Germany last year. I was so disappointed when I had to come back to shitty Indiana."

"Hey, at least you get to see me," I said.

"Thank God, Farley! Oh God, let me hug you again!"

There she went again. She hadn't changed a bit. She was stroking my little lost ego like it was a puppy that needed to be with its mother and finally found an owner to nurture it.

"Oh," I said awkwardly, "this is Sandy. Sandy, this is my old friend Sophie."

"Pleased to meet you," Sandy said cordially.

"Oh, hi," Sophie blurted, "God, I should leave you guys alone before I ruin your evening."

"Nice exit," I said, "Are you staying anywhere or living someplace that is reachable?"

"Right now I'm with some friends, Farley, and I really don't want to tie up their phone lines. You know how it is. But don't worry. I'll be in town for at least a few months. I'm sure I'll see you."

"Well why I don't leave you my number in case you get a crazy urge the next time you drive by a pay phone or something."

"Sure Farley."

I wrote down my number on a cocktail napkin just to make the moment even more nostalgic and cheesy for the both of us. "I hope you don't mind my message paper."

"Oh, Farley, it couldn't be more perfect. I'll probably see you soon." She embraced me very physically one more time, planted a quick kiss on my cheek, and then placed her mouth over to my ear opposite Sandy while reaching into my back pocket on the same side. I felt a hot exhale and the almost silent whispering of what sounded like the phrase "I want you, Farley." Perhaps I was hoping that's what it was, having been whispered so soft. "Take care," I said in what I hope was still a composed manner as she turned around and headed back toward her table. I wondered how long it would be until I could rid myself of this current conversation with Sandy and look at whatever the hell Sophie had put in my back pocket. Then my realistic side kicked in, and I remembered what a tease Sophie was and realized I probably had something better going here at the bar. It wasn't much, but at least it was honest and real – with Sophie the idea of being honest and real was non-applicable. She was always however she needed to be, conforming herself to every situation to fit in just perfectly and play it smoothly in order for her to get exactly what she wanted out of it whether it was affection, friendship, some attention, or merely an entertaining distraction for the moment. I remembered nights of going out drinking, dancing all night, and at the end of the night sharing long passionate kisses. And then there were the days following our excursions when she totally centered her attention on someone else or something else like her precious piano and I was again barely an acquaintance of hers. I guess you can see now why I wanted her so badly.

"Well Farley," Sandy began somewhat teasingly, "-how did you get that name by the way?" "It's short for my last name, McFarland. Calling me by my first name is just too personal for some people. Maybe you should start calling me Farley too."

"Can I call you Jack instead?" she smiled.

"I would prefer that." I smiled back.

Yes, I was doing the right thing.

III

Steve's Advice

I woke up at about six thirty or seven-ish the next morning. My old warning alarm of getting out before the person with me woke up was right on time. I searched and groped around Sandy's dark bedroom for my clothes and personal belongings. Sandy looked quite appealing while sleeping; the sunlight was shining through the curtains on her face. She had a cute, petite-looking face that resembled a pixie when she smiled. Her brunette features framed her face well, with dark eyebrows just the right size and long black eyelashes. Her shorter hair worked well with those small features of hers. Other girls couldn't get away with the short hair look that she had. She also had a surprising athleticism about her that I had not expected. And her demeanor, though usually reserved, had a hidden spice to it – it made me wonder if she might have some Hispanic or Irish blood in her. She was a uniquely appealing woman, and I always liked a girl who could bring out a different kind of beauty from the usual standard super-model issue mold. If I let myself feel to a certain extent, I could even say should looked beautiful, but that would be too personal of a statement.

I quietly crept outside. I left a little note in her kitchen to look for me again at Turtle's. I felt at the very least that this woman could become a good drinking partner.

I was somewhat familiar with the neighborhood I was in. It was quite close to downtown. I figured I might be able to catch a cab or the bus back to my street, but I might as well hang out somewhere for a while first. On Saturday mornings I often would forego the shower, shave, and activities of daily living thing.

I made it to a little coffee shop soon enough. It had a nice feel to it – a lot like the shops in the north central side of town that was quite popular with the college students and earthy types. Once inside, I ordered some coffee and eggs and sucked on my java while waiting for my chicken embryos to finish. The stool I was sitting on felt uncomfortable. It was lumpy or something – and then I realized that it was that thing that Sophie had slipped so sensually in my back pocket.

I took out a folded beige sheet of paper which had been torn off of a piano recital program, probably played by her high and mighty, tight-assed former piano instructor from college who I liked about as much as I liked wedgies with a rash. She had written something quite messily, probably in a rushed manner, but it was still legible. It said the following:

**Meet me tomorrow behind Stray Cat's
-it's important Farley**

Well this was quite odd. Not the invitation part, but the "it's important" part. It seemed like Miss Sophie Mitchell had some sort of serious matter at hand. This did intrigue me. Maybe she needed money –nah- she would ask one of her parents first or some guy who actually had money. It was probably one of those things that were an important matter to her and the rest of the world couldn't care less. I had to admire the way she gave the message to me, though. She certainly made it look to Sandy like she didn't have much of an interest in staying in touch with me. Ha!! This weekend I was the king of female rendezvous!

My eggs came and I slurped them down with my coffee. I was only a few blocks from the library, so I stopped by to listen to some Mingus and Miles for an hour or two before catching a bus home.

Steve had just gotten out of the shower, his goatee dripping like a water fountain. I admired his bulky physique. He had those big, iron-worker muscles. I was thinner and had to settle for more of the lean, chiseled look, and in the past few weeks my chisel work had slightly faded from lack of maintenance.

"How'd you make it with that little brunette number from last night?" he inquired. "Score!" I exclaimed and gave him a very adolescent high-five. "And it looks like I might have another date tonight as Sophie's choice." I was grinning from ear to ear.

"Sophie Mitchell?"

"Yup, she is back in town."

"But you're not going to get anything out of that scene."

"Maybe not, but she left me an interesting message which is how she invited me out by the way, and the end of it said that it was important."

"Hmm, let me see this." Steve took the message from my hand and looked at it as he headed to our little bathroom and took out a razor. "She's jerking your chain like she always has. She just wrote that to make sure that you'd show up."

"You really know how to take the wind out of a guy's sails. You know that? And Steve, don't even tell me that you are going to shave off a year's worth of beautiful facial hair."

"I'm sick of it and so is Jessica. Just yesterday when she dropped me off here, I got it stuck in the car door and nearly got pulled out onto College Avenue chin first – luckily she heard me yelling." "This is sad, man. It's like the end of an era. Oh well.

17

Anyway, I don't care what Sophie's motivation is. It'll be fun just to hang out."

"Just don't get all serious about her like you did that one time," Steve said above the sound of his electric razor.

"Hey, I know what she's like now, and I realize that you have to take everything she says and does with a grain of salt."

"Yeah, and you're really good at that, Jack. Give me a break. You're the original Mr. Obsessive Compulsive."

"Shut up and let me screw up my life if that's what I want to do. It might just be worth it." "I give up on you Jack, oh, I mean Farley." Steve smiled at me while using his girl voice on "Farley".

"Yeah, bite me!" I exclaimed with my usual slight touch of endearment. "So did you make your way into any ladies', eh hem, hearts last night Mr. Cool Bartender?"

"Yeah, Jessica would love that," he said keeping the sarcasm alive.

"Jessica Schmessica, you're a young, virile man – you need to be free!!"

"Hey buddy, I get to be a lot more virile with Jessica than you get to be with your haphazard, occasional flings with who knows what you're sleeping with."

"I don't always have sex with those girls," I retorted.

"There's an understatement! And it also supports my case," Steve had now finished his butcher job and was cleaning up the sink. He had a little ole' baby face just like mine.

"You look so cuuuuuute, Steve," I said in my baby talk voice as he headed to the closet to pick out some clothes.

"You can just cut that out right now, Farles."

"Are you and Jessica doing something today?"

"Yeah, we're going to the park this afternoon I think and then maybe to a movie or something. Whatever, nothing's really set in stone, just some kind of romantic day."

"The park by the library? That's a nice spot."

"Yeah, that's what I was thinking too."

"I thought you had to work tonight."

"I got the night off."

"Huh, so you're going out with Jessica today."

"I think there's an echo in here."

"Well, what am I supposed to do?" I asked half seriously.

"Here's an idea: You could actually follow up with that brunette if your inner child could handle it."

"Naw, I didn't get her number. Besides, I left her a note that I would see her again sometime at Turtle's. Maybe I'll see her tonight – oh no. I forgot, I have to meet Sophie."

"Well Farley, you'll just have to figure out your screwed up babe situation and your screwed up relationship philosophy by yourself. I have to go meet Jessica," he said jangling his keys.

"I thought you weren't going till this afternoon?" I exclaimed.

"Check your watch. It's already twelve thirty."

So it was. "All right. Go on and be Mr. Woman Pleaser. I will keep my manhood and my dignity and stay here."

"What would we men do without you, Jack?"

"Most of yahs don't qualify as men, but the ones who do know that I am their champion!"

Before Steve opened the door to leave, he turned around to look at me. I remember every word he said. It wasn't the words themselves that were remarkable, but more the earnest way he said them to me. "Seriously man, don't forget how much Sophie has messed you up in the past. I thought you were going to drink yourself to death the last time you got hung up on her. I don't want to lose my best bud – and especially not over her." Then he became less serious and was his cool detached self again, "Later butt-head," he said.

"Later Steve."

IV

Kissing the Snake

I scarfed down some Chef Boy-R-D out of the cupboard and decided to take a shower. I wasn't much for making fancy meals unless I was trying to impress somebody. Even then I didn't know how to make anything that great outside of a few lasagna and linguini dishes. The weather was getting warmer to that point where showers are needed more often than once a day – at least for an active young male such as myself. It was late May and up to this point I was still wearing this light brown blazer, very stylish I might add, to help ward off some of the 50 and 60 degree weather we had been having. After this afternoon it looked as if I might not need to wear it again for a while. I threw off my blazer, shirt, and trousers as I usually did in my cluttered surroundings that I called a bedroom and put my dirty socks and underwear in my hamper.

I performed my Baloo the bear back scratch against the side of the doorway. One is not usually allowed to do such things in public. After a refreshing shower (I had not had one since yesterday morning), I put on my favorite pair of boxers, combed my hair, put on some antiperspirant, and fell down on top of my bed for what became a long nap. When I woke up, it was already eight o'clock at night. I was trying to think of what time I should head over to Stray Cat's. I decided the encounter wouldn't be worth it unless it happened around midnight. Now that would be cool!

I noticed there were a couple of messages on the answering machine. The first one was Jessica wanting to know if Steve had left yet. I must have eaten and taken that shower pretty quickly if she had called after I went to sleep. She probably had called when I was in the shower because it was only about a fifteen minute drive from our place to hers. Either that, or Steve took a long pit stop somewhere along the way and was late which didn't seem like Steve but was still possible. Whatever, she would have left a few more messages if he had not arrived at some point. I checked the other two messages. The second call was from my father. I wasn't even close to being ready to talk to him during that time. Two people that I have always been unfairly hard on are my parents. They don't deserve to be treated like that, and my father didn't deserve to be ignored then, but that is what I did. The third call was Sophie. "Hi Jack, this is Sophie." I had to stop and rewind the tape. The first shock was that she called. The second shock was that she had called me so soon after seeing me, and the grand pooh-bah shock that made King Kong's coconuts shake like giant maracas was that she called me Jack. I played it back, "Hi Jack, this is Sophie. Meet me tonight at ten thirty and if you can't make it then try to get there sometime afterwards and if I'm not there, look inside the sewer gratings. Thanks Jack, I appreciate this." "What the hell is going on Sophie?" I said out loud to myself. I slipped on one of Sophie's favorite shirts from what I remembered and luckily it was also a short sleeved shirt which would help ward off the possible heat wave that was supposed to be over-taking the city tonight. The kind of heat wave that this evening would produce ended up being one that I had not expected. I stopped and had a beer over at O'Malley's at about ten o'clock before heading for the Stray Cat area. I made a little eye contact with a little Latin number. I was especially partial to that look since the breaking up with an ex live-in. She was your original girl from Ipanema. My mind wandered as it did too often back then: a Latin looking girl with long, curly red hair and long legs – that would be the perfect looking girl…this girl of course would be a combination of Sophie and the ex, what it would probably have taken to bring me to marriage back then since no one woman had gotten me to officially propose yet...

I arrived at the meeting place at about ten twenty eight. I knew she wouldn't be there yet, but that was OK because I wanted to prepare myself to be my utmost coolest which would take a beer or two. Just then, Sophie turned the corner at the opposite side of the building where she must have been waiting for me. She was walking briskly, even for her. "Thank God you came Farley; I was worried you might get distracted or something."

"Everyone knows that you are the world's ultimate distraction, Sophie." Sophie took my hand and started leading me down the alley where it was dark. "What's going on, Sophie?" I tried to ask. "Shhh," she turned around and gave me a soft kiss on the lips while stroking my cheek with her free hand, "You'll find out soon enough." We went around another corner and she backed me up against one of the buildings. "You're going to have to trust me on this, Farley," she said and pulled out a scarf. She then put it behind my head and proceeded to blindfold me.

"Sophie..." I began to object before she grabbed my head and planted on me one of most passionate kisses I had ever experienced, especially being initiated by a woman. Needless to say, it worked as a wonderful silencer. "OK, you win." I said while catching my breath. She finished the blindfold job, kissed me once again like the way you would kiss your lover, and then started walking, leading me again by the hand. We entered what I thought was a taxi and Sophie whispered some instructions to the driver. From my sense of direction, it seemed that we were headed north or south. We were on a large road and I could not think of any streets in that immediate area large enough that could be heading east or west, so I guessed that we were on Meridian Street. I was hoping we were headed north because the south side can get a little seedy. However, most of the more risqué night clubs were on the south side and I knew that Sophie had a fetish for taking guys to places like that. The environments there aided Sophie in her seduction techniques or teasing session, whichever the case may be. But tonight it seemed like Sophie was acting much differently. It was almost as if she was being honest and sincere – something that I had never seen before.

"What were you talking about on my answering machine when you told me to check the sewer gratings?" I whispered to her.

"It's not important now. I would have most likely left you a message about where to meet me." "Are you in a rush or something?"

"I don't want you to be worrying Farley. You know me. I like to make things exciting and interesting."

"Yeah, you always were big on flash, but you're acting funny Soph, even for you."

"Maybe having been in Germany for a year made me realize how much I missed previous men in my life, especially a certain incredible guy that I overlooked in college."

"This is all too much," I responded.

"Don't worry Jack. I will put your mind at ease."

My magic carpet ride in the Indianapolis cab took a few more turns and came to a stop. We were in someone's neighborhood, possibly close to my own from the sound of the dogs barking. We walked up a few steps and then Sophie put her hands in my pocket and groped around for my keys. "Whoops," she giggled, "that's not your keys."

I pulled off my blindfold and pushed her hand back, "We went through all this mystery bullshit just to come back to my house?!" I was a little irritated.

"Not just to come back to your house," she purred as she opened the door and pulled me inside. She quickly slammed the door shut and pinned me up against the wall with her hips and proceeded to unbutton my pants.

"Sophie, my roommate..."

"He's not here Jack. The door was locked."

"Jesus," I gasped.

"He's not here either," Sophie smiled with intensely glaring eyes, "but heaven will be soon." She again pressed her beautiful red lips against mine. I was completely overwhelmed and frightened. But the way Sophie smelled, the way her lips felt against mine – it was too much to resist. I had never experienced a girl being this forward before, and even though something was telling me deep inside that there was something wrong about it, I just couldn't say no to her. I never could say no to her before then, and there was no reason why this situation would be any different. Her ability to completely entrance me took over. All I could think about was her beautiful face, her hair, her eyes, her perfume, and her amazing body. As much as I was originally offended by her sexually harassing behavior toward me, because it was her, I became putty in her hands.

Not too long from then, in the darkness of my room with just a dull beam of moonlight sneaking in between my bedroom window curtains, I experienced a vision. I didn't know if it was real or not. There was Sophie sitting upright above me while I was lying down. Somehow her hair was glowing, and with this glow, her emerald green eyes seemed to glow also. She flipped her thick mane of hair backwards from her face and the full, ruby-red tendrils cascaded down the soft skin of her neck and shoulders. She looked both beautiful and menacing. To say she looked like a lion would be too ordinary, too of this world. She looked more like the mythical chimera, part lion and part serpent. The bulbs at the end of the tendrils of her hair turned towards me to reveal dozens of tiny snakes hissing at me with tiny forked tongues.

I discovered, months later, that earlier while I had been blindfolded and kissed, Sophie had dropped acid into my mouth.

V

A Threatening Message

I woke up the next morning at my usual six thirty to seven o'clock time but on this day – my sleeping partner had already awakened. I noticed that most of my clothes, aside from a few small odds and ends like ties and handkerchiefs, had been organized and put into my closet. I heard the clanging of dishes and silverware in the kitchen then a "good morning Farley" from her calm, smooth, controlled voice. She came into the room with a tray and breakfast on top of it.

"Holy cow, Sophie," I gave away my Chicago area origins, " first there was last night, and now this morning you tidy up my room and serve me breakfast. If you're looking for a job as a maid honey, then you are hired for sure!"

She smiled but there seemed to be some sort of hesitance or impatience behind it.

"Eat up, Jack." She fed me a spoonful of warm oatmeal.

"Mmmmm, it doesn't get any better than this. So you say that you overlooked me while you were dating around in college, huh?"

"I suppose I did – Farley, where is that jacket that you were wearing at Turtle's the other night? I just love that jacket, and I'm dying to try it on."

"Nice change of subject, love." I snickered.

"Do you know where it is?"

"You mean you didn't find it while you did all this tidying up?"

"No Jack, I didn't."

"Uh oh, you're calling me Jack again. You're getting serious on me aren't you?"

"Jack you need to understand something. I need that jacket. If you are hiding something, I will be willing to pay you good money if that is what you want. I figured last night would have been enough, though."

Even for cool detached me, that last comment really hurt. I tried not to think about it and focused back on the business at hand, but my voice may have stammered a little bit. "Wait a second, what exactly is so important about my jacket? And don't feed me any crap about how you like it and think it's really cool and want to try it on."

"Farley, I don't want you to get mixed up in any of this. Please just tell me what you did with the jacket. Did you take it to the cleaners or something? Did you lend it to somebody?"

"No, when I got home late yesterday morning (remembering Sandy, I briefly stopped and looked at her somewhat embarrassingly), I took care of a few things and then I threw it on the floor."

"What about your roommate? Did he borrow it from you?"

"No, he didn't. He couldn't have because he left before I took it off."

"What did you do after you took it off?"

"Sophie – I want to know what the deal is with this jacket!"

"Jack, if your roommate is wearing that jacket, he could be in a lot of trouble, serious trouble." "After I took my clothes off, I took a shower, and then I fell asleep on my bed."

"How long were you asleep?"

"From about a little after twelve thirty in the afternoon to eight o'clock at night."

"Jesus Farley, anyone could have walked in here and taken that jacket." She paused for some thought, "Where do you think your roommate might be Farley, and does he look anything like you – he doesn't shave his head too, does he?"

"Don't worry, he has this really long, ultra-cool goatee beard -," my heart stopped as I remembered the shaving. "Oh my God Sophie - ...his girlfriend's house, he probably spent the night there. God, I hope he didn't go out in public much...Jesus Steve, of all the times you pick to shave off your beard why now? Is he in danger?! You better tell me if he is!!"

"Let's just get to his girlfriend's house quick."

When we arrived, her door was unlocked. I cautiously proceeded into the apartment. The bedroom door was lodged open and inside was a sight I have never forgotten. Jessica lay dead on the floor. Her half-covered, naked body now had a bullet hole through its forehead. There was also a small piece of paper in her now stiff left hand to "Sophie and her friend":

Sophie and her friend,

I surmise that either you or your friend have what we are looking for. If it is not given back to us within twenty four hours, then this man who claims not to know what we are looking for will cease to exist.

S & L

VI

Sophie Gets Her Gun

Steve was a calm and practical guy. You couldn't tell that by the way he usually looked, but that was pretty much his style. He definitely wasn't someone who deserved something like this happening to him. Neither was Jessica or I for that matter. I suppose no one deserves this kind of situation to befall them, but Steve and Jessica were two of the sweetest, down to earth people I knew. It wasn't all that strange that I had gotten mixed up in another bad situation, which was a mild term for this. I just never thought my somewhat haphazard lifestyle would get me involved in a murder – not only that, but a murder of someone who was very dear to me and sweet and who was soon going to be proposed to by my closest friend.

"I can't believe they didn't find it." Sophie thought aloud, "God, where could it be?"

I sat down on a Lazy Boy in Jessica's living room area. "What the hell have you done to my life?" I looked at Sophie with eyes that were now beginning to burn with fury as tears streamed down the sides of my face. Sophie was obviously scared and shaken, but the aura of her still having control of the situation was there. I was soon going to find out why.

"I'm calling 911 and then the police. She's obviously been dead a long time, but they may want to send an ambulance anyway," I said while heading towards the chair next to the phone. As I sat down and started to dial, I heard a click and then Sophie's voice.

"I'm sorry Jack, but I can't let you do that." I looked over at her and saw the gun. She wasn't totally composed, but she still was aware enough to pick me off if I made a lunge for her. My panic from seeing Jessica dead made me forget that underlying realization I had been having that Sophie was obviously in some kind of deep trouble.

"This is great." I exhaled and put my head in my hand, "Are you going to kill me now?" My heart was pounding like a machine gun.

"I need you to listen to me Jack. I know you are a good guy, and I know you believe in doing the right thing. That's why I am going to trust you with some things. First of all, I'm married. I am married to a very politically active man from the Middle East."

"Oh Lord, you married a terrorist, didn't you?"

"He's not a terrorist, Farley. He does a lot of international investigative work, but he is not a terrorist."

My former impression of Sophie as someone who overall possessed good judgment was disappearing fast. "So what does he have you mixed up in?" I asked.

"The murder of the former Israeli prime minister, Itzhak Halachmi; most of the Israeli Jews think the Palestinians had something to do with it. As crazy as it sounds, they think the Jewish man that shot him was working with a well-known Palestinian group. If this new election in Israel does not go the right way, Israel will turn aggressive again and there will never be a chance for peace in the Middle East. The truth is, Farley, the man who shot

31

Halachmi was actually working for a Neo-Nazi German group that would like nothing better than to see more Arabs and especially Jews killing each other off."

I decided that arguing with a possible fanatic about the unlikelihood that anyone of Jewish descent would ever work with a Nazi organization was not a good idea. So I slightly scaled down my protests: "Nazis?" I whimpered beseechingly, "You are mixed up with terrorists and Nazis now? I thought you were smarter than that Sophie."

"Jack, what's going on is wrong and it could lead to thousands of deaths."

"So what is the deal with my jacket?"

"I put some negatives from a roll of film in the right-hand pocket. These photos will show Halachmi's murderer linked on several occasions to this Nazi German group. Apparently, it even shows him as a member in one of their meetings or rituals or whatever. We need to get these pictures to the people of Israel before they vote for this guy that wants to take back control of the West Bank. If he wins, Israel will start military action against the Palestinians again. Now if your friend was wearing your jacket, then the film must have fallen out before they got to him or something. Maybe-"

"You really think some roll of film is going to bring the Jews and the Arabs together? Sophie, even if the guy was a Nazi, the Jews still have plenty of fodder and excuses in their fire to hate the Arabs. For crying out loud Sophie, ever since the Palestinians were given control of the West Bank, they have been suicide bombing Israel every other day!"

"Those are isolated, extremist groups Jack, and part of the reason they have been doing that is because this German group I mentioned has been sabotaging the peace process. They have been leaking false information to the Palestinians and telling them things that aren't true. They send doctored up proof of events to the Palestinian media that never even took place. They are smart Jack, and they know how to push people's buttons."

"So how the hell is this film going to stop all of that from happening Miss Save the World? God, why can't you just learn to live like a normal person? If those people want to kill each other, then let them. Why do you, me, and my friends all have to die for this?"

"I'm sorry Jack, I really am. But you might as well help me because now both you and your friend are in danger and the only way out of it is to help me get that film back."

"And give it to the Germans, right?" We looked at each other in a stand-off. "Tell me Sophie, how is your husband going to like it if he knows that two American guys know his secret, who his wife is, and have the ability to blackmail him at any time?"

"I know you wouldn't do a thing like that Jack. But for now, I would feel a lot better if you stepped away from that phone."

"All right, all right." As I started to look up, I quickly glanced behind her in a startled manner. She quickly looked behind her and I lunged for her. She kneed me in the groin and I was down for the count.

"You shouldn't have done that. Not only do I have a gun, but I have taken three different classes in self-defense training – and now I don't have as much trust in you," she said very matter-of-factly. I took a few minutes to moan and cough out my pain while laying all curled up on the floor in the fetal position with visions of my testicles floating around aimlessly somewhere in my abdomen. "I'm sorry," I croaked as I got up slowly. "I just think you've lost your head on this one, Sophie. You've lost your perspective. Whatever happened to music and the piano?"

"Look who's talking Mr. Bass Player-Composer turned insurance executive."

"Hey, claims are a lot different from sales…never mind. Look, I'll cooperate; I'll do anything you want. Please just try and do what you are going to do in the best way that can help Steve and me to stay alive, OK? In fact, just please help me get Steve out of this and I will take whatever risk I have to take. I wouldn't be alive today if it weren't for him, and I couldn't live with myself if I did something or didn't do something that resulted in him getting killed. It's bad enough that Jessica is dead. So please, I'll do whatever you want me to do. Please take my wishes into consideration."

"That's why I still love you Farley," she smiled, "you can't help but be a great guy – and you're so damn cute, too."

Nothing like flirting with a guy while pointing a gun at him.

"So where do you think these people have Steve, and you do think it's the Germans, right?" "Yes, I'm sure."

"How did they know that you put the film or whatever in my jacket?"

"They found it missing while I was staying in their house. They confronted me and searched my room. When it didn't turn up anywhere, they suspected the bar from the previous night. That was the only time we all left the house."

"That was the only place you guys went while you were staying with them?"

"Yes, we all stayed together the entire time. It was a royal pain just getting to their safe alone while they were in another part of the house, and then I had to take out the film without making any noise."

"So they obviously suspected me since they saw you hugging and hanging all over me."

"Yes."

"How did you finally get away from them?"

"I just did. I know a few tricks."

"That's for sure. God, I figured those people with you were somewhere from Europe, but it didn't seem that odd to me. You've always been the international type. But Sophie, Nazis? That whole scene we went through at the bar just makes me want to freak now."

"Sorry Farley. I saw you there and I knew you would be a way through which I could get the film safely away from the Germans. I wasn't so sure I was going to be able to escape from them, but I figured I would find some way to let one of my contacts know the film was with you via telephone or something."

"Did you?"

"I escaped the house and I decided it would be better if I got the film back from you and absolve you from this whole mess. I was going to provide you with a place to stay and a new identity and everything. And I can still do that for you. You just have to cooperate with me."

"I don't know if I want to be living in Pakistan or someplace like that. But cooperating with you sounds like the logical choice for now."

"Do you have some friends we could stay with? Your place might not be safe right now." "Yeah, I got some buddies."

"We've got to get your prints off the door and the telephone – I don't see how this murder could be pinned on you, but there's no sense in taking any chances."

VII

A Smokey Night

"Who needs privacy anyway? If I want to do something, I just do it." She looked at me almost flirtatiously, but had enough tact not to dwell on it too long. I looked back at her and almost said something about what a freak she was, but I decided to hold back. At least she had finally put the gun back in her purse. "Were you going to say something, Farley?"

"No, nothing I haven't already told you."

Here I was looking at a girl who had indirectly caused the death of one of my close, personal friends: a girl whom I at one time had briefly dated and who was about to become the fiancée of my best friend – a best friend who now was in significant danger of falling victim to the same fate. Also in this equation was the fact that Sophie had just gotten me involved in this whole terrorist-espionage crap that I couldn't give less of a shit about, at least not to the point of my putting my own life at risk. Yet still, I could see things from her twisted perspective to a certain degree. Perhaps without the influence of her amazing beauty, I would have written Sophie off on the spot as a fanatical lunatic. So maybe a few lives lost were worth the ultimate ends of saving the world, if indeed anything was going to be saved. Sophie had the capacity to allow the same sort of manipulation to engulf her that she was able to get most of her own victims to swallow. I couldn't help but remember her obsessive practicing back when she was in the conservatory. She was in love with her piano professor, or so she thought. People could tell something was going on, but this particular school was too conservative to let professors be open about students they were involved with. This particular professor probably didn't even consider their involvement as a serious relationship. He had a serious girlfriend of significant political influence in his field of competitive concert piano performing and probably considered Sophie no more than a cute, red-headed distraction between his practice sessions.

Sophie would practice a minimum of eight hours a day and eventually ended up acquiring acute tendinitis in both of her wrists. She had to quit playing for six months and could never quite come back to the level of mastery she had reached before her injury. When she finally quit, she told people she "wasn't willing to put in the amount of time and commitment necessary to become a concert pianist," but I knew differently. Her demonic obsession with her professor and her desire to impress him ruined her career. I could honestly say that as a bass player, I was too lazy to put forth the work required to win a big city symphony audition. Even during my most intense practice sessions, I was never so blinded by my desire to win an audition that I ignored my body when it would start to hurt. I had the awareness of when to say when and realize that when pain reaches a certain level, it needs to be addressed before it causes serious damage.

Sophie had already caused someone in my life serious damage. Would Steve and I both come out of this alive? I didn't know. It wouldn't seem very practical to let two people with incriminating knowledge about what she was involved in live to divulge that information.

"I'm going to take us to this one guy's house. He has some weird goings-on now and then, so if I call, he may not pick up the phone or just blow me off. His house is in one of the less well-known areas of town and his phone number is unlisted. I think he used to deal. He doesn't deal anymore, but he is still pretty paranoid about people."

The truth was he was just a pot-head who was usually stoned all the time and turned his phone ringer off so he could just screen all of his calls. You would be lucky if he called you back within two weeks. He was a damn good bass player too, I am sorry to admit.

The bus ride was quiet. We sat near the back and Sophie let me sit back and close my eyes in a feeble attempt at relaxation. The nearest stop to his house still required about a six to eight block walk, so we got a quick bite and I stopped at the corner ATM machine. When we finally began to approach his house it was nearing late afternoon. Don's car was in the driveway, and I sighed a breath of relief. His house was a shabby, brown, one-story ranch that resembled a mobile home in simplicity without the wheels. I knocked on his rusted-out screen door when we reached the top of his porch. I had to knock three times and then I finally yelled, "Don, it's Jack McFarland. I've got a gig for you. It pays $1,000 for three hours work. I had to back out and they specifically wanted you as a replacement."

I heard some movement. The door opened and Don's head peered through. "John!" He coughed for a few seconds, "How are you doing, man." His voice was barely coming out of his throat that was obviously very stoned and very dry. "C'mon in."

"Don, this is..." I looked at Sophie, "this is Stacey. She's a ballerina with the Boston Ballet." "Oh wow," he said, "you should meet my wife; she's a dancer too. She is with the Indianapolis Dance Association."

Sophie and I looked at each other. "Don!" I laughed, "You're married?! Wow, that's great, congratulations! Hey, Stacey's not really with the Boston Ballet, I just like to say that to people because I think she looks like a dancer. Actually, she's just an old friend..."

"I'm actually a secretary," Sophie laughed. She gave me a quick, icy stare. I was not handling the situation very well.

"Whatever man," Don was out of it, luckily, "so tell me about this gig."

"Well there's a condition that goes along with it."

"What?" He looked at me almost soberly.

"Me and Stacey...eh hem, Stacey and I need a place to stay for a few days, man. Let us stay, and I'll give you the gig."

"Hey, that's cool John."

"Call me Jack." I said.

"Sorry man, everyone who hires you calls you John, so I always have said that for the times I've referred you to people to take over my gigs. But hey, you're always welcome to stay here whether you got a gig for me or not."

I knew that wasn't true, but it was nice to hear anyway. It gave me a point to argue with him if he decided he wanted to kick us out before we were ready. Don offered us some marijuana, naturally. I declined, but to my astonishment Sophie accepted a couple of hits. I thought to myself, "How could she get buzzed on weed at a time like this?" Don had us sit down on the couch and was talking it up. I could tell I was way too uptight to pull this social façade off naturally, and Sophie had been giving me worried looks. I reevaluated my thinking, "Maybe I better pretend to get high, and just not inhale," my inside voice reasoned with me. "Aw, what the hell," I said, "give me a hit." We sat in his dark colored, earthy decorated room and proceeded to smoke and laugh. Don talked about good times; times that were a lot more carefree. For a few hours that evening, while listening to Don's amazing stories, I nearly forgot how screwed up my life had become in the past thirty-six hours.

VIII

Surprise Visitor

I woke up the next day on the floor. Sophie was sitting on the couch fixing up her hair and Don was still snoring in his pea-green seventies oval chair. Sophie was trying to decide whether to put her hair up or leave it down or just pull back the front and the sides and leave the back down. "I think you should pull back the front and just the very top of the sides into one of those cool barrettes you have and then leave the rest of the sides and the back down," I suggested casually. She looked at me and then looked back at her hand mirror, or maybe it was Don's mirror, who knows, and she proceeded to do as I suggested. She was gorgeous. There was no doubt about it – at least to me there wasn't. I had heard other men complain of her being too tall and slightly big-boned. I liked it. Her face was big and beautiful and her large, smooth lips could peel back into a stunning smile when she did smile. She also had piercing green eyes. She often inwardly stunned me with her glance. If I could remove her from the moment and transform her into an inanimate picture, I could sit back and admire her for possibly hours on end. I knew that she liked me and that she thought I was attractive, but I highly doubted that she was as smitten with me as I was with her. She represented something to me that I always wanted – a certain freedom, a certain level of carelessness and blind disregard for the status quo. And it wasn't in the way she looked; she was a classic beauty if ever there was one. It was in the way she was, the way she lived. To a certain extent, I envied her. I never had the guts to go live in another country for a year even though I've always been in love with Venezuela. She had done it, and she had done many other things that I hadn't, but I knew there was a price. There was a lack of stability and peace of mind and control over your life. Maybe that is why she liked to control others; her own life blew with the wind. Or perhaps I should say, her life blew with the whims and desires of whoever her new romantic, father-figure was. I had tried in previous times to find out about how her family experience had been growing up. She always changed the subject whenever I brought it up. I do however vaguely remember either someone telling me or just a general feeling when she did discuss the subject that she wished she had been closer to her father. I do know that he divorced her mother awhile back before she came to college and had maintained only very brief contact through the phone with Sophie and her older brother who was a very talented jazz piano player in the Chicago area. At least, that's what I had heard. "Farley," Sophie began after finishing up her hair job. She had gone with my recommendation of the top up and the back and most of the sides down concept, of course. "We need to get a plan going here. I may need to fill you in on some more information, but I promise I will only tell you what I absolutely think you should know for your own safety and awareness of the situation." Sophie was in one of her professional moods at this moment.

"Well," I said, giving Don a little nudge just to make sure he was still fully asleep, "I think you've already pretty much told me the situation and who we are dealing with."

"Our best bet for your friend may be to contact Stephan and Liane, that's the names of the Nazi couple that we are dealing with, and pretend like we have possession of the negatives. I have some other negatives that we can substitute for the real ones as long as we can keep them from getting a good look at them –"

"I don't think that's going to work, Soph." She was somewhat startled with my uncharacteristic assertive interruption of what she was saying. "I think we should try and sneak in and save him ourselves or try and find the real negatives if we want to bargain with these people. I don't see any way that they are going to accept a false set of negatives. They don't seem that gullible to me."

There was a conflict of interest that I was beginning to see. I wanted my friend safe first and foremost. Sophie wanted to get her negatives. "So where do you think the negatives might be, Jack?" She was looking at me strangely.

"What do you think, I am hiding them from you or something? How crazy do you think I am? Why the hell would I want to keep those things anyway?"

She looked down for a moment. Don stirred a little bit, found a comfortable position, and settled back into dreamland. "I am not accusing you of hiding anything, Jack. I just think you could be making a little better attempt at trying to remember where you went with that jacket while you had the photo negatives."

"Well," I started, "after you left the bar, I ended up talking to that girl for a while and well…you know."

"You made love to her."

"No, I mean, we did other things, you know. We didn't go as far as all of that, Sophie, we just…" "Farley, I don't care what you did or didn't do with that girl, just where you went with her." "I ended up spending the night at her place…in her bed." I added the last phrase reluctantly with a sense of guilt as if I owed some kind of fidelity to Sophie. Her expression told me that I was telling her something she already knew and my information only verified her already rock-solid premise.

"So where does she live?"

"I am not sure I can remember. I had more than a few drinks that night-"

"Did you walk to her place or did she drive you?"

"I am pretty sure we walked…yes, we walked. We were too buzzed up to drive."

"So she must live close to Turtle's, right?"

"Yeah, but that still is a very broad area. I think that we would have better luck finding her back at Turtle's."

"God Jack, that is too risky. What if Stephan and Liane are back there waiting for us to show up?"

"I don't think they would expect us to show up there."

"Well by now they know that this roommate of yours is not you, and they have definitely been back to your place and know that you haven't shown up there yet – so they probably have figured out that we have found each other. And their message was implying that anyway," Sophie spewed forth her ideas in a stream of consciousness. I was surprised to see her actually getting a little confused. She rarely showed that trait.

"Yes Sophie, you're right, and they also now know that we know how dangerous they are and how stupid it would be to go back to such a common, popular hang-out where they have seen me before." I rationalized, "It is the last place where we would go. That is probably what they are thinking." "I don't know, Jack."

"Oh come on, Sophie. You are supposed to be the risky one here."

"You didn't get that chick's name or number, did you?"

"No, just her name, but she does hang out there a lot. Maybe someone else might know her." I looked over at sleeping Don and then looked back at Sophie. "I am going to wake him up. I think he might know her. I have definitely seen him talking to her at the bar before."

"So what is our plan if he doesn't know her?"

"We go to Turtle's tonight and try to find her or someone who knows her."

"Some of your other friends might know her. Why don't we try and get a hold of them?" "A lot of my friends are not easy to get a hold of. I haven't been in the insurance field that long and most of my acquaintances still are musicians like Don. We were lucky to find him. We need to take care of this fast so Steve can hopefully spend a few less hours at the shrink's office when all of this is over – that is, if he lives through it."

"OK, wake the stoner up, but if he doesn't know her, we might as well try some of your friends. It would be a hell of a lot less dangerous for us than going back to Turtle's, regardless of whether it is a slim probability."

"You know, you can talk very intelligently when you want to, Soph." I humored with her as a last bit of psychological relief before the ordeal began.

"Wake up your scuzzbag friend, Farley."

I started to put my hand up to Don's shoulder, and then I stopped.

"Sophie, you seemed to have already known that I spent the night at her place and not mine. How so?"

"I've seen your room, Jack."

"Well," I thought for a moment, "that's a good point."

It still seemed to me like she'd have to be quite witty to think

44

that out on her own. My room was a disaster area, though, so maybe I was just being paranoid. Sophie had seen my room a number of times when we were in college hanging out with various friends. I usually had to pick up and rearrange things for a few minutes just so people could sit down somewhere. I started to shake Don's shoulder. He started mumbling to himself, but he was not coming out of his funk easily. "Don, man, you gotta wake up. C'mon Don. I've got to ask you something."

"What is it man?" He gasped sounding like some cross between Cheech Marin and an old man on his death bed. I could actually envision him in a Cheech and Chong movie at that moment.

"I want to know if you know this one girl. She hangs out at Turtle's a lot-"

The doorknob turned and the door swung open accompanied by the jangling of keys.

It was Sandy.

IX

Too Many Names

Sandy looked at me and then looked over at Don. "Hi sweetie," she said and walked over to Don. "Sam!" He exclaimed, suddenly much more alive. He stumbled up to a standing position and they gave each other an endearing kiss. "Oh John, this is my wife Samantha. Samantha this is John McFarland. He is a great bass player in this area – I've probably mentioned him before. We do a lot of substituting for one another."

"Yes, I think we have met before as a matter of fact," Samantha replied.

"Yeah," I said, now getting over the shock of the whole situation. "I think we have met at a jazz bar somewhere. You're one of those avid Indianapolis jazz fans – just like me."

Sophie and I looked at each other. I think we were communicating telepathically at that moment. Just as Sandy, or Samantha I should say, seemed to do with me when she mentioned that we had met before.

"Oh," Don stammered looking toward Sophie, "this is …uh, God I'm sorry, what was your name again?"

"I'm Sophie, I believe we have met, too."

"Yes we have," said Samantha, "quite recently I believe."

Don was looking a little puzzled, "Sophie? Is that the name you told me last night?"

"Sophia is my middle name, and I prefer to be called Sophie. Stacey is my first name, but when I am in social situations, I prefer to be called Sophie," she said, smoothing over her mistake very well. "Well," I said looking leeringly at Sandy or Samantha or whatever the hell her name was, "you two make a charming couple. So Don, I have heard that Turkey is a great place to visit, especially if you like cigarettes."

Don looked confused again, "I guess, man. I wouldn't know."

"You mean you've never been there?"

"No man, that shit would cost way too much."

"Huh, I figured a guy like you might have been there before, oh well. So how long have the two of you been living here?"

"I have been in the process of moving in from my other place," Samantha said. She was looking at me with a stern stare but a sweet voice. "It's a real mess. I still have to pay for six more months of rent unless I can find someone to take over the lease for that place."

"Oh," Sophie chimed in, "so how long have the two of you been married?"

"Well," Don was chuckling like a dumbass again, "we aren't really married, I introduce her as my wife because we've been together for nearly two years now and we are really closer to each other than most married couples – so when we're out and meeting prospective employers and such, I just introduce her as my wife because it looks better and shit. You know how Indiana people are Jack, they can be so judgmental. You might as well just play their game."

Don was weird – he always was. For one thing, he smoked pot like it was an antibiotic and he had scarlet fever. On the other hand, he would go through almost any act of conformity in order to look good in front of people that might hire him to play bass for them or teach their kids music. The thing was, he looked like a Bohemian with wild, curly black hair and these tinted prescription glasses. You could also smell pot on him nine out of any ten days. So any attempt he made to try and meld in with conservative Indiana Hoosiers was beyond futile.

Things were starting to make a little more sense now. When "Samantha" first walked in the door I thought I was in the twilight zone for a second – especially when considering Don's original "my wife" comment.

"How much moving do you have left?" Sophie asked Samantha.

"Oh I am nearly finished. I just have a few things left in my living room area and then my bedroom which I still have to get organized."

"You must need some help with some of your bigger things like your bed and your dresser," Sophie suggested.

"Actually, yes I do – Don and I were just wondering who we might get to help us with some of that stuff."

"Well who better than another bass player?" I said with a disgustingly happy smile of opportunity, "After all, we're used to carrying big things."

"That would be great, man." Don said.

"The only thing is," Sophie said pensively, "we would have to do it today or early tomorrow because Jack and I are leaving for vacation in two days and we will need tomorrow night to get ready and pack." As she said this, she walked up next to me and took my right hand in hers and with her other hand she lovingly rubbed my forearm.

"That's fine with me." Samantha said looking at the two of us together, "I don't have to work today or tomorrow. I don't know about Don, though."

"I just have some gigs to get to tonight and tomorrow night. The rest of the time I am free," Don informed us almost astutely.

"It's settled then," I said, "What do you say we all have some lunch and then start moving?" "Don't the two of you want a shower or something?" Samantha inquired.

"Oh God, not before we get all sweaty again from moving all that furniture. Maybe Jack and I will take one while Don is off at his gig," Sophie responded. She still amazed me sometimes with her ability to improvise her way through any situation.

After we had lunch, I requested that Don and Samantha drive us over to my street where my car was parked. Luckily, I was parked a couple blocks down from my house so I felt safe from seeing the German disaster team. I used the excuse that two cars would give us all the more room for moving more stuff efficiently and I also knew it would be an opportunity for Sophie and me to work out a game plan. Things were getting pretty hairy, and I could foresee a conflict of interest developing. I just wanted Steve and myself safe and out of this mess. Sophie had her big cause to worry about – and she also still had that damn gun. Our discussion began soon after I started the car:

"Do you think she's found the negatives?" I asked.

"No, I don't think so. If she has, I just hope she hasn't overreacted and shown them to someone else, or even worse, shown them to the police. You can never tell how someone from Indiana might react to seeing pictures of a Nazi party meeting."

Putting aside my dissatisfaction with her putting down my state of residence for the umpteenth time in the past two days, I was beginning to wonder about something and I decided to test Sophie on it and see how she would react. Sometimes I felt like I wasn't supposed to think for myself when I was around her or that my ideas were too off base. I was beginning to think this new idea of mine was right. "Did you ever think that maybe the worst thing this German couple could do to ruin their chances of getting the film back would actually be to kill Steve?" I glanced over towards her while I was driving and she looked at me with the furrowed eyebrow look. "I mean, I know what they are capable of doing obviously, and I know they want to show us that they are tough and we shouldn't mess with them. But if they are smart like I think they are, they must realize that Steve is the only leverage they have to get what they want."

"I wouldn't mess with them Farley," as usual in situations like this, her voice sounded as if she was impatiently parenting a lost child. I sensed her eyes roaming around the street as she maintained her mental and emotional distance that allowed her to go into her automatic pilot, manipulation mode. "I don't know how to tell you this, but your roommate's chances don't look so good, even if we do give them their negatives. I would highly suggest that we both play by their rules. They are going to have to be given something - my contacts have some film that would be a dead ringer for the film I took; we may even be able to make a copy before we give it back to them. At any rate Jack, I would not get tough with them or try to play hardball. Our best bet is to make them think that we are playing by their rules but maybe fool them in the process. I would hate for you to be traumatized the rest of your life for doing something that caused your friend's death. I know you'll be smart, Farley. I know that you won't mess things up for your friend or try to incriminate me and what I believe in."

As she finished her press statement, she opened her purse

and checked the bullets in her magnum. I thought her subtle suggestion was now being conveyed in a not-so-subtle manner.

Her reaction to my suggestion made it clear to me that Sophie preferred me to be in fear, as opposed to having a clear head with which to think. But it was more than just that. Being able to think in the moment to deal with anything that comes your way is great. I knew that Sophie was one of the best there is when it came to that sort of a thing. But the fear took away the trust that I had in myself, the kind of trust and security that you have deep inside where you know you are doing the right thing instinctively even if it doesn't make rational sense on a surface level. Call it Transcendentalism if you like. I don't know if Sophie ever had that kind of gut instinct when it came to making choices in her life. She was moved by passions and by what some voice in her head told her what she should do. It used to be her piano teacher that planted that voice inside her. Now I think it was that husband of hers from the Middle East. At that point in the car, I decided I needed to start making sure I was still listening to those good instincts deep inside of me. Sophie talked a good talk and walked a good walk, but I wasn't sure she was so good at navigating a good course.

"So if we don't find this film sometime today, do you think we should ask Samantha if she has found anything?" I continued my attempt at coming to an agreement of plans.

"I think it would be polite to at least wait until her boyfriend is not around. I don't think she's too hip on letting him on to the fact that she fools around behind his back. We need to play the situation. She might have a lot more stuff to move and a lot more uncovered area than what she is letting on. I always tell people that I am almost done moving even if I have barely just started. What other rooms were you in besides her bedroom?"

"I can't remember. I usually don't take off any of my clothes until I am in the bedroom – wait a second, that's right! The next morning I was groping around for my clothes in her bedroom and all of them were in there, including the jacket. So the film probably fell out in her bedroom!"

51

"I hope she keeps her bedroom messy." Sophie said, "Otherwise, we might have one more person involved in this mess and we don't need that."

"I don't think she's found it." I said with absolutely no foundational proof or reason.

Hope springs eternal.

X

Moving and Searching

    Sure enough, when we arrived at Samantha's house the only things that she had moved already were her television, some shelves, and a coffee table. She still had a million little things to put in boxes and get ready to pack. She also had a few large items as well like her bed, a large stereo system...even a fish tank. This girl was way out of touch – she even thought her boyfriend was an international tobacco dealer. Both as a musician and as a part-time sleazy drug dealer, Don was strictly a local phenomenon. I had at least done some gigging on the East Coast and in Chicago a few times. Don of course, did not mention that when he introduced me to Sam as "a great bass player in this area." If one of us was a provincial musician, it was him, not me.

    The moving began and so did the search. We somehow talked Don and Sam into moving a lot of the smaller, medium-sized things first. Then we paired off: Don with Sam and I with Sophie. While Don and Sam were outside putting something in their car, Sophie and I were inside frantically searching through the bedroom which was about as messy and cluttered as my bedroom was. We would then rush outside with something of theirs the moment we heard them coming in and then throw it in my car any old way. Any engineer would have had a fit if he saw our inept loading scheme. I was beginning to build up a sweat with all the behind the scenes running around and Don couldn't resist comments like "Boy, you must be out of shape, Jack!" At least he was still calling me by the name I preferred. I guess as long as I was helping him move and there was a gig opportunity, he figured he might as well put on his brown nose. It was funny how much of a people-pleaser this man could be and still consider himself a true individualist and artist. I guess two faces are better than one.

Nothing was turning up. We searched under piles of papers and behind her bed, in her closet and in her pile of dirty clothes. Two hours had gone by and we had already made two trips from her place to his and it was about getting to be time when we needed to switch our pairings so Don and I could carry some of the heavier things. In actuality, Sophie was probably almost as strong as either Don or I were, but it wouldn't have looked good for a gentleman to say something like that.

"Have you looked through the other rooms much?" I asked Sophie.

"Yes," she said, "I haven't seen anything, and those rooms are a lot cleaner and easier to look through, too."

I looked out the window and saw Don and Sam discussing something about loading ideas outside of his car. "It's impossible." I said, "We're going to have to ask Sam if she found the negatives." Sophie's eyes began to wander in thought. "It was hot that night that you were here wasn't it?" "No," I said, "it was pretty humid, but not hot."

She was still thinking.

"What? What is it?"

Sophie walked into another room and I followed her, "What are you thinking about Soph? Tell me!"

"You're a sweater, Farley. If you left any of your clothes on while you were doing whatever with Samantha, I bet you were sweating."

"And your point is - ?"

She looked at me the way a school teacher would look at a clueless student. "Your sweaty B-O would have gotten on some of her clothes, too." She continued to wander into the laundry room. She opened up the washer and there was a pile of wet clothes – white and pastel underwear, sheets and some other delicate fabrics. She turned off the washer and began to search.

"Go outside and stall them for a while." She instructed me.

If you ever look through a load of wet laundry, you'll probably realize how hard it is to stop in the middle of looking and then come back. As soon as you restart the load, you might as well trash all the progress you made in the last minute or whatever time it was that you were searching. I doubt that Sam would even be aware enough to notice that the washer had stopped running. Don probably wouldn't have noticed if Sophie and I were on the dining room table bleeding to death.

I went outside and started my spiel by suggesting that we put some of the more jagged, bulky furniture in Don's car instead of mine and giving a plethora of reasons and excuses as to why. It became very wordy, and I was quite impressed with my performance.

"It's cool man, it's cool." Don began to impatiently chime in, "We won't even get to that stuff at this rate anyway. We have to make this next trip soon because I have to pick up my bow from the repair shop before it closes today and it is going to take at least another half hour to get this stuff over to my place and unpacked –"

"Wait a second." I retorted, "You said all you had to do today was make it to a gig that wasn't until midnight and now all of the sudden you have to pick up some bow that you're not even going to use tonight anyway so –"

"Farley, Don is right." Sophie was trotting out the front door towards us. "Don't worry; even if Don has to go, I'm sure Sam will be able to manage. You look very handsome with the sun on your scruffy, cute face like that!" She brought her left hand up the left side of my face to rub my cheek as she gave me a romantic, endearing kiss. Her eyes were smiling into mine like two huge flying saucers that had just reached their destination. SUCCESS!!

I put my arm around her waist and she did the same with mine. "Well, you're probably right Sophie. I should just relax and settle down. A couple nicks in my upholstery won't ruin my car. It's not like I'm driving a Mercedes Benz or anything."

"Good," said Don, his desire to take charge of the situation coming to the surface, "let's get this crap over to my place so I can get going."

Don and Sam began to make their way around us towards the house. Sam had a funny expression on her face and glanced at both Sophie and me before she made her way past. "What's up with her?" I whispered into Sophie's ear.

"Who cares?" replied Sophie, her beautiful face still beaming. We embraced and I kissed her on the cheek, "Way to go Soph; I knew you could do it!"

"Oh Farley," she purred, "We might have to take that shower soon."

What a tease.

XI

The Walls Come Back Up

So the negatives had been found. After one more moving trip, Don was off to do whatever and the rest of us headed back towards the house. I mentioned to Sam that Sophie and I were thinking of going out somewhere that night before we began to pack to leave for our "vacation" the following day. Sophie said she had to make some calls to some friends first before we would know what we were doing.

When we got back, Sophie asked to use the bathroom and then disappeared behind the door. "So Sandy, whoops, I mean Samantha, uh, how are things with your ex-boyfriend?" I said very facetiously.

"You are so funny." She quipped back, "Tell me something. Should I dump him for you, Mr. Love'em and Leave'em?"

"Hey, I was planning on following up with you at Turtle's!" I interjected.

"Oh, really?" she said, "Were you planning on bringing Miss Hot Redhead along with you so that you could enjoy a threesome?"

I was shocked for a moment at how she seemed earnestly upset by the turning of events. "Look," I protested, "don't make me into the big, bad guy. I was straight with you and you lied to me about your boyfriend."

"Sandy used to be my name."

"I didn't ask you what your name *used* to be that night we hooked up."

"I was very mad with Don at the time, and I was pretty blown away by your...never mind." Silence.

"So you are a dancer, huh?" I asked politely.

"Yeah, I used to study voice too at the Indianapolis Conservatory."

"How long ago?"

"I started when I was 17 –"

"I might have come in as a freshmen while you were a senior!" I said, letting a little bit of excitement into my tone. "No," she said in a down voice, "I quit after my junior year. But I remember coming back to a couple of symphony concerts and seeing you at the head of the string bass section." "Oh," I said, "you should have introduced yourself."

"Maybe," she said, "my life became kind of complicated after I quit voice."

I laughed, "You mean to tell me it's less complicated now?" I had committed a serious, undercover faux pas.

"It's not all that bad," she said almost defensively. "What makes you think things are so rough?" Her eyebrows furrowed together slightly. We looked at each other for a moment. There was something going on with her; maybe she was on to me and Sophie. I couldn't tell.

"I just meant that compared with life in college, real life is much tougher, you know."

We then heard the flushing of the toilet. Sophie had been in there quite a while. I wondered at the time whether she had been trying to listen to our conversation.

She came out of the bathroom fiddling with stuff in her purse. I hated when she did that. I always anticipated her pulling out her gun when she even looked at her leather-sewn bag of secrets. "I just talked to Stephan and Liane. They are going to meet me at their house, and we can all go out later if you like. The two of them are kind upset with you Farley, but I may be able to smooth things over – oh, and they said Steve will be able to make it too."

"I'm guessing you were on your cell phone all this time?" I asked.

Sophie nodded.

"Good." I said, trying to process all of her insinuating messages between the lines. "If Steve can make it, maybe I can just sort of hang out with him and then Stephan and Liane wouldn't have to deal with my behavior."

"I just don't think that it is a good time for you to be hanging out with them right now. You and Steve will have plenty of opportunities to do stuff together. Why don't you and Sam go out and do something since Don is playing that gig tonight?"

Maybe she had heard a few things through those thin, bathroom walls.

"I suppose if there is no way I can go without ruining Stephan and Liane's evening, maybe we should do something." I said to Sam.

"We could listen to some jazz maybe?" Sam smiled.

"Just not at Turtle's. I am getting sick of that place. My friend Charlie plays at the Jazz Factory on Monday nights. We could go over there."

"So you didn't have to work today or tomorrow?" Sam asked.

"I have to work tomorrow. But I can call off when I need to."

I sensed Sam's suspicions beginning to grow again, maybe not, maybe it was just me. I just hoped she didn't start asking more questions about me and Sophie's peculiar behavior.

"You know, if you guys are holding off on a shower because you don't have any clothes, you're free to use some of Don's or my clothes if you like. I'm sure we could find something that would fit you both."

Sophie and I had both finished taking our showers. I had doggedly made a half-serious suggestion that I should join her with the old "If you need someone to wash your back…" line, but she brushed me off with the even more commonplace cliché, "Not tonight Farley, I think I'm starting my period." I only meant it as a joke, but Sophie sent a clear message about the suggestion through her tone. I was now wearing a baggy, beige colored, hooded top and a pair of heavy denim jeans that were actually too short, but I wore them low around my waist. I was happy because you couldn't smell pot on them unless you put your nose deep in the fabric and took in a really big breath. Sophie was wearing a bright, light red halter top that I especially liked because it was quite tight on her, and it really brought out her nice figure. She also had on some brown pants that I don't think matched her top, but Sophie didn't usually care about that, for she had enough charm in her to make up for any bad fashion statement.

We were all back in the living room now, at least that is what I call the area we were in, making small talk. I was dying inside because I still hadn't gotten a chance to talk to Sophie alone about her telephone call to the German dynamic duo. She had still been able to successfully brush off any attempts I made to calmly suggest I come along to meet them, and I was about to start a serious mock-argument with her in order to insist that I come along. I didn't trust her enough to believe she had it in her to get Steve back. I wasn't convinced that she cared enough about my situation and more importantly, Steve's situation.

Sophie brought up in our "light" group discussion that she was going to have to leave in a few minutes. Sam said she had some clothes for her in the dryer, and she went to go get them.

As soon as Sam left the room, I started in quietly but sternly with Sophie. "Sophie, I'm coming with you and that's final."

"Jack, you are not equipped to handle this situation. Let me take care of this. Your roommate will be back in your apartment by tomorrow."

"I need to know more of what's going on here. What did they say to you? What did you say to them? You've got to fill me in Sophie!"

"Jack, you are going to have to let me handle this and if my word isn't good enough, then maybe my nine millimeter can speak for me!" She looked at me and my face sunk into an expression of dejected acceptance. "But for right now, Farley, you can help me by calling your answering machine and seeing if there are any messages on it. I have already put something in the phone receiver that will keep the calls from being traced. It will also record the messages onto my pager and another device that my contacts have. If Sam sees you on the phone, don't freak, just be calm and say that you are checking your messages. Make something up about that gig if you want to tell her something about the messages, just be cool about it." She caressed the side of my head, "I'll get your friend back to you Farley, I promise." Unfortunately, I was not pacified by her reassurance.

I picked up the phone receiver and I heard dialing. I quietly put the phone back on the hook. "Sam is making a call." I said.

"You should have said excuse me or something, Farley. She probably heard you pick up the phone."

"No, I don't think she did."

"When you get nervous, you act weird. When you act weird, you look suspicious, and looking suspicious is what we are trying *not* to do, so calm your ass down!" Sophie's eyes were intimidating. "Now pick up the phone again and if she is still on it, say 'excuse me Samantha.'"

I picked up the phone again, but this time there was a dial tone. "She's off." I reported to Sophie. On my answering machine there were a couple of messages from some friends of mine that I was going to meet the previous day. Then the calls came in about Jessica. First the police called wanting to talk to Steve, then Jessica's and Steve's parents both called wanting to know where he was and if he was OK. Then there was a message from the chief investigator on the murder: Detective Keyes. That was all. A few seconds after I put down the receiver, Sam walked into the room with our clothes neatly folded. "Sorry I picked up on you just then," I said, "I was just going to check my messages. I wasn't trying to be nosy."

"Oh," said Samantha, I noticed her eyebrows wrinkled together again very slightly. Sophie did the same thing when she fed me a line of bull. "Don't worry about it; I dialed the wrong number or something. I was trying to get the weather. I'm going to have to re-check what the number is." "555 – 8989," I replied. We looked at each other for a moment.

"Well," Sophie began while pulling out a plastic bag from her large purse to put her clothes in, "I have to get going; my ride is going to be here any second."

"Your ride?" I asked. "Of course, sweetie, you know Stephan and Liane always give us a ride," she said joyfully as she rested her hand on my chest. "You two have fun tonight, but not too much fun." She pointed her finger at me in a cute, mock-threatening kind of way.

"If I need to reach you tonight, can you give me their number; they just changed phones you know, and I can't remember their new number."

"You can just page me, Farley."

"You never call me back. What if there is a change of plans with our trip tomorrow that we need to discuss? We could be tied up all day long if we don't make adjustment plans as soon as possible." "Well Farley," she said, "they would be paging me if that came up anyway. Look, why don't you take this extra pager that I bought for you, and I will page you sometime tonight if that will make you feel better." She handed me a pager from her purse that was still in its store packaging.

"You promise you'll page me?" I said as I looked in her eyes.

"Of course." I knew she was lying.

"I'll see you tomorrow then. Don't forget to tell Steve all about our travel mishaps; he'll get a big kick out of that."

"I will."

"OK, bye then." I put my hand behind her head and I kissed her. I could tell it was awkward for her. It was all purely my own impulse, not initiated in any way by her. For once in our strange relationship, it seemed that in this moment she was the nervous one. She was the one who didn't know what to do. I displayed to her an earnest feeling from inside myself. It had no ulterior motive behind it. Sophie looked around startled for an instant, made a tentative smile, and walked out the door. I touched on something that she couldn't handle in those few seconds: real feelings. I watched Sophie walk out the door and continue out to the curb where a black Mercedes Benz sedan was waiting for her. As the wind blew her hair, I noticed one particular tendril waving through the breeze. It had a large bulb on the end that resembled the head of a snake.

XII

Set Up

"All right," I said turning around to Sam, "what did we decide we were going to do tonight?" "Are you OK?" Sam asked, "You look a little flustered."

"Yeah I'm fine. She just acts a little weird sometimes, you know how it is."

"Yeah, Don can be the same way. He gets very secretive and very stubborn. It is hard to deal with him."

"Yeah, it is."

We looked at each other. It felt like two nights ago at Turtle's again. Sophie had just left the scene. Why should I bother with Sophie? For one thing, she's married. I also could never stand the lifestyle that she has. When she is around, she knows how to steal my full attention, but when she leaves, I am always left wondering why the hell I should invest any feelings in her at all. Nothing serious with Sophie could ever lead to happiness or fulfillment. Steve was right about her. She's manipulative, and can't be trusted. No one could beat her when it came to having a good time, or when it came to raw animal attraction. But in all other areas, what could she possibly offer in a relationship? I wondered briefly about Sam. Something was odd about her relationship with Don. I just couldn't see the two of them together. Sam really was more my type of girl, if I had one type. She and Don technically were not married – a point I took very seriously. My Midwestern Chicago instincts were still strong, and if a man truly knows he loves a woman – he would be leading the relationship towards a marriage. I could not envision Don proposing to Sam, or anyone for that matter. I also felt that Sam could do a lot better than Don.

"So," I began again, "what do you want to do?"

"How do you feel about a little Tango?"

"Tango?"

"Sure, I have some old Tango records here that we could warm up with before we go out. I bet you're a natural, though. Most bass players are good dancers, I think it is because they have such good rhythm. Wait here while I go get those records." She walked out for a moment and came back with a few Tito Puente and Jobim records, a bottle of wine, and a hot red dress on. The records were authentic LPs, and there was a phonograph player in the room. In those days, when someone offered to share a bottle of wine, I almost always accepted. I suggested the Jobim because the Puente would be better for a faster paced Samba. I was able to meet Jobim once when he came to visit the conservatory. Sam and I each consumed two glasses of wine during this musical conversation. Sam then put on a tune with a good bosa nova beat to it and we started up. She was a very physical dancer, even for a tango. We danced quite close and as she seemed to get more involved with the music, she would often rub and caress my back in broad, circular strokes. Ordinarily, I would have enjoyed it very much, but presently I was having trouble getting my mind off of Steve.

"Whoops," Sam fell into me and caught herself by grabbing my behind. I looked at her and she smiled followed by an embarrassed-sounding giggle. She was acting kind of strange beyond just the flirting, but I was now starting to crumble under the wine and her wiles. When a girl as cute as she is rubbing your back and grabbing your butt, you tend to get your mind back into the immediate moment. "There's one more move I want to work on before we go out," she said hurriedly as she ran to the record player to top on another tune. This song was a little slower. "All right," she said while running back to me, "now you know when we usually take the fifth step back towards me? This time you are going to stay there and I am going to take a step back and do a slide maneuver under your legs." We came to the fifth step. I spread my legs apart, and she stepped back as we brought our hands together. She jumped downward and I pulled her toward me. When she was halfway through my legs, she let go of my hands and clutched my legs to keep her from hitting the ground. I had done what I was supposed to do, but she had purposely sabotaged the slide move, forcing her to clutch onto me. She then began to feel up and down my legs and even up around my crotch as she frantically pulled herself up. She stood in front of me and brought her face close to mine. It was pretty clear what she was trying to do, and my will power was fading fast. "What is that, a gun?" She almost sounded serious as she was grabbing something that may have felt like a gun, but was something different. "Yeah," I chuckled, "hands up!"

She raised her arms and I began to lift up her red chiffon dress that she had changed into while retrieving her records as she simultaneously began to murmur, "Kiss me Jack."

The phone started ringing…talk about irony. "I better get that," Sam said in a script-like fashion and nearly lunged toward the phone. She deftly managed to reach behind her and make sure her dress was pulled down to its starting location.

I began to get scared. Something weird was going on. "Yes… oh, hi Don. You're where? What happened? All right, all right, I'll be there as soon as I can."

She hung up the phone. "Don has a dead battery down at the

Murat Theater. He needs a jump because he has another gig to get to tonight. I'll be back soon. It shouldn't be too long."

"Sam," I said as she grabbed her coat and headed towards the door. "Look, I'm sorry about just now." I wasn't sure what to say. She had obviously initiated most of what had just happened between us. I just suddenly sensed some kind of negative vibe, and in past situations like this I found that the best thing to do was to apologize, even if you didn't think it was your fault.

"Look, I'm sorry about just now. It seemed like you were coming on to me just now. I may have pushed it too far. I mean, you were trying to start something, weren't you?"

"I gotta go right now, Jack. We can talk about it later."

She walked out and shut the door behind her. I plopped down on the nearest chair feeling worried, tense, and flabbergasted over the whole situation now at hand. "Why the hell was she touching me like that?" I said aloud to myself.

Like a flash of lightning the door flew open. A countless number of men in black body suits and masks stormed the room with automatic machine guns. "Hands in the air and feet apart!!! Get up against the wall, **NOW!!!**" I then heard the stern voice of Samantha coming from somewhere behind the men in black. "Sorry Farley, but the party is over."

XIII

Debriefing

"He may have a gun hidden in his underwear; I frisked him very thoroughly," Sam chimed in as two black-clad grunts searched me.

"That's not a gun...," I tried to explain nervously.

"Shut up, scumbag!" The big one screamed in my face. I looked up toward the ceiling as I felt rough, large, male hands grope around my most private area.

"I don't feel anything," another voice said.

"Don't take this personally, but Sam is a little more inspiring than you are." I said snidely. "SHUT UP, TERRORIST PRICK!!" said Big Guy who followed up his cheer with a crushing blow to my side.

"Arrrrwwwwhhhh!!!" I screamed and fell to the floor in pain.

"All right, take it easy Carl." A new voice was on the scene, "We don't know that yet."

I looked up between gasps of air to see a big, round, smiling face of a gentleman somewhere between forty-five and sixty years of age. I guessed this from his salt and pepper colored hair and slightly raspy voice. "Hurst, Patrick Hurst." He announced to me while looking down at my pathetic condition of agony. He had a very confident air about him, and I could tell immediately that he was no dummy. "I apologize for my friend Carl's lack of hospitality, Mr. McFarland."

"Patrick Hurst?" I repeated curiously as the pain began to subside. "You were in the news, weren't you?"

"Very good Jack, I can call you Jack, right?" He again made a professional style smile and continued to speak as he pulled out an apple from his overcoat pocket and took a bite. "Yes, I was quite popular for a while. Now the news is on one of my colleagues, but that is beside the point. I am surprised Jack, that you didn't know who I was right off. I mean, considering that you have been cavorting for the past few days with the wife of the man against whom I and my fellow colleagues in the CIA have been accused of plotting an internationally, illegal assassination attempt."

"Emile Bajaj?!" I nearly froze, "Sophie is married to Emile Bajaj?"

"That's right, jack. The guy who wiped out fifty thousand of his own countrymen because he believed they were insincere Muslims. We haven't seen dictators like him before with family origins from India, but he certainly is living up to the title of dictator and tyrant in the country he has been ruling for the past decade." I was trying to remember what country he had fled to after being kicked out of India in his earlier years. I didn't want to ask and sound stupid. It didn't really matter to me what country he was ruling now, anyway. I had heard enough about him to know he was one of the world's most hated and feared dictators. At that moment the pressure completely overtook me.

"Oh my God!" I began to cry. I brought my hands to my head

and buried my face in the floor. "No, it can't be! No, God, why her! Why Sophie, Why!"

Hurst held back and let me cry for a minute or so.

"They were married around ten months ago. He has many mistresses, but she is his favorite. So, he married her to set an example for the other upstanding men in his country to marry and have children in order to populate the country and make it strong like China. China actually hasn't been doing so well in recent years, but apparently everyone in his country is too afraid to remind him of that fact." "I didn't know she was married to *him,* honestly I didn't." I cried to him.

"I believe you Jack, I do." Hurst was still in his mental zone, I figured he almost always was. "No one who has knowledge of the insides of these matters and is involved in this stuff would make the kinds of boneheaded decisions or act the way that you have if he or she was anywhere near his or her right mind. Failing a psychological assessment right now might be the only thing for you to worry about Jack, but I can tell just from talking to you that you are not crazy. From what we have seen of you and heard from you on our tapes, the only thing we could possibly indict you on is ignorance and stupidity. Unfortunately, there are still no laws against acting under those influences in this country."

"She said she was married to a political activist from the Middle East."

"Well, calling Mr. Bajaj a political activist would certainly be up for one of the most hyperbolic euphemisms made in this millennium." I understood the gist of what he was saying, but I ended up looking one of those words up in the dictionary at a later time just to make sure. Hurst then took another bite of his apple and began to walk about a bit, gazing at the room's décor and occasionally fingering a plant. "These things are something I thought you should know Jack, and we may be able to help you – especially where your friend Steve is concerned."

"I'll help with anything I can sir," I nearly stammered, "I will, you have my word."

"That's good Jack, that's good. Now, Tracey here has been following your friend Sophie for quite some time." He put his hand on Samantha's shoulder, "I know that it gets confusing keeping up with all these different names, but you can still call her Samantha. Samantha is actually her real name, but we just call her Tracey because she is our best tracer specialist. Now then, we want you to spend as much time with Tracey as you can. We know that you have a history with Sophie and that you can help Tracey in following what her next moves might be because we can tell by the way that you talk to her that you know Mrs. Bajaj pretty well, even as deep as a certain subconscious common instinct that you both seem to detect from each other. We know that eventually Sophie is going to get together with her husband at some point of interest. Sources have told us that he is indeed somewhere here in the U.S. By tracking her, we can get to Emile and hopefully make an international arrest and try him under international law. Now, I know that Sophie has undoubtedly told you the same story that Emile has been telling his countrymen and all his followers…that he is not responsible for the death of Itzhak Halachmi, that it was a Nazi terrorist association or something like that. There is no evidence of any Nazi affiliation with the murder of Halachmi. In the days before his murder, there were countless numbers of Bajaj's men that were within a mile of Halachmi's whereabouts. There is no evidence that this so-called Nazi terrorist group even exists and if it does, it would be so small and so low on funding that there is no realistic chance it could have the intelligence to get anywhere near Halachmi, much less murder him. We believe this roll of film that she talks about was produced by Bajaj and has superimposed pictures of this supposed, Nazi, 007 looking character firing shots at Halachmi from a building that would have been the same trajectory as the entrance of the bullets into Halachmi's body. This photograph has already been shown to many people in Bajaj's home country. He just wants to come up with a set of original negatives to use as further evidence to support his claim. Bajaj has chosen a new unified German organization called Herr Schlangenstein which

most closely translates to Mr. Serpent or Mr. Snake in English –
which one is it, Gus?"

"Schlange means snake, sir, and Schlangenstein would be the
German word for serpent." Gus replied instantly.

"There you have it. It makes a lot more sense than our
English language, I hate to admit," Hurst critiqued. "Anyway, this
organization has more capability than most other new German
groups, but is still grossly incapable of pulling off what Bajaj
claims. At this point Jack, I will go ahead and ask if you have any
questions. We may or may not fill you in on the answers, and we
may or may not have the knowledge to do so at this time."

"What do you plan on doing with Sophie after you get to
Emile?" I asked.

"If she helps us put Emile away with testimony and important
corroborating evidence that we need to try him, she may get off
with nothing more than some international educational duty for
six months or perhaps civil service here in the U.S. If she stays
loyal to Emile, we could bring her down also because we have
evidence of her committing at least one murder for him by her
own hands."

"Can you provide some kind of protection for Steve and me
when this is all through?"

"We can give you new identities, new homes almost anywhere
you like, and new jobs in the same fields that you have now with
at least as much pay as you're getting now."

"Then I guess it's time to start being a good American."

XIV

Gadgets for Jack

Over the next couple of hours, Hurst filled me in on some more information that puzzled me. The "quite some time" that Sam had been following Sophie was actually only a few weeks. Sam had been on clerical duty for the agency on a computer downtown until a couple of months ago when they heard about Sophie coming to town, so they thought Sam would be a good one to put on her. I thought it was a pretty big gig to give someone her first time out, but Hurst explained that a new-comer would be better in this situation because Sophie and Emile had already studied and familiarized themselves with many of the agency's veteran investigators. The German couple that Sophie and I had been dealing with was actually two former members of Herr Schlangenstein that left Germany to come to America. Mr. Hurst then suggested much to my disbelief that Sophie had actually been the one who killed Jessica and had friends of hers kidnap Steve in order to scare and pressure me into finding the film faster. The film did have some incriminating photos of the German group and of Stephan and Liane, but killing innocent women was not their style; that was something that Bajaj's organization would do. It was also highly doubtful that the couple would know who Sophie really was and what her intentions were with the negatives. Sophie spoke fluid German and befriended many people even to the level of spending days and nights in their homes.

"So," I asked, "you planned to have Sophie find the film in Sam's washer, right?"

"Actually," Hurst paused and pursed his lips as he scratched his head somewhat embarrassingly, "Sam here, in her rookie assignment, unfortunately misplaced the film after getting it from you that wonderful night that we all got to listen to the two of you breathe and grunt, among other sounds." Sam and I both brought our heads down in embarrassment.

"The film ended up buried down in one of her dirty laundry piles. It is probably quite fortunate that Sophie found the film when she did, seeing as how a roll of film in the clothes dryer would have turned into syrup." He gave Sam a stern glance. "It is also very fortunate that the film was in an air tight, vacuum sealed, aluminum container and the water temperature in the washer was set on cold. Overall, we would like to have choreographed her finding the film in a bit more controlled manner, but this scenario is actually working out well."

The shock of the whole new situation that had fallen upon me slowly began to start sinking in. I was now involved with the CIA. Most all of my activities in the past two days had been monitored in some way: either filmed or audio recorded. Almost everything I had said had most likely been heard by Hurst and God knows how many more agents and worst of all – another woman whom I thought I had won over with my male charms was just playing me to help out her professional situation.

Hurst told me a few more details that I stored back in the reserves of my brain because I didn't feel they were as urgent to keep in mind as what he already told me. I wondered about his plans to make an "international arrest" of Bajaj under international law. I suspected that more than likely they would try to kill him. I wondered if the assassination would include Sophie and if Steve and I would become casualties in the crossfire. It never helps a situation to think about the worst, but in the back of my mind I knew that the chances were there. Hurst told me in a couple of days, if I cooperated and helped out Sam, they might let me carry a weapon for my own protection. He said he would leave the ultimate decision up to Sam.

Sam and I decided to make up a story for everyone that we had been to Canyon Jack's that night for a little while and then decided to come back to the house to watch television. Canyon Jack's was one of the better decorated bars in town that usually didn't have a great number of distinguished young people there. It was attached to a restaurant and had a little more of that Midwestern, family appeal to it. Hurst had taken me down the block a couple of houses or duplexes, I wasn't sure which they were, to a van where he brought me inside and showed me some of the camera shots and audio bugs they had inside Don's place and Sam's old place. The pictures were very vivid, high-definition quality for back then. He then played an audio recording for me.

"Farley!" it was Sophie's voice and there was a lot of chatter and rustling in the background. "Sophie, how are you?" That was my voice.

"My God, I haven't seen you in so long. You look so good. God, I love what you've done with your hair!"

"Yeah, I decided to clean up that awful mess. Didn't you go away to Austria or something?" My voice asked in a somewhat commercial tone.

"Oh Farley, I had the most awesome time in Germany last year."

Hurst then cut off the tape. "That conversation came from Sam's body microphone from the bar you Indiana folks affectionately refer to as Turtle's. We have a few microphones we would like to supply you with, Jack. This one here has a small, dark blue fabric casing with the mic carefully woven inside. This mic is undetectable by most any electronic device. I would recommend putting it inside the collar of your shirt or inside the flap of your fly – for *you* the collar might be the better choice since it is usually not being manipulated nearly as often as the other spot." Hurst had his way of getting in brief editorials when he so desired. "Let me see your keys Jack...thank you. This leather emblem usually works phenomenally well. As long as you are not wearing too many thick layers of clothing over it, it will do very nicely. The weather is warming up, so I don't see why you would need any thick clothing or winter coats in the near future. The last mic I am giving you is a band aid that is still packaged in its box. My advice to you is to tell people that you have a blood condition which deters your ability to clot or scab very easily when you get cut if anyone asks why you carry around band aids. If you don't have either of our other mics for any reason or if you think they may not be picking up very well, you find a way to cut yourself or pretend to cut yourself and put this on."

The leather key chain emblem was the only mic that I wasn't impressed with. I wasn't into big key chain fixtures and this one had the old hippie ying-yang symbol on it. Anyone who knew me well would know that I was too much of a no-nonsense, straight-minded guy for that kind of new age bullshit. I had a short period in college like that, but those days were over. "Could we possibly get a key chain that didn't have this symbol on it?" I asked Hurst.

"The symbol is the microphone, Jack. Hurst informed me, "Would you prefer a smiley face painted over it?"

"How about a Van Halen insignia?" I suggested hopefully.

"We will try and work on getting one." Hurst exhaled impatiently, "For now, just tell people you lost your other key chain and are using this one that a friend gave to you. Improvise a little Jack. You need to be able to do that better. Wasn't that part of your musical training, improvisation? There will be a lot of things in your behavior and actions over the next couple of days that may seem odd to people, especially those that know you well. You are going to have to learn quickly how to smooth these situations over and put people back at ease."

He somehow knew that I was worried about what people would think of the key chain and how it didn't fit my tastes. I figured he would have just thought that I didn't like it. He had a good idea of how my mind worked after listening to me from his little van the past two days.

XV

Cloak and Dagger

I didn't know who to believe anymore. What Sophie said made sense to me, but I suspected that her husband had her brainwashed so she would believe what he wanted her to believe. The trouble was, she had brainwashed herself her whole life, so it wasn't hard to get her into that mode. The things that Hurst told me all made sense too. I guess the question was whether the German group was behind the murder or whether Bajaj was behind the murder. But, I didn't really care that much. I just wanted my life back, and I wanted to be free to not worry about being killed or being watched constantly. I wanted to see my friend alive. Living life on the edge just isn't worth it. As a musician I had felt the pressure when I went to classical symphony auditions. I met people from all over the world, and each one was one of the best bass players in his or her country. I was able to make a decent showing on the audition scene for a while, but I never won one. There was something inside of them that I couldn't match: intensity and a drive that overshadowed my own coming from very focused individuals that frankly scared me. A lot of them didn't seem happy, but they buried themselves in their music like someone addicted to pain killers. I felt the same feeling now with Sophie, Hurst, and the other players in this international game of murder. I didn't care enough to get caught up in who was right and who was wrong and how to justify it all. I just wanted my peace of mind back – my little safe world where I could work, have fun, and spend time with friends and loved ones. I was scared that I was about to lose all that and possibly lose it for the rest of my life.

Sam slept in Don's room that night, and I attempted to sleep in their living room area on a maroon colored futon. I watched Don's dark silhouette as he opened the door and drunkenly stepped by me into his room with the accompanied audio of a few mumbles and burps. I turned my head to watch the clock ticking to my left… three, three-thirty, no page from Sophie yet…four, four-fifteen… darkness.

The men in black suddenly ransacked the room again. Four intensely bright lights were shining in my face. Hurst's face suddenly appeared in the middle of them. "All right Jack," he said holding back certain fierceness, "now we are going to see what you're really made of. Go ahead Carl."

"You're going to tell us where Bajaj is or we are going to carve you up for turkey dinner you terrorist prick!" The thick-necked Carl sneered at me.

He pulled out an electric knife and turned it on. "NO!!" I screamed as I watched him slowly move it toward my thigh. I could even feel its vibrations as it inched closer. "NO! Please! I don't know anything!"

- The light of the sun illuminated the room and I groggily looked down to my pocket where Sophie's pager was softly buzzing and vibrating in my pocket. "Jesus," I gasped. The men in black were all gone, for now. I looked to the clock and saw the time as six-twenty five.

I looked at the number on the pager. It was a Chicago number: 312 865-9310. "What the hell… she's in Chicago?" I muttered. I went to Don's phone on the wall and used an expensive 1-800 line that would save him a whopping two cents a minute from the most expensive rate on earth. After two rings I heard a voice that sounded like hers. "Hello." As I began to speak, I took note of the microphone that was placed under my collar and the van that was still parked down the street. "I got your page." I responded.

"I'm glad Farley," Sophie responded and I sighed with relief.

"Where are you?"

"I can't tell you that over the phone, Farley. We need to meet somewhere, though."

"I only asked because you called from a Chicago number."

"That's my cell phone's home calling area." She giggled, "I'm still in Indianapolis silly, and I have good news: your friend is alive and doing fine. You'll probably be able to see him sometime today." "Where do you want to meet?" I asked, hoping that Hurst's thought-police had their pencil and paper ready.

"Same place as before," she said.

"When?"

"In two hours, no...wait...," she discussed something in the background with someone, but I couldn't make out the words, "make that three hours."

"Three hours it is." I said.

"You better bring your pistol Farley," she laughed again. "I have to give you a proper good-bye, you know."

"Don't worry," I played along, "it's cocked and has plenty of ammo."

"Mmmmmm."

"See you soon."

"See ya."

Sophie's tone of voice was very relaxed, almost lackadaisical. She had no idea what was going on. I suddenly realized that I was now the predator who was keeping her in the dark, not vice versa. There was no time to feel sorry for her. Survival now depended on my ability to put feelings and attachments aside.

When nine-thirty rolled around I was hanging out behind Stray Cat's I had told Don and Sam that Sophie and I had to do a little shopping before we left for our vacation. I didn't have to give much of an explanation because the only person to convince was Don, and as long as he had that gig coming, everything was either "cool" or "whatever, man."

As I walked out of their house towards Stray Cat's, one of Hurst's cronies threw me something the size of a grape but pinkish and cream in color. "Put it in your ear," he remarked as he continued to walk nonchalantly past me.

I discovered the device was a skin-colored ear piece. I placed it in my ear.

"Hello Jack," it was Hurst.

"Hello Hurst."

"I just wanted to let you know that we will be following you very closely."

"That's nice to know."

"I should hope so, Jack. I would be on my guard if I were you. You may be walking into a lion's den."

"I think I'm already in one."

"Jack," he abruptly interrupted, "we have decided not to give you a gun yet. So be careful. Always make sure you have one of your microphones within hearing distance of what's going on. Otherwise, we won't know to come in and help you if something goes wrong."

"Okey dokey"

"You are a pretty good bass player I hear."

"Is there a reason for bringing this up?"

"Yes there is – musicians are cool, or at least they know how to be cool when they need to be. I suggest you use your musician skills today if you think you need them."

"Thank you, sir."

"No problem Jack, we'll make an agent out of you yet."

I wished he was there next to me so I could punch him in the nose.

XVI

Snake Trap

I was still in the alley at 9:45 when a black Mercedes Benz limousine pulled up in front of me. The door opened and Sophie came out.

"Come on in Jack." She smiled, "I want you to meet some people."

"Where's Steve?" I looked at her intently.

"Come in Jack, you'll see." I stepped inside and sat down next to Sophie and in front of three other people facing me, one of whom was Steve with his hands and feet tied to one another. The mystery of my jacket was now solved, it was on Steve. It fit tightly over Steve's bulky arms and shoulders, helping him to show off his muscles. I could now see why he came back to our house to take it with him to Jessica's – he looked pretty good in it.

"Steve," I said as I leaned toward him.

"Easy tiger!" A German man said next to him pulling out a gun and pointing it towards Steve's head.

"Farley, this is Stephan and Liane."

"The pleasure is all yours," I replied foolishly.

"My, my," the woman named Liane replied, "not much gratitude from the spoiled American is there?" She taunted.

"Your friend Sophie here has been kind enough to give us back what was ours so we have decided to let your friend go."

"This should put you on par with Mother Teresa." I replied trying hard to hold back my anger. "Are you okay Steve?"

Steve paused and glanced first at the German duo before he replied, "I'm OK."

"We are not concerned about what you know," the German bimbo proceeded, "because now that we have back what is rightfully ours, you have no solid evidence to prove anything."

It was dark inside the limo and it was difficult to see their faces very clearly. The only light was a small, over-head light that was conveniently pointed right in my face. The German couple seemed to be thin and fair-complexioned with blonde or light brown hair. There was a wall between our seats and the driver so the only view out was to the side and the tinted windows made that sight difficult to see as well.

"You don't need to look out there." The man named Stephan warned, "You will see where we are going soon enough." His voice was authoritarian and arrogant as well. *I am just glad that Steve is still alive.* I thought to myself.

We finally got out of the car in a wooded area. We walked down a gravel road for what seemed like a few minutes until we reached a large white house with brown and red trim. Next to the front door was a small statue of a Bavarian milk maid happily churning butter. She had a blue dress and a blue bonnet on. The house's style of architecture was old, probably turn of the century.

As we walked up the front porch, the steps creaked and moaned. Sophie held my hand and massaged my arm, which she had been doing ever since I uttered my Mother Teresa comment. In front of us, Stephan held Steve by one arm with the gun pointing in his side and Liane surveyed the whole scene from behind with her own pistol.

"As I was saying earlier, Mr. Farley," she couldn't even call me by my entire last name even in formal conversation, "Stephan and I are not concerned about what you and your friend Steve know about our international behaviors because you have no evidence of that now. But, unfortunately your friend Steve put up quite a fight when we tried to get our film from his jacket and as a result we ended up killing his friend whom I believe is named Jessica. We did not know the film was in actuality not in his jacket, nor did we realize that he was not you, Mr. Farley, until we had a chance to talk to our good friend Sophie here. So we will have to discuss a few things about these matters inside our little house before we let you all go."

"Can I ask permission to speak without you using your gun on my friend?" I asked with my head downward towards my collar to make sure Mr. Hurst and his buddies knew the situation.

"I just said I prefer we discuss these matters inside." Stephan replied while turning around to glare at me as he pulled Steven even closer to his side and his gun.

Now I was freaking out. Did these two share the same brain or something? One of them says one thing and later the other claims he was the one who said it.

We were greeted at the door by a six foot ten, three hundred-fifty pound German henchman named Simon. He was dressed in all black, tight-fitting clothing just as Stephan and Liane were, aside from a pair of colored gloves and scarves merely for fashion sense. I half expected Deter to pop out from behind Simon: *"And now is the time on Sprockets when we dance!"* I also considered asking Stephan if we were in a Calvin Klein commercial, but glancing at Stephan's gun told me to shut my trap and watch my smart mouth. The inside of the house was predominantly white and decorated with some reds and blues and other solid colors. It had a similar Devo feeling to it: that 1960s, Euro-modern flair with impeccable cleanliness. I glanced around trying to find the lava lamps. We passed by a bathroom and I took note of its location.

We entered a small, narrow hallway with mirrors and banisters on both sides with a large metal black door between us and the next room. It would have made a for a perfect small ballet studio. "You will have to take all of your clothes off now, Mr. Farley." Liane said to me.

"What?" I asked pleadingly.

"You must remove your clothes; we cannot risk you bringing in unknown items at this point." "You won't need your clothes anyway, Farley." Sophie smiled at me.

"Please," my voice was choking. Having all these guns around was bad enough, but no clothes and no contact with Hurst was too much. How would I be able to let them know when it was safe to come in? We already had a confession to their killing Jessica, but the current situation simply made it impossible to make a bust.

"Sophie, why don't you take your clothes off too." Stephan smiled, "It might make him feel better."

"Let's all take off our clothes!" Liane chimed in

Sure enough, everyone but Steve stripped naked. I guess they figured that Steve had been through enough already. Simon was left to watch him in the ballet studio while the four of us went into a room that I will never forget.

A dim red glow filled the entire area. A humid wet mist gently blew through the room and came to the center to spin into a small, miniature funnel cloud that spun upward into a large black hole in the ceiling where I guess it was recycled out to come back in though the walls. There were four or five large round beds with dozens of pillows on them and two Jacuzzi whirlpools at the back of the room. The whole area was about thirty-five by forty feet. There were four alcoves evenly spread inside the walls of the room that contained naked statues of Greek figures. In one alcove there was a large bong at the feet of the statue and a salad bowl filled with marijuana or some other hash or hemp-type drug.

"Would you like some opium, Mr. Farley?" Stephan asked as he reached into a drawer under the alcove containing the bong. He momentarily set his gun next to the bong, but he was a good twenty feet away from me at this point.

"If you want to know what I'd like, I'd like for me and my friend to go home."

"Patience," Liane chimed while looking my body over. At the other side of the room I noticed a large red dragon painted on the wall and a picture of some odd-looking plant underneath it.

An ominous feeling inside me knew what was coming. For a moment, a pang of sympathy shot through me for all people around the world who had been abducted through human trafficking and then used for horrible, unscrupulous purposes. They were slaves, treated like animals, made to do anything for the amusement of their captors. I was now the slave of this German couple. How long would they keep me, and what would they make me do?

They did make me do things with Sophie, and it was while a gun was being pointed directly at us. I remember Sophie saying, "It's going to be OK, Farley; you'll get out of here soon, I promise." Sometime after that I remember crying. And then sometime later Sophie said, "Just try to relax, Jack. Focus on me and try to forget them." When I had a moment of clarity, I made a small request, "I want to go over to that bed," and pointed to a bed that had a cupid-like statue over it that was holding a bow with a sharply-tipped arrow.

Much later on, I was able to recall some more of the things that

Sophie told me during this ordeal, sometimes through a whisper, and one time when pulling me aside to emotionally comfort me. Stephan and Liane's organization was involved in the drug trade, among other things. Their organization was slowly dying, but they still had some delusional idea that they were going to annihilate the Palestinians and the Jews; the Jews because they hated them and the Palestinians because they wanted to take over the oil and the drug trade with the Middle East. They were somewhat entranced by my "Midwestern straight-forward earnestness and innocence".

After I had requested the bed below the cupid statue, I saw the excitement in the German couple's faces, and they followed Sophie and me from a safe distance to this new location. "Pick me up and carry me; they'll like that," Sophie suggested. I picked her up and carried her. While I carried her, Liane quickly trotted up to Sophie's ear, whispered something to her, giggled, and scampered back to Stephan's side. Sophie looked up to me and whispered, "She wants to join in pretty soon." I knew I had to act fast to get out of this situation.

On this new bed, after taking a few instructions from the German couple, I put my plan into play. I jerked my body up at one point towards the Cupid's arrow, and its sharp tip gashed into my forearm.

"Arghhh!" I yelled and jumped back from Sophie.

"What is it darling?" She asked me as if hypnotized.

"Damn it. I'm bleeding!" The blood was trickling down my arm and through the fingers of my other hand as I pretended to try and subdue the flow but in actuality squeezed my arm to cause more blood to come out faster.

"It's not a huge cut," I said, "but I have a blood condition. My blood is thin and it doesn't clot properly."

"Oh scheisse!" Liane cried, "We're going to get blood all over our clean white house and all over my silk sheets!"

"Where's your bathroom?" I asked Stephan already knowing where it was.

"On the other side of the house."

"Damn, that is going to take too long." I made a very short pause, "I have some band aids in my right-hand pants pocket."

"Will that be enough?" Sophie asked. "It looks like you're bleeding a lot."

"It's my condition. My band aids have a special chemical on them that helps my blood clot. My doctor prescribed them to me. Why don't I just go get them, my pants are right outside the door." Stephan looked at Liane. "No," he put his arm up in front of me, his gun lying close to his other hand. "Let Simon get the band aids and bring them."

Stephan walked a few feet over to a white pillar and pushed an intercom button, "Simon, look in Mr. McFarland's pants pockets for some band aids."

"Right hand pocket," I interjected.

"Right hand pocket. Bring them in quickly."

"What about the man I am watching?" Simon's voice came through faintly through the intercom.

"Just make sure he is tied to the chair, fool. We need those band aids. There is blood all over here."

Simon came in with the small flat box of band aids. I picked out the one that Hurst demonstrated to me just to be extra sure. I put on the band aid and raised my arm to my face and began to moan, bobbing up and own, "Oh it hurts, ummm," I then put my mouth directly over it while my head was down and whispered incredibly fast, "Come in now, come in now. We are in the northwest corner of the house, we are in the northwest corner of the house. There are two, possibly three with handguns, come in now."

"Are you OK, Mr. McFarland?" asked Stephan.

"Herr Schlangenstein, do you want me to go back and watch the prisoner or -?" Simon began. "I told you not to call me that in front of new company, stupid ass!"

"I am not trying to be an ass with Mr. McFarland, sir..." Simon was pretty dull.

"What did you say about me?!" I yelled with testosterone and took the helm.

"With all due respect Mr. Farland, I did not mean..."

"That's McFarland, idiot. If you're such a big man then let's see what you got, wuss!!" I had to keep the distraction going; otherwise, Hurst and his men would not be able to take them by surprise. So, as masochistic as my charade seemed, I knew it was necessary. I stepped down off the bed and started to shove the giant's shoulder. I believe I even noticed a smile on Stephan's face as if he was enjoying the drama. He sat down on a padded round green chair and prepared for his own private Jerry Springer show. "Go ahead," he said to Simon, "but be easy on the poor fellow."

"Farley!" Sophie pleaded.

Before I knew what hit me, I was lifted up and brought down on one of Simon's knees right in the middle of my back. I felt like I was immediately paralyzed. Somehow I managed to get up and grab one of his legs. I lifted it up, pushed him off balance and he fell to the floor. I ran up to his head and cracked him one right across the jaw. Simon did not even flinch and shoved me back into Stephan who pushed me back into the fight. I backed away from the giant and kept my person within a few feet of Stephan, noticing his gun now pointing downward in his right hand.

With my ears perked and my senses piqued, I then heard the sound. The door was broken in and as the first vibration of the sound wave hit my ear, I lunged for Stephan and wrapped my arms around him, knocking the gun from his hand.

"Hands up and against the wall! Keep your feet spread apart!!" The men in black announced over a megaphone. Liane fired a shot into one of the men's body armor and she was immediately showered with bullets - so much for her clean house. So there we were: three naked people against the wall with their hands and feet spread apart, one naked woman dead on the floor, and one giant, former pro-wrestler whimpering his innocence to the whole affair.

XVII

Turtle's Revisited

The CIA did not want us to give testimony to them at the Pentagon, so we were directed to the FBI. At the Midwest FBI headquarters in Chicago, Steve and I identified the German couple via photograph and signed and swore to countless different testimonies for a period of three days. I was allowed to work half days in the morning for those three days and they even sent me back and forth from Indianapolis to Chicago by private jet.

I tried once to talk to Hurst, who had become nearly impossible to get a word with since the time of the bust, about what was going to happen to Sophie. From my knowledge, she and her alleged terrorist husband had nothing to do with the matters of Jessica and the murder of Halachmi in Israel. I suppose I couldn't be sure about the latter fact, but I did hear that the German couple had become the prime suspects for that murder as well and that before she finally died on the floor, Liane had admitted it to one of the CIA operatives. I don't know if she wanted to gloat or what, but my guess is that she wanted Stephan to suffer at least a little bit too.

The same night as the bust, we were all flown by helicopter

to Chicago. Just after landing – while we were both being led separate ways, me walking freely and Sophie handcuffed, Sophie looked at me with very sad eyes. "I'm sorry Jack." I looked at her with a sense of deep pity and she added, "Stay the way you are. Stay innocent."

No words came to my lips. I simply watched them take her away to who knows what fate.

A couple of weeks later on world news, I saw a report on the capture and trial of Emile Bajaj for a long list of international terrorist crimes and activities. Sophie must have given the CIA or the FBI the information they wanted. "You did the right thing, Sophie," I murmured to myself. I did not make it back to Turtle's for another two months. It was hard for me to get comfortable enough to be my old self again. Steve quit tending bar and enrolled at University of Bloomington for a communications degree. He was getting ready to move down to Bloomington in a few weeks. The night when I returned to where the whole ordeal started featured a young talented saxophonist who had a killer drummer. The drummer even played with the Indianapolis Symphony Orchestra, so this saxophonist was knocking on wood. They opened up with *Body and Soul.* I closed my eyes and let the music wash over me. I am not sure how long it was, but the last solo in the song was nearly over when I heard, "Excuse me sir, but if you need a place to sleep, there is a homeless shelter down on Massachusetts Street."

I opened my eyes to see Samantha sitting on the bar stool next to mine. "Hello!" I blurted out, somewhat startled.

"Aren't you going to offer me a cigarette?" she smiled.

"I quit smoking, but I have a light if you need one."

"That's OK."

"How's Don?"

"I don't know. I left him."

"I'm sorry to hear that."

"Don't be. He's on probation now as we speak."

"You two guys did make an odd couple, him being a musician and you, well, you know.

"Yeah, I know. I guess opposites attract."

I thought for a brief moment and looked down at my drink. Then I looked up at her again, "You look great."

"Thanks, so do you."

"We should maybe get together and do something really, really boring sometime."

"Boring sounds great." She smiled very wide and sighed. I took her by the hand and rubbed her first knuckle with my thumb. She reciprocated with one of her fingers. I smiled and turned back to the band. They started up on *Don't Get Around Much Anymore.*

I smiled at Sam: "Let's make this our song."

THE END

PART II
Charming the Snake

I

Classical Music

He placed his bow on the string. When he made his first down-bow motion, a smoky puff of rosin rose into the air. Edgar sawed on that string, but the sound that came forth was not that of a saw. It was strident, laser-like – having the quality of a great muscular wrestler who was now wowing his audience by doing an intricate quickstep on the dance floor with the adroit dexterity of a seasoned professional ballroom dancer. Such was my experience as I watched the great Edgar Meyer play his bass violin at the University of Bloomington. Then the other half of the duo stroked his magic-wand bow across his violin strings. The world-renowned violinist Joshua Bell was actually playing the static, accompanying music for Edgar's solo. We all watched in awe as the grand duo played piece after piece in front of all of the music students in the top-ranked Jordan School of Music at the University of Bloomington in Indiana. I was a graduate student at the time, having already skipped and swapped between two different graduate school programs. No one said a word during that performance. There was absolute silence as the two musicians played. It was fall in 1996, and I had already completed my first year of playing requirements toward a master's degree in bass violin performance at the music school. People can argue back and forth about which school had the highest ranking. Usually the argument was between University of Bloomington, the Eastman School of Music, and the Julliard School of Music. A bass player in our program at Bloomington had won the most recent big city symphony audition for the St. Louis symphony orchestra, so we currently had the bragging rights. I had no intention of actually receiving a master's degree, unless it happened by accident. I just wanted to be enrolled in the program so I could receive bass instruction from the two most highly rated bass teachers in the world who both happened to teach at this school. Of course, there were other reasons why actually completing a degree was far down my list, which we will find out about very soon. In the meantime though, this beautiful scene deserves a little framework in modern history to explain to the reader why it was really so incredibly remarkable:

Just ten years after this performance in the very first decade of the next millennium, Joshua Bell, still considered by many the best violin soloist in the world, would play in a Washington D.C. subway – no one even noticed it was him. People walked by him in the hundreds, and eventually by the thousands after a couple of hours passed by. Only a handful would stop to listen to him play. Hardly anyone knew who he was. Most of them were too busy going to where they needed to be, or they were already locked into their own world of electronic music with their cursed lousy iPods. I believe after playing for three hours, he had collected about forty dollars in his violin case. This was not because Joshua had lost any of his talent. It is because our country and the world had lost its sense of what performance art is – especially fine performance art in the area of music. This beautiful time in history – the 1990s - will never even remotely return to our culture. The computer giants in technology, graphics, service providers, search engines, and whatever other Big-Brother corporation system that justifies itself as the future in technology has ensured our country and the world that the days of experiencing live, acoustic, fine music or going in person to a music store to pick out albums based on the beautiful creativity of the album cover art are gone forever. I pity all young people today who think that watching something on YouTube is anything like listening to it in person. I have played inside a symphony orchestra. I have heard the beautiful sounds all around me being played by dedicated musicians who took time to practice and tune their instruments. I even hear the little beautiful mistakes – YES MISTAKES - that occur whenever you are listening to real live music. *There* is something you *never* hear with any of the computer generated, overly engineered music that is put out so rapidly in our ever-so-enlightened new millennium. How about that machine that changes the pitch the singers sing while they perform, auto-tune? That in itself is a microcosm of what the new millennium and giant computer corporations have done to the fine arts. Everything will be played by machines. Anything less might actually produce a mistake. *Oh no! Not a sign of being human!* Of course, with the machines we lose all the little subtleties like inflection, crescendo, diminuendo and anything else that a human musician can provide spontaneously that a machine cannot. How does the modern music industry get around that? Simple – nothing is spontaneous. You really think that when your favorite pop singer tells the band to quiet down and starts "jamming" that the band is being spontaneous? The singer and the producers have planned and rehearsed that jam hundreds of times already. And when the singer isn't feeling up to snuff, turn on the pitch changing machine and then he can just talk the words while the machine makes the correct pitches. So back in the 1990s, before computers had completely taken over our culture and the way everyone communicates with each other, beautiful interactions took place. People got off their lazy butts and walked to music stores or walked to their local bar to hear someone play live music. Blues, yes blues was popular in the 1990s. Stevie Ray Vaughn, what a guitarist! Let's hear a machine play like him! People followed the Grateful Dead again in the 1990s, a band who became well known in the 1960s because everyone valued how spontaneous the music was. No one can say that the Dead always sounded good, because they didn't. They let their human side shine. Some jams were not so good, but other jams were brilliant. That is the way it is supposed to be when music is played and performed live and spontaneously by human beings. Now we have all become too lazy. Too lazy to walk to a performance – it's easier to click on the iPod. Too lazy to walk to a music store – it's easier to buy music on Amazon. Artistic experiences that have real depth to them typically require the listeners or viewers to challenge themselves or stretch themselves in some way. It requires some patience to listen to a full symphony. Hell, a Mahler symphony can push close to two hours, maybe even longer. Good luck accomplishing that with a population that won't do anything that requires more patience than clicking a mouse! I hope no one injures an index finger or gets carpal tunnel. How will they click their mouse? Oh well, such is life.

So, why am I back in music school? Well, after the whole ordeal with Sophie and the missing microfilm and the German terrorist group and the CIA and all the other international intrigue stuff that I had no business being involved in, I felt a void. Yes, I felt a void. I had a nice relationship with Samantha which yes, is the name she actually uses. I believe we were in love, or as in love as I could be at that time in my life. I was slow to mature in many ways, but I reached a new level with Samantha. The phrase "I love you" was exchanged many times between the two of us, which was something that had not happened for me before. I meant it when I said it, too. I cried in front of her and shared things about myself and my past that I had never shared with any woman before. As the summer ended in 1995, Samantha had a great opportunity to train to become a top level operative with the CIA, although she had to go to Baltimore to do so. I was also making plans during the end of that summer. I couldn't face another year of insurance work after having experienced another taste of living life on the edge with Sophie. I wasn't looking for dangerous work, but more exciting work. My bug to play music on a higher, more serious level took over me. I was fed up with the recording industry, but the purity of classical music appealed to me. I saw it as the best of both worlds. Playing in a big city symphony like Chicago or New York offered musicians the opportunity to play regularly, and to stay in the same place. Those musicians always played in the same music hall. They could buy houses and raise families. And, they had time to spend with their families. I was thinking about things like family now. I couldn't provide a family opportunity for Sam – not that she was interested in a family – but being with her gave me a desire to want to have a family. So, I applied to the country's top music schools, one was in Baltimore where Sam and I had a suspicion she might get stationed. The best bass teacher at the Baltimore school would not be available to me. This had been probably my worst audition when I auditioned for schools. Baltimore offered me another bass teacher who was essentially a nobody. None of the best bass teachers in Indianapolis had ever heard of the man. As much as it hurt the both of us, we knew that it would ruin our relationship if either of us was held back from our dreams because of it. Sam's dream was to have a bigger role in the CIA, and going to Baltimore would help her accomplish that. My dream was to win a spot in a big city orchestra, and my best opportunity to accomplish that turned out to be going to the University of Bloomington. So, in fall of 1995 when the internet had barely just begun, we attempted to stay together under those impossible restrictions that occur within the realm of a "long distance relationship". We did communicate by email, which was still very new but still very underutilized by most of the population at that time. I even did some technological trailblazing and learned how to have a live chat – text only of course back then – which we enjoyed very much. But missing each other's company and touch turned out to be too difficult. For these reasons and a myriad of others, we ended up drifting apart and breaking up around three months after she left for Baltimore.

But that is not all that was going on during the end of the summer and the beginning of fall. I had already picked the University of Bloomington by the time August rolled around and paid for the first semester's tuition, but I could have made another one of my infamous transfers to the Baltimore school later in the year. Something else kept me in Bloomington. Sam had already left for Baltimore in the last week of August and I was packing my things for Bloomington when a not-so-old acquaintance paid me a visit in my little rented house on College Avenue in Indianapolis, Indiana. There was a knock on my door a little after lunch time, and I went to answer. I opened the door.

II

Seeing an Old Fiend

"Good afternoon, Jack," it was Patrick Hurst, the director or assistant director of the CIA. I did not remember his official title, but he was one of the biggest wigs in the agency. He had been the director earlier in the year, but he received some kind of partial demotion for not operating under agency rules. I was not pleased to see him.

"Mr. Hurst" I offered him the obligatory hand shake and we commenced with the ritual. "What are you doing here?"

"Jack, how have you been, my boy?"

"I have been with Samantha all summer, you know, 'Tracey' as you call her. I thought you would have known that."

"No, she doesn't share all the details of her romantic life with me. I only pry into agents' lives if there is reason to suspect their romances are detrimental to the agency." I did not believe his words. "Well, we have been together. She already left for her Baltimore training, but we are going to stay together. Our programs are only two years at most and we should be able to make it through that."

"We shall see. I hope the best for both of you. May I come in and sit down, Jack?" I had been blocking the doorway from him.

"Oh, certainly. Come in." What else was I going to say to a man like him? After we both sat down at a coffee table and I brought out a beer for him, he stood up and began to walk around the room in his old pacing mode. I knew a long speech was coming. I was afraid to hear what its objective was.

"Jack, you're absolutely right to let Sam – and I do call her that when we are not on an assignment – go to Baltimore and receive some better training for upper level CIA work. But you know, there is someone in this room who has the ability to execute upper level CIA work without that training."

"You must be talking about yourself," I responded.

"No Jack, I'm too old for field work. Even though you're right about my abilities – my body is just too old now to execute the work." There was a pause. I gave him a look that must have looked like either a lost puppy or a deer in the headlights. He continued, "You amazed all of us on that Herr Schlangenstein assignment when you took on that ex-wrestler and called us in on your Band-Aid hidden microphone. And you and I both know what else you were doing during that time that makes it incredibly hard for any man to think clearly."

Hurst was referring to an incident that I had actually been trying very hard to forget. Two members of a German rogue terrorist organization had abducted and then driven me, Sophie, and my roommate Steve to an isolated house in the woods where they forced Sophie and me to do very private things in front of them at gunpoint. I was able to begin the act with Sophie because I still had many feelings for her at the time, but before the Germans could join us, I had found a way to cut myself, put on my Band-Aid microphone, secretly call the rescue team, and fake

105

a fight with their giant henchman to distract everyone while the swat team made their way into the house to surprise the terrorists with a gun barrage and finally arrest all the survivors. "What about it?" I said. "I had to do it. I had no choice. It was either do that or die, basically."

"I know Jack," he responded, "but that is a mentality that CIA agents have to tap into as well. And the way you did it was masterful. Most men would have ended up dead in a situation like that, and by most I mean 99.9%."

"What are you getting at, Hurst?" I was either losing my patience or becoming desperately scared, "I don't care if I am good at it. What difference does it make if I am good at it?"

"Do you want to know what ended up happening to Sophia, Jack?" I put my head down and took a long breath. I *did* want to know.

"Yes, tell me."

Hurst smiled conservatively. "She works for us, Jack. She gave us more information than what we needed to put away her husband Emile. Her skills were too good to pass up. She is serving out her domestic service sentence by working for us. She is an agent for us for about the next two years, and guess where we have placed her."

I didn't want to know. "How about Terre Haute, Indiana – lots of espionage there."

"You're not far off, Jack. She will be at the University of Bloomington, about an hour and a half away from Terre Haute. She is enrolled in the graduate music program for piano performance. She has been practicing for the past two months and her skills are back to what they used to be. She was easily accepted into the Jordan School of Music. They even gave her a scholarship!"

I was dumbfounded. I stood there with my mouth open. Why? I thought. What the hell is he trying to do to me?

"Sir," I said, "with all due respect to you and your high position in the United States clandestine services, what in hell are you doing to me? Why in God's name would you station an agent there, and of all people why Sophie, and I know that you know I am enrolled in that school this fall, and what kind of sadistic game are you playing with me?" I ended my stream-of-consciousness rant with a frustrated exhale.

Hurst took another short walk to one of my windows. His demeanor changed. Maybe he was waiting for my emotional outburst to change it. "Well, Jack is pretty unappreciative isn't he? Does little Jack know that we have been protecting his name for the past two and a half months from terrorists who were affiliated with Emile Bajaj? Does he understand that my agency does have other very important matters that we could be spending time on and engaging agents in? Does he know that we are at no obligation after ninety days to protect him and his name any longer?"

"What do you want from me, Hurst? You obviously want something."

"You will work with us, Jack. We have an issue going on right now at the University of Bloomington. We suspect a physics professor there to be recruiting young men from around the world and training them to commit violent crimes against our democracy. He could be divulging military secrets to these men and doing it under the protective umbrella of the University. We think he might be plotting terrorist attacks against the U.S."

"Mr. Hurst, for once you have not done your homework. That is a huge school and I am going to be in the music department which is halfway across campus from the physics department."

"Ah, so it is. But, this professor comes over to the music school three times a week because he is also a professor of music who conducts the top orchestra and also directs the chamber music department's piano ensembles."

"Oh," I replied very unintelligently.

"You and Sophia will work as a team. You will win a spot in the top orchestra. You don't have to be the first chair bass Jack, you just need to get into the section. Sophie will get involved with chamber music. You know, Jack, one of the chamber groups is playing Schubert's *Trout Quintet*. This requires both bass and piano along with three other string players. You and Sophie will be in that chamber group."

"How am I supposed to work with Sophie? Hurst, you must have an idea of what I have been through with her. I am trying to forget her. She is not a good influence on me. Could you maybe assign another CIA agent who is good at music or physics instead of her?"

"No Jack, the two of you work together like no two agents I have ever seen before. It's like one of you can tell what the other is thinking. It's remarkable. Jack, don't you see the greater good that you are serving here? What higher calling can you have than this? You are serving and protecting your country and your way of life. The group that this professor is rallying up is primarily men from Muslim countries. Do you know what life is like for people in countries like that? Do you know what life is like for women there? America does not need extremists from those countries terrorizing us. We will never succumb to their way of life. We will not tolerate it. To put it bluntly Jack, using some of your favorite words, we must kick their ass before they can kick ours." His word choice startled me. You rarely here old conservative guys like him talking that way.

"And besides," I added, "I don't really have a choice, do I?"

"Now Jack, don't think that way. It is very negative, even though it's true."

"I thought your agency was going to provide me with a new name and identity and all that." "Well Jack, you chose to keep seeing Samantha after knowing she was involved in the German assignment and even started living with her – in sin I might add." Hurst was showing his old-timer values again. "That made it difficult to redefine your identity as did your decision to go back to playing bass and staying here in Indiana. People are going to recognize you, Jack. You're playing the same instrument, you haven't changed your name and it would do no good to change it because too many people will know who you are anyway in this state. So we have had to work extra hard to protect you. When you land a big audition somewhere away from Indiana, changing your name and identity will probably be easier. But, your choices this summer have made it impossible for our agency to furnish you with a new identity at this point in time."

"What will I tell Samantha about this?" I remarked.

"You won't tell her a thing about this," Hurst replied.

"But she's in the agency –" I stopped.

"You know as well as I do, Jack. *You* tell *me* why."

I paused for a moment then recited like a Kit from *Knight Rider*, "Because any information given to her that she does not need to know might jeopardize the mission."

"And…"

"And it could put her in danger."

"Exactly."

"Still, it will be hard to lie to her. I love her, Hurst, I really do."

Hurst became tender for a moment and put his hand on my shoulder.

"I know you do, Jack. So, because you love her, you will do what's best for her and protect her." I looked at him with a small tear in my eye, "Yes, I will."

"And that's how we feel about our work here in the agency, Jack. We love our country and our families that live in this country. We will do anything to protect it and them."

"This is going to be weird."

"Aww, Jack. This is your weakness, you know. So you have a history with Sophie. And yes, I may be old, but old men also have the ability to recognize beautiful women, you know. She is a strikingly beautiful girl. You have great taste when it comes to who you are interested in. But, you have lousy judgment when it comes to controlling when to think and when not to think about the powerful beauty that such women possess. A beautiful woman can be like a bomb, Jack. You have to know when to let it explode, how to handle it correctly, when to diffuse it, when to run from it, and perhaps even when to let it explode on someone else," he gave me an odd sideways glance. I didn't quite get his last analogy in that list.

"When to let it explode on someone else?" I repeated questioningly.

"Forget that last comparison. I mean learn how to control what your mind thinks about, Jack. You ever hear that quote 'your mind is a field ripe for harvest'?"

"Of course, I live in Indiana, don't I? My father used to say that to me all the time."

"Well start applying that when it comes to the powerful physical attraction that some women have."

"Hurst, look, if a beautiful woman like Sophie or Sam was making passes at you, I'd like to see you resist."

"You sound like the people who are defending Clinton." The Jennifer Flowers scandal about President Clinton had just subsided and the new Paula Jones scandal had just started to arrive in the media. "Jack you basically had a gun to your head forcing you to have sex with someone – but of course, we both know it was not all that forced. Just imagine that someone has a gun to your head, but this time they are forcing you NOT to think about sex."

"I don't want to think about someone having a gun to my head, period."

"Well," Hurst said as he put his fedora hat back on his head – talk about an old timer, "my young friend, as you get further in life and wiser, you may find the times when you are acting as if a gun is to your head are the times when you get the most done and perform beyond your wildest expectations. I watched him head towards the door. There was more I needed to know. He pacified me on that somewhat while he opened the door and turned around. "We will be in touch Jack. Go ahead and move into campus. The graduate residence hall you will be staying at is actually perfect. Maybe you didn't realize it, but this residence hall's knick-name is the United Nations. You'll find out why. I think you will easily audition into the top orchestra, but if you don't, we will work with the school to put you in there anyway. Also, you will be automatically enrolled in that chamber music group with Sophie. Auf wiedersehen, my friend. Remember, you're a cool musician. Stay cool, and don't get too hot under the collar."

He left. The bastard.

III

Getting Acclimated with Bloomington

The first week in Bloomington was filled with signing documents, reviewing schedules, finding instrument locker combinations, getting keys, moving items from my rusty van into my dorm room, getting parking passes, finding out where one can and cannot park, finding the buildings and rooms where classes and rehearsals take place, and many more very uninteresting but necessary details. Parking in particular was a complete pain in the ass. Not since I had spent time in New York City had I ever seen so many parking restrictions. There was basically no other place on campus where I could park my van other than the residence hall parking lot. Every other street and building on the over 40,000 humanly populated campus had strict parking restrictions with threats to tow within twenty minutes of parking there. And people WERE towed all the time. You saw tow trucks several times a day pulling away cars that were parked in a restricted area, or those yellow tickets under the windshield wipers of such a car. There goes about $75.00 for that car owner. Basically, the only way to get around campus was to take the bus or to ride a bike. I purchased an old ten-speed at a local bike store for the warmer months. When winter rolled around, I was forced to take the bus. It was just like a city bus. No one talked. Hardly anyone ever knew each other. Of course, if you were going off campus, then you could find some reasonable place to park in the city of Bloomington. However, when you would return to campus, you would have to wait and fight for an available parking spot in your designated lot. These waits could be twenty minutes or longer depending on the day. So, I would use my ten-speed that fall to go from building to building in the music school.

Hurst was correct about my residence hall. It was a graduate residence hall, which is what I wanted. There was a meal plan in the hall so that I would not have to cook and therefore have more time to work on my music. But I soon discovered what his "United Nations" comment meant.

I was literally one of about twelve people in the entire eight story residence hall that spoke English as a first language. Students from Germany, Spain, France, Jordan, Egypt, you name it, all lived there. They mostly would sit together during meals according to which country they were from. Of course everyone COULD speak English, but conversing with someone who speaks English as a second language is not the same as talking with a native speaker. I had always enjoyed the subtleties of conversation such as sarcasm, humor, hyperbole, etc. No such qualities existed when talking to these exchange students. I ended up beginning to feel quite lonely. I was able to latch on to a young Jewish man who had grown up in of all places, Baltimore. Melvin ended up being one of my closest friends at Eisenberg Residence Hall. I might have had a chance for a closer relationship with women there, but of course, I was still in that long distance relationship with Sam. The first few weeks at the hall, I noticed some women looking at me and even smiling at me during meals. I would smile back, but I would not sit with them. Some of them were quite attractive. It seemed the girls from the Germanic countries were the ones who took interest. Germany, Austria, and also Switzerland, Sweden, Denmark. I think they liked my light brown hair that I had grown back out and the red tint to my new goatee facial hair that was emerging. Of course, I do also have those dreamy blue eyes – but enough about me.

So my eating group ended up being Melvin, a girl from Jordan named Palak, a girl from Russia named Dyena, a girl from Germany named Diana (and of course I had trouble pronouncing the difference between the Russian girl's and the German girl's names), and sometimes a young man also from Germany named Ludwig. Dyena and Diana were both on the cute side, but none of us flirted. The cultural gap made that difficult anyway. We were all there to get an education and we were all very serious about what we were doing. As the year rolled on I would invite this group to of all places, my parents' house over the next summer and drive them all to Chicago to show them around. I really enjoyed their company. They were all great people.

So at the end of the first week, I had been familiarized with the campus and had auditioned for my orchestra placement. There were four orchestras, the top one being the Philharmonic. I learned a day after my audition day that I had indeed made it into the Philharmonic. I believe I made it solely on my talent, but perhaps Hurst made a call to the Dean of the University – I will never know. I held my own during rehearsals though, and no one ever questioned my abilities or gave me odd glances during rehearsals. There were eight bass players in that orchestra. I was seated fifth for the first concert. Apparently, the first through fourth chair would rotate for each concert and the fifth through eighth chairs would rotate as well. So I would be sixth for the second concert, seventh for the third, eighth for the fourth, and then back to fifth chair for the fifth concert and so on.

Just as Hurst had said, I was enrolled in the chamber music program as well to perform Schubert's *Trout Quintet*. To be honest, I was not a big fan of the piece even though it appears in one of my favorite movies, the 1970s version of *The Great Gatsby*. I was even less of a fan of having to rehearse with Sophie. At the end of the first week, I received a phone message in my dorm room from none other than the international woman of mystery herself.

I returned the call that Friday night; to my shock, she was home and actually answered the phone. Enter now one of my life's most awkward conversations:

"Hello."

"Um...hello. Is Sophie Mitchell there?"

"Yes Jack, it's me."

"How did you know it was me?" I did not think my voice was that distinctive.

"It's a relatively new device called caller ID. I'll show you it sometime."

"Oh." A long pause ensued. I am sure it was probably only a few seconds, but it felt like ten years.

"Um, how have you been?" I gave in and began a very slightly friendly tone.

"Good. All things considered. How about yourself?"

"Oh, about the same...about the same."

Ok, I had asked her how she was, she had asked me how I was; now I wanted to get down to business.

"I was returning your phone call, Sophie. What's up?"

"We need to get together this weekend."

"Fine."

"My place would be the best."

"I agree. I am cooped up in this little dorm room."

"There are other reasons. You'll see when you get here, Jack." Her voice was serious and business-like just like mine. But also there was just a shade of tenderness. She gave me her address and made a time to meet the next evening. That was fine with me. I was not going out anywhere. I certainly wasn't going to have any dates. I could practice my bass violin Saturday during the day. My practicing sessions now lasted anywhere from four to eight hours depending on whether there were any auditions or performance exams approaching. I was quickly learning the downside of becoming a serious classical musician: the practicing never ends.

IV

The Snake Sheds Her Skin

For the remainder of Friday night I talked to Samantha over the phone. Our phone conversations were becoming longer and longer. As the weeks would later roll by, this pattern would continue. Twenty minute conversations gradually morphed into two to even three hour conversations. This made developing friendships in my new environment very difficult. About an hour or more each evening had to be reserved for my phone conversation with Sam while everyone else on campus was being social with each other. Sam started to become that horrible adjective used by many men known as "clingy". Like me, she too felt lonely and isolated. She said she needed to go out and meet more people. I agreed. I felt like saying to her that having less phone conversations at night would actually allow both of us to do that – but I knew that was out of the question. Truth be told, I enjoyed the conversations most of the time as well. I just felt they dragged on too long. The best parts of the conversations, of course, would be when we would talk more intimately with each other. This often kept me going nights. But sadly, it still wasn't anywhere close to being as satisfying as actually being together in the same place, able to hold each other's hand and look into each other's eyes. Sam and I agreed that I should try and fly out to see her in person at least once every two months for a weekend. I scheduled a flight for the middle of October. That visit mostly went well. But, things began to crumble soon afterwards. When I went to visit Sophie the first Saturday of September, Sam and I were still very official and very much a couple.

I arrived at Sophie's house. It was as normal as normal can be: a one-story ranch house with a small back yard within a chain-link fence. It had a small basement that I could see from the outside, nothing extraordinary. It was a beige-tan color with a cedar exterior. The trim was dark brown. A small three step front porch led up to the front door. I rang the doorbell and waited.

Before leaving for her house, my goal was to look as normal as I possibly could. There was no reason to dress up or do my hair any better than I usually did. There was no reason to purposely look bad. Either extreme would give too much credence to Sophie's former power over me. I wore a very average shirt, pants, shoes, and socks. I put on exactly the same amount of after shave as I always did. Never have I tried so hard to not look noticeable.

Sophie came to the door. She opened it. Our eyes met for only an instant as she said, "Hello Jack, come in." After this quick message, both of our gazes stayed low. Eye contact seemed to be uncomfortable for both of us.

"Come downstairs with me. I have to show you some things." Her tone was business-like, matter-of-fact, but not harsh or authoritative. I liked it because overall it felt like she was talking to me as an equal. It also started to make me feel a new emotion that I had rarely felt for Sophie – I felt a little sorry for her. She was probably even lonelier here in Bloomington than I was. I didn't let this sympathy take me over though, not by any means. I was going to apply Hurst's recommendation: consider that there is a gun pointing to your head. I imagined this and told myself I was not to think of Sophie in a romantic way, nor was I to engage in overly deep emotional feelings such as sympathy with her.

Any sympathy must be very minimal. This Vulcan mind-meld technique seemed to be working, so I went with it.

We entered into what looked like a control room. There were twelve different TV screens that I counted. There was a sound control board. Each TV was labeled either with the name of an intersection or the name of a building on campus.

"Watch this, Jack." A TV labeled Eisenberg now showed the parking lot and bike rack there. People were coming and going. Out I walked of the building. I unlocked the lock on my bike, stepped on, and rode off. "Now look at the TV under that one." This TV showed me biking down Jordan Avenue, one of the main arteries that went through University of Bloomington. "Now look at this one." She pointed to another screen on the other side of the room labeled "Stevens" where a salt and pepper- haired professor somewhere in his middle forties was lecturing to a class. I couldn't make out his face that well. I could only see that he had a darker complexion. I couldn't make out much distinction in his voice either because of the reverb effect in the room. She turned the volume up and I then I heard some of the authoritarian tone in his voice. He was talking about physics concepts that I didn't quite understand, and did not care to understand. "That's our man, Farley." I was actually glad she deferred to my old nickname. Calling me Jack felt uncomfortable and too personal.

"So I can see the agency has already set up some basic surveillance over the critical parts of campus that we need."

"Indeed," she responded. She almost sounded like Hurst. Maybe he was having an effect on her.

"We think his secret meeting place for terrorist recruiting is somewhere in the basement of the physics building, or worse yet, at his house off campus. We have not been able to get a camera or microphone in either place yet. That will be our first mission."

"OK," I said, "we need to befriend somebody in the physics building then."

"That's what I thought too, but it turns out we don't really have to go that far."

"Please explain." I replied.

"There is a bass player in your orchestra, he sits seventh chair right now. He is an undergraduate who is double majoring in music and physics. His name is Ryan Kleinschmidt."

I made a mild frown. I had become somewhat acquainted with Ryan over the past week. My appraisal of the undergrad at that point was that he was a complete asshole. Getting friendly with him would not be fun. "OK, I will try and practice in rooms next to his. I should be able to start talking friendlier with him this week. I'll see if he is in some kind of physics club."

"He is," Sophie responded, "Stevens has a physics club that was just scheduled and it meets once a week. You can still sign up for it Jack, you don't need to get friendly with Ryan. You can just spontaneously run into him at the meeting."

"They let non-physics majors join the club?"

"No, but you can try and sign-up at the meeting. This will draw Ryan's interest to you. It will seem less suspicious than you trying to insincerely befriend him."

I thought it over a moment. Is this Sophie trying to control and manipulate me again? No, how could it be that? We are working together now, not against each other. Her idea made sense. I was not really a social guy unless I had a couple beers in me, and you can't really do that inside a college academic building.

"OK," I said, "Show me the time and place." Sophie wrote it down for me on a small note pad and tore off the page. She handed it to me. Our eyes looked up and met each other again.

"How often should we meet?" I said.

"We can continue to meet here Saturday nights," she replied, "I can call you if we need to meet in between times."

"You don't think anyone might tap my phone, do you?"

"I check your phone in person in the mornings and once again digitally in the afternoons each day. So far, no tampering. Besides, look at this screen over here." The screen said "Jack" under it. Sophie pushed some buttons and performed some rewinding. The screen showed my dorm room hallway. She showed me entering and leaving my room in the morning and evening of each day. In between times, she fast forwarded the whole day through. It was funny watching the walking people dash this way and that on the higher tape speed. No one entered my room the entire time for all five days that week besides me and Sophie, who disguised herself in a maid's outfit of all things.

"Looks good." I said. I turned around and started to walk out of the basement.

"Wait," Sophie said a little bit energetically. She then calmed down a little, "Uh, let me walk you out."

I shrugged my shoulders a little bit, "OK." She walked alongside me on my right. We walked up the basement stairs, to her front door. She opened the front door and then turned around to me. "Jack," she said. There was now a noticeable sadness in her voice. "I am so sorry about everything in the past." Tears were actually coming down from her eyes. "I know I caused harm to many people, especially you and your friends. I...I don't know what to say. I thought I was doing the right thing...I...." She totally broke down. She stood in front of me sobbing. The small bit of mascara that she wore was beginning to run. She tried to wipe her eyes with her sleeves and then her runny nose that was developing with the tears. I was not made of stone – I never was. I walked up to her and put my arms around her as she cried into the top of my shoulder.

"I am for leaving past things in the past." I said. "I know you

James Matthew

thought you were doing the right thing. Don't worry about me, I'm OK."

She kept crying and I held her tightly against my shoulder. God, Hurst did not give any advice about this. She was not seducing me, and she was certainly not showing off her amazing physical attractiveness – she looked horrible while she cried. Now I was starting to feel things for her because of this first-time view into her emotional world. The human side of Sophie Mitchell was even more alluring than the seductive, mysterious side. There was finally a break in her crying. She seemed to have finally cried herself out. I let go of her. She looked at me. "Thank you, Jack." She placed her hand on my chest. It was on the left pectoral muscle. I focused not to try and flex like I usually would whenever a pretty woman touched my chest.

"Sophie," I said, "do you have anybody to talk to? I mean *really* talk to.

This might have made her a little nervous. A small semblance of a thin wall seemed to come around her.

"I'll be fine," she said while wiping off a few straggling tears that were left over from her sobbing.

"Are you sure?"

"Yes Farley, I'll be OK."

I wasn't going to push it. If I were her professional therapist at that moment I would have told her that she had already made an amazing break through. Why push it too far? This was great to see from her. Hopefully her emotional side would continue to develop further.

"OK," I said as tenderly as I could. "I will see you next Saturday. But Sophie, anytime you need to call me for anything, call me – it doesn't matter if it has to do with the assignment or not. I will be your friend; I would be happy to be your friend."

"That's very nice of you to say. Thank you, Jack." I could tell she had had enough of the group therapy stuff. I walked out her door and headed back to my van, and then drove back to my dorm. I did not know it, but a small gray car followed me back to my dorm.

V

Stalker

I arrived back at my dorm. I parked in a spot I found immediately available – talk about luck! I got out of the van, locked the doors, and headed up to one of the dorm's side doors. As I unlocked the door to go in, some man yelled, "Please wait!" I turned around. It was already dark. I saw the outline of a young man in a hooded sweatshirt. I could not make out the face. The hood made too much of a shadow from the shining street light. There was something funny about the voice, but I didn't think much of it. "Please hold the door for me. I forgot my keys."

Again, I didn't think much of this either. I had been in the man's situation myself a couple of times. The buildings on campus all required keys to enter after around eight o'clock. People held doors open for others constantly. Remember, this was back before 9/11, and people were much more trusting.

I held the door open and he came in behind me. He stepped into the elevator with me – again, no big deal. I felt it was a little bit of a coincidence when he stepped out onto the eighth floor with me. But, when he walked up with me nearly to my door – the coincidence was up. Right before I had walked all the way up to my door which was one of four rooms at the end of the hallway, I realized he was not a resident of any of those other three rooms. I had already seen those people several times over the past week. I turned around. "Can I help you?" I said in a stern, mildly threatening voice. He pulled down his hood and took off a pair of mirrored sunglasses.

"Hello Jack." I remembered him well, Armande DeJesus. Armande had had a mildly long-term relationship with Sophie back in Indianapolis when I was an undergrad there. He had impressed many women because he was an exchange student from Columbia. He had even impressed me. He fell into a little bit of a social trap, however, when people started to learn that most of all the high accolades he bragged about when referring to his life in Columbia were lies. Sophie had been impressed with his tall tales, not realizing how tall they were, and had a relationship with him. From what I understood, Armande fell madly in love with Sophie and after about six months of dating, proposed marriage to her. Sophie said no. The proposal had prompted an investigation into his past by her and she became one of the primary myth busters when it came to disproving all of the great titles that Armande claimed to have achieved in his homeland. She comically started calling him Mr. Mafe, which was a backwards pronunciation for Mr. Fame. Sophie soon dumped poor Armande, and his demeanor around the conservatory became much more humble from that moment on.

"Armande!" I said startled. "What are you doing here? Why didn't you just tell me who you were earlier?"

"Looks like you're getting along well with Sophie, aren't you?" He said it in his thick Columbian accent. His tone was very threatening.

"Armande," I said, "I sense something is bothering you. Why don't you tell me what it is?" "You are more insightful than you used to be, Jack." He said with an increasing snarl in his otherwise smooth Spanish voice. I felt the muscles tense up in my back. My mind became a lucid thinking machine. It was as if I was thinking ten times more efficiently than I usually did. It was as if I was thinking as if "someone had a gun to my head." I looked at him squarely in his eyes, but my peripheral awareness of his two arms, legs, and even the top of his head was acute: if he came at me with his right I would block it with my left arm and upper cut him with my right which he probably would not be able to block, if he came at me with his left I would make the same move with my other arm, if he kicked with one of his Ju-Jitsu style leg kicks I would lock up the leg in the crook of the elbow of my arm and throw him off-balance to the floor, if he tried to lock up my two hands and give me a head butt I would kick his testicles into kingdom come. Head butts, to me, were out of bounds, so I did not think kicking in the nuts was an out of proportion response. All of this went through my mind in less than a tenth of a second.

He rushed me. He held back his right as if he was going to punch, but I saw with his eyes that he was targeting a spot on my stomach where he was going to kick me. I moved slightly to my left, caught his leg with the crook of my right arm and blocked his right fist with my left arm and then pulled up his leg so he'd fall to the floor, and then I pounced down on him in a sideways manner enabling him to only get a half guard defensive position instead of the more protective full guard. This allowed me to pound two rights into his face which also had the effect of banging the back of his head into the hard carpeted floor.

I put my forearm far down into his throat. Armande coughed and choked. I checked his pockets with my other arm – I didn't find any weapons. I shoved my face down into his, "Are you done now? Or do you want some more?" It surprised me later when I replayed those words in my mind. I never heard my voice growl in such a mean way my entire life. "I'm done," he said barely able to get air out of his throat, "I'm done, I'm done."

After coughing on the floor a little while and catching his breath, I let him get up. Surprisingly, I was hardly winded at all.

"Do you want to talk about what's bothering you, Armande? I would like some kind of explanation. Maybe it will help your case when I report you to the Bloomington police and the campus police."

"You always wanted her. You couldn't stand it when she gave herself to me, could you?" He spoke in half cries and half scolds.

I decided to give him a little credence. After all, he was partially right about that last fact. "You're right about that, Armande. But did I ever stalk you and attack you?"

"No," he said, still breathing heavily, "but you did get horribly drunk was sent to the hospital."

His English-as-a-second-language grammar was starting to show in his present state of duress. "Again, you're right. But let me tell you something. You're assuming things that aren't true…" I thought for a moment. If I were to tell him that I am NOT dating Sophie, would he actually believe that? It was obvious that he had followed me from her house. How would I explain being at her house? He probably saw us hugging while the front door was open too. How would I explain that? How would I explain it other than to tell him that I was working an inside CIA job with her? *I am going to have to pretend as if I AM having a relationship with her; otherwise, Armande is going to be suspicious about what is going on.* It was the easiest lie to tell, and also the most believable.

Armande butted in while I paused for that moment, "what am I assuming?"

"Be cool" I mentally told myself. I needed to think on my feet. I needed to be a good agent. "Armande," I said, "you assume that being with Sophie is a great experience, and maybe it was for you. But let me tell you what you saw while Sophie was crying in the doorway. Sophie has cheated on me, Armande, and I don't know if I can forgive her. If you read her lips in the doorway you would have seen her say 'I'm sorry' to me over and over."

Armande was transfixed on my words, "She was not facing me, but those were the only two words I was able to hear from my car: 'I'm sorry...'" He looked away and off into the distance as if processing the whole situation. If he was an orthodox Catholic as I knew many of his countrymen were, this trait in a woman was absolutely unacceptable. After all, if the Virgin Mary could control herself, then today's women ought to be able to do the same. "Jack," he said now forcing himself to stand up while whisking off some dust from his clothes and wiping away the blood from his nose, "I owe you a deep and grave apology." Armande put his hand on my shoulder like I was a lost brother. "I too know how deeply that woman can hurt a man, and she has hurt you deeply." He put his hand down and looked out into the distance again. His gaze returned to me and he brought himself to a military-style attention with a proud and formal voice. "Such women, my friend, are not worth honorable men such as us. And certainly, she is not worth fighting over. I have been deeply wrong in this whole ordeal." He clasped my arms and I returned the clasp. The scene was completely surreal. His demeanor seemed to be a cross between Captain Kirk and Buzz Lightyear. I was now his "brother"; *alrighty then.* I was surprised to learn that he too was in the Jordan School of Music graduate program for violin performance. He enrolled five days late and lived off campus. This meant that Sophie and I were going to have to keep up the charade of being a couple. By sheer coincidence he lived at the far end of the block that Sophie lived on. He drove past her house every day on the way to school. He surely would spot us together again on Saturday nights. What were we going to say then? When he finally left to go home, I called Sophie to fill her in on the details. She agreed that for at least a little while, we would have to pretend to be a couple. I was very happy to hear her laugh about the whole thing. "Oh Jack," she giggled, "it's just like old times, isn't it?"

"It is." I said, and allowed myself one small little laugh.

VI

Steve

My old roommate Steve, the one who had been kidnapped and whose fiancée had been murdered, had begun working on his business degree also at the huge University of Bloomington. I figured it was unlikely that I would run into him on such a large campus and that we would probably drift apart as he began to associate with different circles. After his kidnapping, I tried very hard to apologize to him and make up for everything that had happened. I felt it was indirectly my fault. He had always criticized what he called my "haphazard lifestyle" even though he also enjoyed a good party, a drink, and staying out late just as much as I did. But he was correct if he were to compare the two of us and state that I was the more unreliable one. He also flat out told me many times to stay away from Sophie and that she was bad news. I never listened. So, when his fiancée Jessica ended up dead at the hands of one of Sophie's rival terrorist groups, I felt a good portion responsible. I had the most heart to heart, tear-filled conversation that I have ever had with another male when I said how sorry I was about the whole thing. It was about two days after Jessica's funeral. Steve looked at me and told me it wasn't "really" my fault. The word "really" kind of stung, but he was correct in putting that in his sentence. He patted me on the shoulder and told me that it wouldn't do any good to worry about it. I wasn't expecting 100% forgiveness from him, and he did not give it to me. But, I was hoping we could stay friends. Even though Steve assured me that we were still friends, I felt a bigger distance grow between us as each week of that summer rolled by. I ended up moving in with Samantha partially because of that. She became my new "best friend" in many ways. Steve had been making friends with the other business students whom he met at some summer pre-orientation meetings. It was ironic because I was getting further away from the business world in my lifestyle and Steve was getting further involved with the business world. He had lost a girlfriend and I had gained a girlfriend. It was like we were switching places in many respects. I called him one time during the first week of school and left a message on his cutting edge voicemail – he then called back and left a message on my primitive answering machine: our first round of phone tag. Hopefully it was phone tag and Steve was not figuring out ways to avoid me. I hoped that I could get my strong friendship back with Steve, but with everything that happened in the past, and now this new assignment that Hurst forced me into, it seemed like the distance between Steve and I would only grow. I was becoming more and more surrounded by women, and now had to embrace the roll of a "ladies' man".

Sophie and I decided to act out one very mildly dramatic scene outside of a classroom of Armande's as his class was leaving. We sat in a sort of waiting-room style group of chairs and tables that existed I suppose for people to be social. Music school people were predominately not predisposed to loitering and usually used this area for a lot of upper level networking and subtle messaging to one another via code words and facial expressions. No one ever stayed there very long. So, as Armande's class got out, I was already sitting there and Sophie then walked up and sat at a chair across from me at one of the tables. As soon as I saw Armande starting to walk by, I gave Sophie a slight raise from my left eyebrow as her cue, and she started up in just a slightly above-normal volume: "What else can I do, Jack? Tell me, I'll do anything." She had a tender yet controlled voice. I stared back at her like a laser, completely in character, "You've done enough, haven't you?

Oh, and you can take both the words 'done' and 'enough' to have as many extra meanings as are applicable!" I had intensity and emotion in my voice, but again, not overly loud. Too loud is not music school style. She looked down. In my peripheral vision, I saw Armande's silhouette. He was around fifteen feet away from us. He had stopped to listen in the hallway – *what a rubber-necker.* Our dialogue continued. "I think I have a solution," I stared back at Sophie, "I am now allowed one free pass, am I not?"

"I didn't do it just to spite you, Jack," she retorted.

"No," I responded, "but *that* will be the reason *I'm* doing it."

"It meant nothing, Jack." We looked down and away for a moment. I cleared my throat and gently wiped my nose with my index finger, a sign that I felt we had gone about far enough and to draw the scene to a conclusion.

"We'll have to talk about this later. I am going to lose my practice room window if I wait any longer," I said. Practice rooms were strictly timed because so many musicians wanted access to them. If you were over ten minutes late for a practice room, someone else could take it. I stood up and she got up with me and walked up to me, "Jack, before you go, I want you to think about this. What we have is too good to just throw away because of one mistake, even a serious mistake." She put both her hands on my two cheeks and softly gave me a kiss. She touched her lips to mine and held them there for a few seconds. Then she added something after ending the kiss, "I love *you* Jack, you and *only* you." Her intense green eyes looked hard into mine.

That last line had not been rehearsed. She was supposed to say something like, "don't just throw what we have away". The word love was not part of the plan. She said it loud enough too so that it would easily be heard by Armande. It almost threw me off. I started to feel myself get a little light-headed and even weak in the knees. I got back in character quickly though and gave out my last line, "I have to go now, Sophia. We'll talk later." I walked away and left her standing there.

131

VII

The Pre-Meeting Meeting

"So…what are you wearing."

"Well, I'm wearing a pink nighty. It's a light, shear fabric."

"Mmmm…so it shows off your figure?"

"Yeah, spaghetti straps too. And you?"

"I've got blue boxers on, that's it."

"Mmmm. Bringing out your blue eyes."

"Yeah." We paused for a little bit. The silence increased the intensity.

"You know what I'd do if I was there?"

"Tell me." Then there was a knock at my dorm room door. "Shit, there is someone at my door. This never happens. Who the hell could it be? Stay on the line, don't hang up." I walked over to my door without opening it. It had a peep hole and I looked through. On the other side was the big fat head of Patrick Hurst.

He had mirrored sunglasses on. I went back to the phone. "Hurst is at my door. I have to go."

"Noooo."

"Yeah, it's him."

"I wonder why he's there?" Sam remarked. I quickly realized that I may have slightly compromised my secret mission.

"He has been trying to convince me to change my name and to wear a security tracking device. I don't want to do it. I told him I could take care of myself. I don't think those old Germans could track me down. I don't think they even *want* to."

"Call me tomorrow, same time?"

"Yeah baby, same time."

"I love you."

"I love you, too."

"Good night."

"Good night." I went back to the door and opened it.

"Hello Mr. Hurst."

"Hello Jack. May I come in?"

"Of course." He stepped in. There was a single small table in the room with exactly two chairs. The only thing else I had was a closet, a single bed, and a single chest of drawers. I had to walk down the hallway to use the public showers and bathroom. That part had been difficult for me to adjust to. "Tomorrow you will be going to Stevens' Physics Club meeting," Hurst started right in. "You have studied up on potential energy and the Steven Hawking book?"

"Yes."

"Still, if people try to make physics conversation with you, keep it general. Be honest that you just recently became interested in physics. Relate it to the physics of your instrument, the Double bass. You do have some expertise about that."

"Yes."

"Did I interrupt your phone conversation with Sam, Jack?"

"I thought you didn't get involved with agent's personal romantic lives unless it affected the agency."

"It *is* starting to affect the agency."

"How so?"

"Two days ago, a bass player in your section tried to call you from one of the complimentary practice room phones located at the corners of hallways in that building. Your phone was busy. He tried to call you again an hour later, your phone was still busy."

"I saw him the next day. He had a question about one of our bass parts. It was Mahler's 2nd." "And what did you tell him about why your phone was busy?"

"I thought these phones had call waiting."

"These dorm phones don't. So again what did you tell him?"

"He didn't ask why I was busy. Most people don't. People around here aren't nosy like that." "What if he had asked you?"

"I might tell him it was none of his business, or I'd say I was talking to Sophie."

"Aha!" Hurst's eyes narrowed. "The first response is much too defensive and puts suspicion into the other person. We don't want people to start wondering about the mysteries of your life. And as far as the other response, do you know what Sophie was doing when he called?"

"No, I don't."

"She was practicing on the piano in the room right next to the hall phone, easily visible through the window in her practice room door."

"Jesus."

"Yes, Jack." I breathed out to help myself relax.

"What do you want me to do, Hurst? I don't think it is that bad of a screw-up. I could say I was talking to my family if anyone asks. That would work."

"Every night, Jack? A grown man in his twenties?"

"I love my family very much." I said very unconvincingly.

"You need to limit your conversations with Sam to shorter lengths."

"How short?"

"Less than an hour. Let's start there. And if that causes us problems, we'll have to shorten them further."

"Damn you, Hurst! She is lonely and so am I."

"I'm sorry, Jack. I have to think about the mission. I think your acting abilities are pretty good. But to start acting out another rift between you and Sophie where she discovers your secret conversations with another woman seems to be drawing a little too much drama to the two of you. I'm sorry that you have to pretend to be dating her. No one foresaw this man Armande moving into the house down the street from hers. A relationship between you two is the only way to explain some of the longer visits that you will be making to Sophie's house. No one will think twice or wonder about that. When I was in my twenties, we didn't do that. But your generation sure does."

"Fine." I said, "Fine, fine, fine." God, did I hate him at that moment. I didn't want to be on a CIA assignment. I didn't want to be pretending to be dating Sophie. I wanted Sam there with me. The only thing I was truly enjoying in my new environment was the music. The music was magnificent. There were hardly any untalented musicians at this school. They were all good. When all the musicians in an orchestra are good, the sound is divine. The one other thing I had been enjoying was my conversations with Sam, and now those were being restricted.

"Anyway, we need to be able to contact you at any time. So, I am giving you this cell phone. It has a vibrate-only ringer. This should keep people from knowing that you have it. When it vibrates, excuse yourself to the bathroom or say you have to get to a rehearsal and then go find a safe place to answer your call. I don't want people to be asking why you have a cell phone. It is not like you are the president of a business or something; you're just supposed to be a graduate student. We would only call you in the event of an absolute emergency."

"What would that be?"

"Most likely that your or Sophie's life are in immediate danger. Sophie will be able to reach you as well. She has strict instructions to call you on this phone only in such circumstances as I have just told you." I put the simple black phone into my pocket. I was impressed. I had never seen a cell phone that was small enough to go into one's pocket before. Remember, this was 1995.

"Do I get a number for you or Sophie?"

"Yes, your agency back-ups are the green button. Sometimes I will be able to answer it, sometimes they will answer it. Sophie's number is the red button."

"Sophie has green eyes, shouldn't she get the green button?"

"You know," Hurst smiled a little, "I actually hadn't noticed her eyes. But you are right, they are green. No, we gave her the red button because of her most distinguishing feature, her hair."

"Oh yes, her hair."

"Did you know that most men could not tell you what a particular woman's eye color is, Jack? Men usually only notice such things when they are with a woman who they find to be remarkable in some way."

All I did was stare at him. After that little pause, I said, "Is there any more CIA related information that you need to relay to me?"

"No. Just remember, you are like a great reporter. Keep your eyes and ears open at all times during the meeting. You're like Earnest Hemingway. You're going on an adventure and we want you to be able to tell us volumes about it once it is over." I didn't know much about Hemingway at the time. I became acquainted with the author later in life. Hurst was correct, though. It was a good analogy. Hurst put his fedora back on and left my room. "I'll tell you this much about Sophie, Hurst," I said after he had left my room and safely walked down the hallway out of hearing range, "She looks a million times better in a fedora than you do."

VIII

The Meeting

In the back corner of the basement of the science building was a large room. It had rows of folded up tables, some against the walls and a half a dozen or so opened out on the floor. There were iron reinforced plastic chairs for everyone at the meeting and many extra ones stacked up high against the walls with the folded up tables. There were about six concrete brick pillars reinforcing the ceiling spread evenly throughout the sixty by ninety foot room. There was a hallway at the back of the room that seemed to lead to a series of maybe four to six medium to large sized office rooms. It was not ornately decorated. There was brown and black vinyl flooring and the walls were a creamy beige color. The ceiling had the typical rude lighting fixtures and visible air ducts that you usually see in the bottom floor of an academic building.

The people in the meeting were another story. I had anticipated seeing a predominance of young Middle-Eastern looking men. Although young Middle-Eastern men had the largest representation in the meeting, they did not constitute the majority of the population of attendees and probably even amounted to less than half of the people there. There were men and women, Middle-Eastern and Caucasian, young but also old. I'd say there were three or four men that were in their sixties and seventies. The old men did not look like professors, and many of the younger people struck me as people from around the Bloomington area who were not necessarily students at the University. Most did seem to be students, but many did not appear to be. The entire group seemed to be separated by newcomers, who represented the majority, and about twenty veterans who stood up in front of the newcomers seated in the chairs. The newcomers were all told to stand up and put all the chairs against the walls. While we did this, I noticed that the leader seemed to be a red-headed man in his thirties with glasses, not Stevens. I still had no idea if Stevens was there. When he conducted my orchestra, I noticed what I thought to be a middle-Eastern accent, but I always sat far away from him back in the bass section and never really got a close look at his facial features. I just saw his dark complexion and the long salt and pepper hair. A close look at his professor photo revealed him as a darker looking man whose race looked unidentifiable – perhaps of Mediterranean origin, with long black and gray hair that was hanging down his back in a ponytail. He had bushy black eyebrows, a prominent Jewish-looking nose, and full dark lips with a pointy jaw not quite as extreme as Jay Leno. The leader of this meeting obviously looked nothing like that. His red hair was cropped short like a business man, and he had smaller elfin features possibly depicting a leprechaun-like Irish heritage. All of the veterans were immaculately dressed as well – some of them in three piece suits and the four or five women among them in elegant dresses.

While we finished moving chairs, the first event that took place was called "atmosphere". It was not explained to us, but shown to us. I interpreted it at first as just hanging out and talking. Then I noticed the serious look that many of the veterans gave a group of newcomers whenever they mixed into a conversation. We were being asked questions and being sized up. The conversations being led by the veterans also did not revolve around physics.

"How do you think the world is going? Are you happy with the direction your country is going? What is your opinion of the distribution of wealth in this country and the world? Are you aware of the amount and proportion of rich and poor in America and the world today?" The questions were like this, and they were asked with very serious looks and demeanors from the veterans. I finally got up the nerve to ask one of the female veterans a question because she looked a little more open and friendly than the rest. She looked about my age, maybe slightly older. She was Asian, maybe Korean or Japanese. She was attractive both in the body and the face.

"I thought this was a physics club? No one is really talking about physics."

She looked at me thoughtfully and mysteriously. "I've heard other newcomers make this mistake before. We are a *civics* club, not a physics club. However, if you show leadership qualities, you would eventually learn that our leadership circle is called *Aerodynamics.* People make an automatic connection between that and physics and then mistakenly call our club a physics club." All the veterans' voices were very sophisticated in sound. No matter what nationality they were, their speech barely hinted at any kind of accent. They spoke as a news anchor would speak.

"Interesting," I replied, "May I ask why the leadership division is called aerodynamics?"

"You must qualify as a leader first. But let me tell you," her eyes now narrowed and she slid her arm halfway around my waist while moving her face closer to mine and whispering in a dramatically serious fashion, "becoming a leader in this organization will bring you more power and riches than you could ever imagine, and it will give you the power to change the world into the beautiful place that it was meant to be. And," she added while looking around to see if other newcomers were watching or listening in, they were not at the moment, "we have lots of *fun*, too." On the word "fun" she patted my buttocks while flaring her nostrils at me and then suavely walked away to another newcomer group. This was not my only secretive dramatic encounter with a veteran. A man also spoke to me in a whispering fashion about ten minutes later:

"How would you like to be earning six figures before the end of this year?" He gave me that intense, secretive look. "All you need to do is to become a leader in this group."

Atmosphere lasted nearly an hour. Then the leader, who I learned was named Chris Conrad, spoke to everyone in the middle of the floor. The entire group respectfully circled around him. I'd say the whole group was comprised of a little over sixty people.

"Many of you have voiced your concerns about where this country is going and where the world is going. You can all have an opportunity to help shape that path this weekend. We are going to march on the state capitol in protest of the Indiana Assembly's recent decision not to pass the law that would have restricted book selling giants like the Ferdor's stores and the Aims and McKinnon stores from selling incredibly lewd magazines in their open aisles that celebrate drug use, promiscuous sex, homosexual lifestyles, and a lack of direction and faith. The assembly has also neglected its responsibility to require magazines with lewd covers to cover their filthy images with an outer black plastic cover. Little children can walk through aisles of these stores and see tattooed homosexuals romantically holding each other or women showing their entire nude bodies while only taking the effort to cover their nipples with their palms and crossing their legs to hide their most intimate area. We all know what these magazine publishers want to do to our world and society. They want to tear everyone away from God and lure us all into their artificial world of idol worship. There is no room for people to worship and learn from Jesus, Allah, or Moses while the publishing giants from the mega-conglomerate corporations poison their minds with sex, drugs, and irresponsibility. And our current president does nothing to help us either. He is one of them; one of the powerful oppressors who is lost himself in a never ending pursuit of immoral sexual gratification while constantly demeaning worship and religion. Who is he directing his most intensive CIA and FBI investigations towards? Evangelist churches in South America. Yes, religion. Our own president is in a war against religion. Whatever your faith, people of faith know that having a strong, loyal connection to

God is something that non-believers will always be jealous of and hate. Unless of course, they change the error of their ways and join us. People of our country, people of our world, the president of our country, none of them see the terrible direction where the world is headed if nothing is done soon. It is now up to us. We can do something this very weekend. We can march at the state capitol and tell the press about our concerns for our country. But, I need you newcomers to do it. I need you novices now to show that you can be leaders. We need leaders in our organization. A few of you heard about our 'physics' club by word of mouth," *(So, I was not the only one who was misled by the physics club rumors)*, "most of you new comers were brought to this meeting by one of the veteran leaders. The more people you can bring to these meetings, the more leadership and responsibility you bring to and demonstrate for our organization. Show your fellow leaders this weekend what you can do by organizing among each other. Organize the transportation, the signs, and the message. Tell the press and the world that there are people out there who are concerned about our people and our society. The riches of the world do not solely belong to the huge corporations. We can have a slice of the pie, too. And, we *do* have a slice already, but you newcomers first must prove yourselves before you can get some of that slice. Start organizing now. The veterans will come with you to Indianapolis, but we will be doing the watching. You will be doing the demonstrating."

As the meeting morphed back into an atmosphere mode. About ten to twelve people left – God how I wished I could be one of them. But remarkably, most of the newcomers stayed. People indeed started organizing. Veterans attached themselves to small groups and were overseeing what was going on. I was in a small group and in my peripheral vision I saw a leader dressed in some kind of impressive navy blue pin striped suit walk up to our group to supervise the session. I turned my head toward him. It was Ryan Klein Schmidt, the seventh chair in my bass section.

IX

Back at Mission Control: Sophie's House

"Start organizing now. The veterans will come with you to Indianapolis, but we will be doing the watching. You will be doing the demonstrating." We sat and listened to the end of the recording. I had been wired the entire time during the civics club meeting. I was with Sophie in her basement and Hurst was listening in over Sophie's speaker phone.

"It sounds like a pyramid scheme," said Hurst. "They use it to help weed out people for whatever reasons. Some might be too dumb, some actually too smart. Some might be too independent-minded and would not be easy to brainwash. They also want to see who is the most motivated and who is willing to do the most for them. Being able to bring in new people is always a big part of these schemes. Jack, you will have to find a way to bring in at least a few new recruits over the next few weeks." It was slightly past the middle of September, so I figured I had until the end of the first week of October to figure that out. "Conrad is obviously not saying anything illegal or incriminating at this point. I am sure that

143

we will have to get further into this inner circle of the aerodynamics division before we can get any real incriminating evidence."

"Hurst," I said, "At some point, I cannot agree to everything they tell me to do, right? I mean, if I am asked to take part in a crime or to kill someone…well I guess, we would then have it on tape and we could make a bust."

"Yes Jack, that's right. But now that you mention it, you need to pooh-pooh any small stuff like ripping off a drug store or someone's purse. We want them to save you for the serious stuff. If they want you to do a small crime, you will have to just do it. When they ask you to do something violent, that's when we can get some real charges against them. I am not sure whether they are directly involved in drug trade or not."

"Based on Conrad's speech, it sounds like they abhor drugs," Sophie chimed in.

"That means nothing," said Hurst. "That is their way of appealing to the religious right. I can guarantee you that they get some kind of funding, either directly or indirectly, from drug trading. Don't forget the two whispered messages to Jack: six figures in less than a year and the woman's comment to him about fun. Jack, I believe my grown children would refer to you as a chick magnet."

"She was just saying that to get me interested in the group," I replied embarrassed. The tone of the woman's voice at that point in the recording was obviously suggestive. I did not want to talk about the ass-patting that she gave me. Thank God we didn't have a camera in there.

"Jack, your first recruit into the group will be none other than Sophie. It is so easy and so perfect I can hardly believe it. See if you can get her into a separate division within the group once she's in. We don't need two identical reports after each meeting. Spread your resources around as much as you can. Just tell them that the two of you argue too much whenever you are paired together in an assignment. Any people who have been in a long relationship can understand that."

Hurst continued, "Sophie, I am sending in men right now to construct a secret passageway into your basement and to hide the current door that goes down there. This terrorist group might want to visit you at your house. Under no circumstances are they to ever learn about this basement.

"Jack, it is Friday afternoon and the big rally at the statehouse is tomorrow. Make your daily call to Sam before dinner and then take Sophie out somewhere to eat so you guys can relax, and have fun. Keep any discussion about the mission to a minimum. I want people to see you out somewhere together. You need to look like a happy couple. Sophie can come with you to the rally tomorrow."

"I don't know if they want brand new recruits at the rally," I chimed in.

"Trust me, Jack. They will love it. It shows initiative on your part. This will show all the control you have over your girlfriend too. Groups like these like to see that the men can rule over their women."

Since the clock was ticking, I didn't want to waste any time. "OK, I'm going back to my dorm now and calling Sam. Sophie, I'll pick you up at 5:30? Is that enough time for you to get ready?"

"Sure," she said and looked at me. Her expression was still something I could not get used to. She was a little sad and looking at me with that lost child look. Maybe I was just reading into things too deeply.

"Sounds good," said Hurst. "I will contact you guys tomorrow night after the rally."

X

The Date

We went to a popular restaurant that played Salsa music. Sophie looked nice. She had a conservative purple and red dress on. It was a soft fabric and not too thick in its texture. We ordered our food. We talked, not too much about the mission. I was careful as I talked to her. I didn't know how deep we should get. I felt bad about her pretty obvious depression, but I did not know what to do for her.

We were aware that there were some people in the restaurant from both my dorm and from the music school. Still, we were not really acting up the relationship besides just sitting and talking. A half a dozen or more couples had gone onto the dance floor and were obviously enjoying themselves. We both longingly looked at them. "Let's order one or two shots of tequila," I suggested.

Sophie looked at me – her eyes perked up a little, "Are you sure, Farley?"

"Yeah, we need to loosen up a little."

We each took a shot and then ordered one more. It really did the trick. I pulled Sophie out onto the dance floor and her face lit up the room with that smile of hers that makes the sun itself look dull. Neither of us were good technically, but we had a blast. I led her across the floor, I dipped her. A member of the band shouted out that the man with the redheaded girl looked like a 1920s dance couple, so they were going to play the Charleston for us. That was a dance that we both actually knew. We did the little two step move. We did jazz hands. I flapped my knees back and forth alternating a hand on one knee and sliding my hand to my other knee with each knee-flap.

Then the band played a slow romantic song. "We better dance this one," I whispered to her. It turned out to be a bad idea. There were only two emotions that I could choose between while holding her close in a romantic dance: extreme passion or extreme discomfort. I could not allow the first one, so the second one kind of took over. I did not show it. I acted like I was loving the slow dance. I think Sophie was going through something similar. We did not look at each other in the face except for one time during the dance. That was much too strong for both of us. We both immediately looked away. After the dance we continued smiling but only glanced at each other. I did not think that acting out a kiss was necessary. There are lots of couples who don't kiss in public. Sophie felt differently. Just before we sat back down at the table, she put her right hand upon my left cheek and leaned over to my left ear.

"I see people from school looking. We should kiss just once."

"OK", I said softly.

Sophie leaned in to me. Her emerald green eyes gazed into mine. I don't know if I have ever had such conflicting emotions going on at any other point in my life. I leaned into her face. Our lips softly came together. She put her other hand on my right cheek with both her hands on either side of my face. I put my arms around her waist and our bodies leaned in against each other. I felt her torso pressing up against mine. My thin silk shirt made it very easy to feel that. We kissed for maybe two or three seconds, then our lips separated and I instinctively gave her a second very soft short peck on her bottom lip. She then did the same back to me on my top lip. Our bodies separated from each other just in time as I was beginning to feel a sensation of light-headedness.

We sat down, which helped to remedy my slight dizziness. I was not facing anyone from my side of the booth except one of the walls of the restaurant. Sophie was the one facing the whole room. I must have been the one who looked distressed now. Sophie gave me a very subtle look of concern through her eyes while she kept her mouth smiling.

"Jack, are you OK?"

"I'm fine." My voice cracked.

"Take this." She handed me her table napkin.

"What for?" I said again with a raspy voice, and with some confusion.

"You're crying," she whispered. I looked up at her eyes more intently, and then looked down. I lifted my right hand to my cheek. There were tears there.

"I need to go to bathroom." I slowly and carefully stood up holding her napkin and walked to the men's room.

XI

Sam's First Visit

Samantha could not wait until mid-October to see me. She flew into Indianapolis during the last weekend of September and arranged a place for us to meet – Don's house. Yes, Don the stoner bass player. I was shocked that the ex-boyfriend would let her use his place to shack up for a weekend with her current boyfriend, but I sure wasn't going to complain. In a way, I have to give Don a lot of credit for not holding a grudge and staying on friendly terms with Samantha.

This spontaneous visit was just what both of us needed. Don had actually been nice enough to pick her up at the airport. When I arrived at his house, he was still there. I walked up to Samantha and we just couldn't contain our joy. I put my arms around her and kissed her affectionately.

"Don't worry guys," Don said, "I'm on my way to a gig in Chicago. I will be there all weekend. The place will be yours. Never mind me while I pack up my things. I'll be leaving in about two hours." We of course insisted that he stay for an hour with us while we ordered some pizza delivery - on us. We laughed and talked about the past summer. After dinner, Don excused himself to one of his two bedrooms and said he really needed to start packing. The other bedroom was for Sam and me.

We walked into the room. Sam shut the door and locked it. I can barely remember what the room looked like because my entire soul was focused on Sam. All I remember about the room was that the bed had a pink comforter and pink sheets.

She looked beautiful. Her hair was starting to grow down her neck and shoulders, finally growing out of her shorter cut she had at the beginning of the summer. She had on dark purple lipstick, some dark brown eye shadow, some black eyeliner, and the effect made her look exotic as if she was Hispanic. She reached down and pulled up her loose-fitting crimson shirt. It came right off. 'How could I ever ask for more than this?' I wondered to myself many times that evening. 'Sam can match Sophie any day.' And that was easily true, if Sam could just be in the same time zone as me.

But as wonderful as that weekend was, I could not get rid of a conflict deep inside me. I knew it had to be resolved. I was determined: *I would not let my assignment with Sophie ruin my relationship with Samantha. I had waited too long for a healthy relationship like this one. This relationship was open with no games.* But then I caught myself – was it really open? Were there really no games? That wasn't entirely true. I was now the one hiding things and playing games. The fact that I was being forced to do this did not alter the effect of its reality. And then the horrible seed of doubt planted itself inside me: *I might lose Samantha because of this CIA assignment, and there might not be anything I can do about it.* The mind is a field ripe for harvest.

XII

The Vision

It was a tearful good-bye when Sam had to leave at the end of that weekend. I drove her to the airport Sunday afternoon right after Don returned from his Chicago gig. We hugged and kissed in the airport terminal. She looked deep into my eyes, "You know I love you, Jack." "I know," I replied, "I love you too." We shared one last kiss with a strong embrace. It was long and felt so good. Then I watched her pick up her bag and walk into the connecting tunnel that led to her airplane.

The weekend before Sam's visit had been the big rally in Indianapolis. It went smoothly from what I could tell. I brought Sophie along and she assimilated very well into the group. The name that the group went by when dealing with the press was Christian and Islamic Vision In Community Service or CIVICS in acronym. Their "vision" was obviously an extreme right-wing view of the world in almost every aspect with exception to their own compulsive drive for power and control. If the group acquired more power and control in the world, that was just fine. When another force such as the government, a corporation, or an individual was powerful or influential, that was labeled as part of the problem or the "wrong direction" in which the world was headed. The largest proportion of Islamic people were in the high leadership positions. Sophie, Hurst, and I concluded that the reason for naming the group the *Christian* and Islamic Vision In Community Service was because they needed numbers and opening up the group to the mostly Caucasian Christian population allowed them to always have enough beginner and novice members to perform the leg work and sometimes dirty work that needed to be performed. So far, the dirty work had been a couple of small things: 1.) Standing in front of a local abortion clinic and making it very difficult for anyone to enter. And 2.) Going into a Ferdor's bookstore as a large group and chanting in front of the risqué magazines "The wages of sin is death" loudly until the police came and escorted us out. The important events actually seemed to be the meetings in the basement of the physics building. They had held two meetings since the first one, and I had been able to bring in two more people besides Sophie. I piggy-backed off of the bookstore idea and would hang out in the coffee shop watching people walk through the magazine section. When someone would scowl or frown at a picture of a nearly naked woman, a homosexual magazine, or a marijuana advocate magazine, I would then walk up and start a spiel like, "It makes you just sick doesn't it? What is this world coming to? You know (sir or mam), you don't have to sit and be silent about filth like this. I belong to an organization that is actually trying to do something to stop this rampant hedonism… etc., etc., etc.

Ryan Kleinschmidt from my experience turned out to be a dud. I really didn't need him to infiltrate into the organization. He didn't speak much and mostly just encouraged me in what I was already doing. There wasn't any major plan as of yet from either of us to target fellow musicians as recruits. The most noteworthy experience within the group during that first full month happened during the weekly meeting following Sam's visit. Ryan walked me back to one of the small office rooms that occupied the small hallway at the back of the large meeting room. I was taken inside. I was now wearing a suit to the meetings even though I was not considered a leader yet. Anyone who stayed in the group for more than a week was rather harshly advised that if they wanted to ever become a leader, they had to dress like one. So I always wore a suit and tie, and Sophie always wore an elegant dress. Seeing Sophie dressed so beautifully so often only twisted the conflicting emotions going on inside me even worse. So during the entire first two months, my stress levels just seemed to increase with every passing day.

Once Ryan had taken me inside one of the medium-sized offices and closed the door behind me…in the dark I might add, a small chord was pulled on a ceiling light that hung over a small table. For the first time, I saw Professor Stevens up close. Up until this point, Chris Conrad had been the highest level leader I had seen. I finally had Stevens in front of me. We recognized each other from music rehearsals; he had been conducting the Philharmonic for the first two weekly concerts. Conductors rotated from group to group and he was now conducting the Concert orchestra. He was indeed of Middle Eastern descent. You couldn't exactly identify it from his look which to me seemed Italian, but you could hear it in his accent. Even though he was listed on the schedule as the director of the Chamber Music group, he only showed up every three weeks and that was to observe a Master's or Doctoral student conductor conduct our group. Chamber groups don't really need a conductor anyway. Stevens looked at me and spoke:

"McFarland, Jack Sebastian," he knew my middle name. "Jack, I am impressed with your leadership abilities. It is exciting to have someone new take such charge in our group. How do you like it so far?"

"Dr. Stevens, I have been looking for something like this my whole life. I had thought that only music could offer the direction that I was seeking. Now I know that something else can as well." "That is good to hear," he replied. "But first Jack, I do have some questions. You realize, there are a few other music students in our school who attended your undergraduate conservatory. I think there are about ten, actually. When members of my group asked these people about you and what they knew about you, they all had a common description." I became a little nervous. I had an idea what he was going to say. "Jack, anyone who knew you closely said you were quite active in the drinking scene, the party scene, and the dating scene. And by dating, I mean multiple women at the same time." "Ahem, sir... like I was saying, I have been searching. That is why I was drinking too much, partying too much, and even dating too many women. I would add, though, that at only one time in my undergraduate years was I dating more than two girls at the same time and that was only while I had just begun to date one while I was breaking it off with another."

"So you're saying that you limited girlfriends to no more than two at one time?"

"Sir," I decided to play the confident male and silly female card, "women have the ability to delude themselves to the utmost degree. When breaking off a relationship with a woman, she sometimes refuses to accept the break up until you actually start dating someone else. I can assure you that in *my* mind, I have always only been having a relationship with one woman at a time.

This really was ridiculous. Only in conservative Indiana would people think that you are in a serious relationship just because you took someone of the opposite sex out somewhere. God forbid you might actually kiss the person – then people would probably say you are married.

"Well," continued Stevens, "honestly, this does not bother me. After all, women should be more prudent about the men they date and not allow the man to date multiple women while in a relationship. We both know that our anatomy makes it difficult for us to deny ourselves."

"Absolutely." I replied. I didn't want to say too much. Overdoing it might make him suspicious. "We are going to make you a leader, Jack. Your job will be as a recruiter and trainer. We think you can influence others very well. You do not have the kinds of skills to execute the highest mission that we are seeking to accomplish, but you can train others to do it with your powers of language and persuasion."

Sophie would get this same meeting with Stevens a week later. He viewed her exactly the same way he viewed me – as a trainer and recruiter. This was actually good. We would be working in separate places most likely. Why put two recruiters in the same place at the same time? Spread us out and we can get more done. We were also able to get more evidence recorded for Hurst that way. Now that I was a "leader", I still felt that all I was really receiving was a title. Was there any pay? The kind of aura this group projected to members was one in which it always seemed dangerous to ask any questions. Therefore, I didn't. I did not want to look like the buffoon who "didn't get it" because I actually did get it. I had learned to read subtleties in communication very well since working with Hurst. But, even more important than the title I just received, I had a more serious question; a question that most likely would take me, Sophie, and Hurst to the root of our quest

What is the highest mission, Dr. Stevens?

XIII

News of the World

"O.J. Simpson has just been found not guilty by a Los Angeles jury. This nearly year-long trial has finally come to an end." The Indianapolis reporter then deferred to one of his colleagues on the streets who was asking people's opinions about the verdict. Most white people didn't like the verdict, and most black people liked the verdict. Not much of a surprise there.

It was about the middle of the first week of October, and I sat in a Bloomington bar on campus known as Bull's, watching the World News on the TV screen behind the bar. Bull's was across the street from the music school and about two buildings down. I reflected on how President Clinton had sure seen his share of worldly events in his first three years in office. After the fall of the Soviet Union, when people thought there might actually be some peace from all of the ominous threats of war, it seemed like we were now getting new kinds of threats. Racial unrest – the L.A. riots, the O.J. Simpson case, and a strange new kind of terrorist threat right here in the U.S that would be labeled domestic terrorism had emerged. In Waco Texas, a religious cult shuts itself in a compound and refuses to let anyone out. The government raids the compound and many deaths result. A bombing at the

World Trade Center, the building does not collapse, but many killed yet again. And most recently, the Oklahoma City bombing kills scores of people there earlier in the year. A religious zealot known as Timothy McVeigh is charged in the bombings. Maybe Conrad had a point, or maybe he was missing the point. Could Clinton's focus on investigating Evangelism in South America be inciting these kinds of domestic attacks, or were these groups already incited and that was why Clinton was looking into them? But why South America? It had been nearly twenty years since the Jim Jones cult, and I had not heard of any dangerous religious groups down there since then - plenty of dangerous drug cartels, but not religious cults. Hurst gave me an earful on his opinion when Sophie and I connected with him via speaker phone in her basement during our meeting later that week:

"Clinton's liberalism is inciting these attacks. There was a bill in congress to ban late term abortions – abortions that clearly occur after any healthy baby is already viable and could survive outside of its mother. Clinton vetoed the bill. And I'll tell you about his foreign policy as it relates to the CIA. He doesn't have a damn clue. Look at any other president since Truman created the organization. They all met with the CIA director at least several times within the first year. Clinton did not meet with me once during his first two years in office. And when Schwarz was named the new director earlier this year, I did not hear of any plans for Clinton to meet with him either. It is very possible that after three years of ruling the most powerful country in the world, Clinton has not met with the highest level CIA officer yet." Hurst rattled off his rant, and I nearly expected him to end it with a 'humpf' or a 'so *there*, you young liberal idiots'. The more I learned about Hurst's conservatism, the more I could see why Clinton might not want to meet with him. Hurst wasn't a complete zealot, but he was pretty far on the right.

Events on campus, in Bloomington and sometimes in the capitol of Indianapolis would continue over the next couple of months. Sophie and I were both leaders. We did indeed recruit more people in CIVICS. I played my role, and she played hers. As a pretend couple, we would go out together about once a week to someplace where everyone could see us. We kept it business like around the music school; this was college and we were graduate students. Public displays of affection are not needed then. And we kept our displays conservative when we went out: maybe we would hold hands for a while at a dinner table, a short kiss when leaving or entering a booth. That was all. We didn't dance again for a while. I was glad for that. I also watched my drinking with her. One or two light drinks – that was all. No heavy stuff. Sophie's depression seemed to lessen from a deeply sad state to more of a general light gloom. The 'midwestern blues' you might call it. Yes, we had the great music and we had the intriguing assignment. But the assignment was actually getting boring and frustrating while the realization that anything non-college or non-academic around here was pretty lame. The bars were all college bars. The social events were littered with what I would call anti-Hursts. The campus itself was extremely liberal. Women's rights, gay rights, animal rights, the environment, get rid of your aerosol cans, etc. I was pretty sick of the far left and far right in general. How about people just getting together and NOT talking about social issues? It was ironic that Sophie and I were infiltrating the one group on the entire campus that seemed to be a conservative group. I secretly wished there could be some more conservative groups – just not nearly as extreme as CIVICS.

There were more CIVICS demonstrations at liberal places like the bookstores, and another sit in at an abortion clinic. One event that bothered me was a funeral. For this event I made sure I was standing behind a tree when the press took a photo of us. It was a funeral for a former army captain who had recently come forward in what he knew was his last year in this world and announced that he was homosexual and was actually dying because of complications from HIV. Well, we had to come with our damn signs saying that the captain was going to hell and not going to die in a state of grace because "God hates all homosexuals". Even for the sake of my own survival, this was a hard event to pretend to get angry about - unless you count getting angry at my fellow CIVICS members. Thank God, when the pictures made the papers and the film footage made the TV news, my image was not visible enough to be identified.

Luckily, no one on campus or at my dorm had identified me with the controversial organization. People who kept up with politics and social activism knew about the group. Many people still were stuck on the misinformation that it was a physics club. That probably helped the club avoid direct criticism – no one knew exactly what we were about unless you came to a meeting. The club was now restricting new members to recruits only. No one could just walk into a meeting anymore without being invited by a veteran leader. I was a little startled during lunch one day when one of my eating partners brought up the group.

"Eh," Melvin was always trying to be very intellectual and very cautious, "has anyone heard about this group on campus called CIVICS?" I kept quiet. Melvin's Jewish inflection came through in a sort of Richard Lewis-like tone.

"Oh yes," Diana chimed in. She tended to be freer in speech and less cautious. "Zsay are *horribool*. I zink zsay should be banned from campoos." It was a little funny hearing the thick German accent after hearing the East Coast Jewish one.

"Well, we have awul of these liberal groups here. Why can't there be a religious one?" Palak's accent was very light. I didn't know she was from Jordon until she had told me.

"Oh," replied Diana, "Zsay are not religious. Zsay are joost extremist!"

"I agree," said Dyena, "Dey are too extreme. What dey deed at szat funeral was just awulful!" Her Russian inflection was not quite as thick as Diana's German one.

"What do you think, Jack?" Melvin turned the conversation to me.

"I don't keep up with local politics. I'm too busy at the music school." I hoped that would satisfy them. Just then Ludwig came to the table. Thank God; they would probably turn their attention to him "What is up? Posse?" Ludwig liked to try and talk like an American. He felt that Arsenio Hall was a good model.

Melvin cracked a smile. "We were talking about this CIVICS group that was in the news. But now, Ludwig, you have just reminded me of how much I can't stand the Arsenio Hall show."

"Don't look at zme. *I* didn't let the dogs out! Wuf, wuf, wuf!" Melvin, Ludwig, and I all laughed. Then Melvin explained to the ladies what the Arsenio Hall show was. Ludwig apparently was in a good mood because he had just been awarded another grant. Thank God, the conversation then turned away from CIVICS.

Sophie and I were frustrated with CIVICS because although we were now called leaders, there was still at least one more inner circle where we were not allowed access. This was *aerodynamics*. I quickly learned that asking about how long it takes for a member to get into aerodynamics yielded no fruit whatsoever. All I would get is silence and an occasional "when a member is ready for aerodynamics, they will be alerted" from a couple of the friendlier, warmer veterans. Julie was the name of the young Asian leader to whom I had spoken at my introductory meeting. I liked her. She was nice. She had tried to get me into her small division, but Ryan had kind of stepped in with a possessive demeanor as if to say "keep your feminine whiles away from my group." She did use her sexual attractiveness a lot too. She wore skin tight dresses with plunging necklines, sometimes backless. She always wore very high heels. I had never dated an Asian woman, and she definitely made me wonder what it would be like. For a conservative group, she sure dressed provocatively.

And she was flirtatious too. Even though Sophie was in the club, Julie would turn me around and use my back to write something on a document. She would put her hands on my shoulders and then whisper in my ear, "Turn around". After signing the paper, she would give my back a couple of rubs. "Thanks, Jacky." She gave me long looks too. I would look away and then glance back a few seconds later, and she would still be gazing at me. I decided to bring something up to Sophie and Hurst at our CIA meeting after

Julie actually licked her lips at me. Hurst was communicating to us via speaker phone as usual.

"The Japanese leader, Julie, is making some passes at me. How should I handle that?"

"For Christ sake, Jack, leave it alone. Keep your pants zipped," Hurst scolded me, "you're supposed to have a girlfriend in the organization and they like men with conservative values. Ignore her! I've discussed this kind of situation with you before, Jack."

"I don't buy the conservative value thing when it comes to the members that are higher in command," I replied. "I think the inner circles don't practice what they preach."

"So what," said Hurst, "you are not into the highest levels, yet. So behave yourself."

"Jack might have a point, Hurst. And this girl might be his way to actually get in those circles." Sophie added. I looked at Sophie.

"I had not thought of it that way," admitted Hurst. "It could show your willingness to do anything they ask you."

I thought to myself, *"Why did I bring this up? This was not necessary. I have a girlfriend in Baltimore who loves me. Why am I volunteering to prostitute myself?"*

"Hurst, I think you're right. I don't know why I brought it up."

"I am going to have you trust your instincts, Jack. If you think Julie might be the key to get you into the inner circles, then maybe you should let her pick your lock."

"Nice innuendo there, Hurst!" I chuckled and so did Sophie.

"I may be old, but I'm not dead!" He laughed back at us.

I was still torn, though.

XIV

What Does Jack Want?

Hurst hung up his connection and I sat in the basement for a little while with Sophie.

"Jack," she had a friendly voice at the moment, "would you mind looking at me for a second?" What an odd request. "Is something wrong?" I turned to her. She looked at me sincerely, honestly and seriously, and asked me the following question: "Are you in love with Samantha?"

I looked away from her.

"Jack?"

"OK, I know. I am not looking at you." I turned to her, and said as if answering a job interview question, "I love Samantha."

"That is not what I asked you."

"Excuse me?"

"I asked if you are *in* love with her."

"She loves me too. It is not a one way street. We both feel it."

"But are you totally in it? You can love someone, care about them, even be strongly attracted to them, but still not be in love with them. Don't tell me that you *love* Samantha. Tell me that you yourself are *in* love with Samantha."

As convoluted as it may sound, I actually understood what she was saying. I understood it a little too well. Samantha had been wearing on me. The nightly phone calls, the plane tickets, I was supposed to fly out to see her in about ten days, and then I had booked another flight to go visit her exactly one month later. Samantha had insisted on it. 'We needed time to be with each other in person' she would say. I was beginning to resent her and her demands. Is that the way you feel when you are in love with someone? When you are in love, isn't seeing that person more wonderful than anything else?

"I...I...," my voice was starting to crack and tears began to come from my eyes, "I'm not in love with her, Sophie." I dropped my head down to my chest and sobbed. It was Sophie's turn to console me. She slid her chair beside mine and put her arms around my shoulders. She leaned her head in on the side of mine.

"Farley," I didn't mind the knick-name any more. I kind of liked the familiarity that came with it. "I have been able to see that for nearly a month now. You notice other women. You don't really talk about her. You talk about having to call her like it is an obligation. Being in love is not supposed to be like that. You might just *want* to be in love so badly that you are forcing yourself. I call it *being in love with love*. Being in love with love might feel nice for a while, but from my experience, it doesn't last." "I can't think very straight right now." I replied. "I am not going to deny that things don't feel so good with Sam right now, but that doesn't mean our relationship is over. I definitely *was* in love with her this past summer. I want that feeling to come back again." I paused slightly, "But even this past summer I..."

Sophie embraced me tightly and I embraced her back.

"Sophie," I looked at her seriously now.

"Yes."

"I want to talk about us."

"Yes?" Her voice stammered a little bit. "I think that right now, no matter what happens, we need each other. No matter what happens, we both have an idea of what the other person has gone through, and we can be there for each other. No matter what happens, Sophie, I want you to know that I will be there for you, and I will be your friend for you. I don't mean the "friend zone" that everyone complains about. I don't know anything anymore about love and romance and who I will end up with and whether I will stay single or get married and have a family and any of that shit. I want someone who will be *there* for me. Sophie, I will be there for you. And however you want to define it – it will be as your true friend. I want to be someone you can trust, someone you can cry to, someone of whom you are not afraid to put your life into his hands. And Sophie, if you could ever feel that way towards me, that is what I need from you. Sophie, I need a friend like that now. If you can't keep that up very long, then fine. But if you could be that for me while we are going through all this spy shit with Hurst and the CIVICS club that would be enough."

Sophie lunged farther into my arms and held me. "Oh Jack." She cried in my arms and I cried in her arms. We cried together. Everything had become too crazy, too hard, too haphazard. We needed this moment. "I will be your friend, Jack. I will be your true friend. And when this is over…" "Shhh," I put my finger over her lips, "let's get through this first. We are going to *bear* down and *take* down this sick terrorist group. And I am going to do whatever it takes to bring them to their knees.

XV

Death of a Doctor

Something had been going on the past two weeks. It was the end of October, and during CIVICS meetings, the inner circle had been having their own private meetings back in the private rooms. Julie was in the circle, and because of this, I had not had much of a chance to flirt and schmooze with her. I found out what they had been planning when a story made the news. "Abortion doctor found murdered in her Bloomington home." The woman had been slashed and stabbed over one hundred times. A message in blood had been written on the wall of her kitchen: "Millions of dead babies and one dead doctor – score still not settled." I had to start working fast. This could not continue.

I had visited Sam in the middle of the month. It renewed my faith in the relationship. We *were* in love. How could we not be? When we were together, the passion continued all weekend. We longingly looked at each other. Sometimes it had seemed that Samantha was a little distracted. Once she said, "We do need to talk about something, but let's wait until the end of the weekend. Then when it was time for me to board my plane and go back to Bloomington, Sam actually laid a bombshell on me. "Jack, I can't do this again next year. You have to find a way to transfer to Baltimore."

I was quiet and then I said, "We can talk about this over the phone. Let's not ruin the good-bye."

Then came another bomb, "Jack, if you can't commit to coming here next year...well, I just think you should know that someone asked me out."

I froze. I was pissed, scared, shocked, dumbfounded. I had been working my ass off to stay true to her. Now *she* is the one asking for some permission to have fun on the side?

"Has Hurst been telling you something?" I had already begun to make some verbal mistakes and didn't even realize it.

"No Jack, but.."

"But what?"

"I think Hurst is getting old. After one of his lectures at the academy, he put some papers into his briefcase, but he didn't notice that a couple fell out as he left the lecture room. I picked it up for him and was going to hand it back to him, but he was already out the door and down the stairs. The papers said classified on top, and I shouldn't have read them. But, I saw a mission labeled 'Destroy CIVICS' and the names of the agents who were assigned to it. I saw your name and Sophie's name on the list. I also read on the other sheet a background of the beginning of the mission which said that you and Sophie are both posing as graduate music students in Bloomington."

"What else?" I asked her.

"That's all. Another professor saw me with the sheets and ripped them out of my hands. Are you working an infiltration job with Sophie, Jack?"

"I can't talk about it, Sam."

"If Hurst is making you do this, why didn't you tell him to assign you another job or another partner?"

"I did ask him that."

"Did you try hard Jack, or did you give in at the very beginning?" Her eyes became accusatory. "Sam, I am going to say this one time. *Nothing is going on between Sophie and me.* We are both being forced to do this by Hurst. Someone at Bloomington went to the Indianapolis Conservatory with us and lives down the street from Sophie. He sees her house every time he drives to or from school and I have to meet her there for meetings with Hurst via speaker phone. He is going to see me there quite often and that is the main reason why we have to pretend to be..." I just realized how badly I screwed up. I did not need to tell her that.

"You have to pretend to be what? Lovers? Oh, how perfect for *you* huh? Your old red-headed obsession is opening herself for her country and also for you! Why don't you two just make a video tape and sell it around the school? Then everyone will know how hot of a couple you are!"

She had her arms folded and looked down and to the left of me. It was the last boarding call for my plane. "Sam, we will talk about this over the phone."

"What about the boy who asked me out."

"Ignore him and see if he asks you again."

"Hmpf," was all she said.

"Or", and this was when I either consciously or subconsciously began to sabotage our relationship, "you can just *'give in at the very beginning'*" I said to her using a snide womanish tone at the end.

I walked away and boarded my plane. Damn, it had been such a great weekend up until then.

XVI

Reflection

Boy had I messed up. I should have just denied everything. But Sam actually saw those documents. How could I deny that? We did talk on the phone, and our next conversation was not fun. "You have to be careful Sam. Don't tell *anyone* about this mission. Not even other people in the agency. This could put *you* in danger."

"I know that. I can take care of myself. You do a good job of taking care of *yourself.*"

"I am *not* doing anything with Sophie!"

"That boy did call me up again."

"Do *you* want to go out with him?"

"Do you *want* me to?"

"I am not trying to hold you back. If two people are in love, they don't need to chain each other down." I said it, but I really didn't mean it. I felt that was what I was supposed to say. Maybe the truth is that when two people are in love, they hold on to each other as hard as they can.

"Ok, then. I am going to go out with him."

Later that weekend, after she had been out with the boy. I made another mistake on my already long list of relationship blunders. I asked, "So, did anything happen on your date?"

"Do you really want to know Jack?"

I took a deep breath. "Yes."

"Yes," was all she said. I hung up the phone on her.

Over the next two weeks, Sam tried to call me constantly at first and left messages. Then the second week the calling trailed off. Her messages varied from, "Jack, please call me back. I don't need to go out with this boy. Please talk to me. I can't stand this. I need you to talk to me," to, "Jack you need to call me back *today.* I am not going to wait much longer to hear from you." After two weeks, somehow I was suddenly ready to forgive her for her date, and I sent her two dozen roses through the mail. I received another call from her after not receiving any for about four days. "We need to talk, Jack." Then I called her that night.

I called her. It was the first time I had dialed her number in over two weeks. "Hello, is Sam there?" Her roommate had answered the phone. Sam came to the phone, "Robert?"

"It's Jack."

"Oh, Jack. We need to talk."

"Yes, Sam, I was wrong. I just needed a little time to think-"

"You shouldn't have sent the flowers, Jack. Jack, I am with Robert now. We have been friends for a couple of months, and

169

now it has blossomed into a relationship. I am sorry to do this over the phone."

I can't remember the words to the rest of the conversation. I asked questions like "why" to which she gave very inadequate responses that such inadequate questions deserve. At the end of what was probably not longer than a ten minute conversation, she hung up and I was left with the realization that our relationship was officially over.

How could this happen? I was deaf to the voices inside myself that reasoned: "Jack, you have been noticing other women, you even admitted you were not in love with her." None of those voices helped. I was only aware of a terrifyingly deep void inside that I simply could not deal with on my own. I went outside and started my van. I drove to the liquor store. I bought whiskey, vodka, and rum. I didn't really even take notice except to make sure that the proof was strong in whatever I purchased. Thus began about a week of oblivion.

XVII

Scraping By

Darkness.

A phone message: "Jack, we missed you at rehearsal the past two days....yadayadayada" Ring, ring, ring, "Hello. St. Anthony's"

"I'd like to see a doctor."

"Are you a new patient?"

"Yes."

"The next available appointment is December 3rd."

"It's only October."

"I'm sorry, that is the earliest spot we have available."

Go to Hell! "Thanks a lot, bitch!" *Click.*

Some more days go by or maybe just hours, can't tell.

Another message: "Jack, this is Hurst. I know what's going

on…you know why. I'm making an appointment for you to see a psychologist. It's tomorrow at 2:30. Here is the address…"

Pencil, paper. 935 Peabody Lane….can't wait until tomorrow.

Back in the car. Can't start. Wrong key. Wrong key again. Put in reverse. Now, put in drive. Drive slowly. Don't let cops know you're drunk. There's the hospital. Go to internal medicine. Walk in building. Third floor. Dr. Jones – sounds nice. Go inside office.

"Do you have an appointment sir?"

"No."

"I'm sorry but you can't see the doctor unless you have –"

"I WANT TO SEE DR. JONES NOW!!! RIGHT NOW!!!"

Security guard comes into room. "Yes, that's the man."

"I'm sorry sir, but you have to leave now."

"Hold on." Man in white doctor's coat.

"Come inside, Jack." Knows my name – must be pretty smart.

Shuts door. "What's wrong, Jack."

"Girlfriend left me…broke up with me. I need something. I can't sleep. I can't sleep one minute even."

"Do you feel suicidal?"

"Yes, but I won't do it."

"Tell me why you won't."

"Because I believe in God, and God did not put me here just so I could destroy myself!"

"OK, alright, that's good."

"I need something."

"Jack, I don't want to give you anything until you've seen a psychiatrist."

"If you don't give me something now, I *will* kill myself, and it will be on *your* head when everyone finds out I came here first."

"OK, Jack. I am going to give you something called Zoloft."

"Thank you, thank you."

"But you can't drink alcohol while you take this."

"I won't" *That was a lie.*

"And I want you to promise me something, too. You just said that you believe in God. I want you to promise me and promise God that you won't kill yourself tonight. Can you do this?"

"Yes." That one was the truth.

XVIII

Slow Recovery

It really took about four months before I was in a completely normal state again. That first night I lied in my dorm room bed, limbs shaking with terror tremors. I understood being sad, but why the constant feeling of panic and utter *terror*? I had become one of Edgar Allen Poe's tortured characters with unbearable thoughts racing through my brain. With the help of the anti-depressants, anti-anxiety pills, or just drinking until blacking out, I was able to get small naps in of about one to three hours after a few days. Luckily I was able to keep from mixing the alcohol with the prescriptions most of the time. I am sure that I accidentally might have mixed them at least a few times. I had a helper, though, that kept me from doing that. The angel appeared that very first night of my panic.

Knock, knock, knock. "Who is it?" No answer.

Knock, knock, knock. "Who is it?" I got up. It could have been after a few seconds, or after a few minutes of more knocking. I opened the door but left the chain-eye latch connected. I looked through the opening. It was Sophie. She was carrying some big duffle bag. My powers of perception during this time were very low, and my interest in the details of the world around me were even lower. "What do you want, Sophie?"

"Let me in."

"No." I started to close the door. It wouldn't close. I pushed a little harder, still nothing. I looked down. Sophie's foot was in it.

"I'm going to break your foot if you don't move it."

"That won't work. These boots have steel-reinforced tips."

"Come in then. Close the door behind you and lock it." I undid the eye latch. She walked in. "Why are you here?" I lied back down on my bed. I had not taken notice, but Sophie would later tell me about the two liquor bottles already lying on the floor, the vomit, the horrible smell, and how she battled to keep my room in a decent livable condition over the next few weeks.

"I'm here because I am your friend," she said very uncharacteristically in my mind.

"Hah," I said, "Sorry, but I'm not in the mood for any sociable sex."

She let my cynical comment simmer a bit, "Maybe you don't remember it right now, but I made you a promise, and I am going to keep my promise. I am going to be here for you."

I am sure her tone was very sensitive and sincere. I imagine there may have even been some tears in her eyes when she said that. I was too out of it at the time to notice any details except the constant terror, panic, and feeling of utter lost oblivion that Poe might say 'pervaded the core of my soul'. But I did hear the words themselves.

"No one is ever here for me." My self-pity was beginning.

"I'm here now. And I am going to stay for as long as you need me." She then opened up the duffle bag. She cleaned the floor, threw out the bottles, and began to fill up an air mattress. After the mattress was full, she put a sleeping bag on top of it.

Sophie stayed with me in my dorm room. She was easily able to sneak food up from the cafeteria to make sure that I was eating. She confiscated my car keys. I was not to go to any liquor stores. I was too tired. My moods swung from a total depressed fog back to the terror panics. Either mood prevented me from having any kind of lucidity. I made some of my classes and rehearsals. My academic grades plummeted. By the end of the semester I was on academic probation. My playing progress stagnated. I would later hear recordings of my playing during this period when I thought I was playing well. The pitch was not good. It sounded like a drunk person playing Bach. We made little progress with the CIVICS operations during these months. Sophie carried the weight for me, and covered for me. Someone in Chicago named Mary McFarland had died a week before my panic started. She was six years my senior and had a younger brother named Jack. Sophie started the myth other students that I was *that* Jack, and that I was completely traumatized by the death of my sister. When I slowly started to emerge out of my dorm room to eat in the cafeteria, people seemed to know about my "sister".

"I heard about your sister, Jack. And you have my deepest condolences. If there is anything I can do, just let me know." Melvin was a nice guy. Honestly though, our friendship was more on a superficial acquaintance level much like my relationships with my other lunch mates.

A very unfortunate opportunity arose - a bass audition for the Baltimore Symphony. I had actually noticed it a week before the break-up. I didn't think much of it because I didn't feel ready. After all, I had only been working on my orchestra excerpts at the University for a little over a month. But now I envisioned a pathetic opportunity: *Win the Baltimore Audition, move to Baltimore with my awesome bass job and sweep Sam off of her feet. A marriage would soon happen and then the house and the kids and everything else.*

I told my bass teacher I was going to take the audition. He advised against it. I didn't care. Sophie never told me not to take the audition, but was not very enthusiastic about it either. Without being able to recall the exact wording, there was a conversation between us similar to this:

"Jack, if she doesn't want to be with you now, and then would change her mind because you land some great bass job, I don't think that is the kind of girl you want to be with."

"The reason our relationship fell apart is because we are too far away from each other. With a job in Baltimore, I could support myself and even partially support her. We could be together. Everything would work out."

Samantha also unfortunately gave me hope in the form of not dismissing the idea when answering a phone call. It was a little over a week after the break-up. "Sam, if I won that audition and could move to Baltimore with a steady bass job, do you think we could get back together?" It was very pathetic, but that was the state I was in. "I could then change my name and quit working for Hurst. What do you think? Do you think we could get back together if that happened?"

Her answer was the most evil, sinister, and hideous answer that a woman could ever give to a man in a condition like mine. She paused for a moment and then said: "Maybe."

XIX

The Audition

I could not afford the cargo charge of shipping my bass on the airplane which amounted to even more than the cost of an extra ticket. So I drove from Bloomington to Baltimore for the audition. It was only early November, but there was snow coming down in Pennsylvania. Driving through the snowy mountains of Pennsylvania in my condition was something I should have never undertaken, but I somehow made it through without getting into a wreck. After driving twenty hours, I stayed in Baltimore at Melvin's parent's house. That was the thing I had suggested he could do for me after he made his 'if there is anything I can do' comment. They lived in the middle of a Hasidic Jewish neighborhood. A detail that would have struck me much more if I were not on anti-anxiety and anti-depressant drugs would be the long beards and large black hats of the Hasidic men and the pilgrim-like attire of the ladies. Melvin was actually very cosmopolitan and Americanized when compared to most of the people living in his neighborhood who seemed to cling to their old-world Jewish customs. I ended up parking right across the street from the performance hall where the auditions were taking place. I was actually a little surprised that I found a parking space so close in a big city like Baltimore. I later found out why that space was available.

I remember seeing and hearing amazing players all around me. I went in for my audition behind the screen. I played well. I was told to wait until the afternoon, it was morning. When the afternoon came, I had made the cut to the second round. The second round was without a screen. Who knows if the lack of a screen was a cause or not, but I did not make the next cut. Forlorn and nearing a total blackout, I headed back to my car carrying by bass by leaning its weight on my hip. Then I saw my car. The windows were shattered. All my luggage had been stolen. Tapes I had been listening to on my tape player were gone. And along with my luggage, all of the photos I had taken with Samantha were stolen. *Why did they have to steel the pictures?* It was as if it was not convincing enough to merely make me lose the audition, someone had to erase all my wonderful memories of Samantha to twist the knife in me and in effect say, "In case there was any doubt, Jack, your hopes with Samantha are now one-hundred percent dead."

I pulled myself together just long enough to stay at Melvin's parent's house a few days while a dealership fixed my windows and charged me about a million dollar bill for it. I remember filing a police report. Nothing came of that. About seven or eight days after leaving Bloomington, I was finally back. If Sophie had not been with me in my dorm room after that, I probably would have needed to be checked into a mental hospital.

I constantly tried to get liquor. Sophie was too smart, too quick, and always one step ahead of me. One time I really lost it and concentrated my total effort to use the one advantage I had over her: my strength. I finally got a hold of her and pinned her down. I reached into her pocket and got my key chain. "Got em'!" I cheered to myself. I sprang up and ran out of the door to the parking lot. I went as fast as I could, but Sophie seemed to let me get away. She was easily able to out kick me, out punch me and out maneuver me partly because of her fighting skills but also because of the constant fog my mind was in. She could have probably run me down. I found out why there was no need when I got inside my van. My van ignition key had been taken off of the key chain. The agency had not taught me how to hotwire a car yet. I was not going to make it to the liquor store after all.

I walked back to my room. Then a good sign happened. The first glimpse of my old wit reemerged. "Well, Sophie. You got me again. I guess this is what they call 'tough love' isn't it?" "Yes," Sophie's face lit up because she saw the reemergence too, "that's right, Jack. Tough love."

XX

Moving On

"It's time to move on now, Jack." Sophie was sitting down on my little dorm bed next to me. She held both my hands in hers and looked at me directly in the face. It was a week after the failed audition trip. "It's time," I repeated faintly and returned her glance for as long as I could. Then my shallowed-out soul reached the limit of its depths and my head fell downward again. Her words had registered though. They registered deep within me.

It is easier to remember lighter conversations we had later while I was walking up the ladder of improvement. "Jack," Sophie said one time, "one thing I find amazing about you is that you can handle bullets, three-hundred pound henchmen, a South American Jiu-jitsu expert, performing sexual acts with a gun pointing at you, and God knows what else without hardly blinking an eye. But, when a woman breaks your fragile heart, you come completely unglued."

"Yeah", I said. "I've got a lot of Billy Ray in me."

"Billie Ray?"

"Billie Ray Cyrus."

Sophie still looked at me confusedly.

"'Achy Breaky Heart'? Never heard of it?"

"No," she said.

"That's because you've never had to play a gig at an Indiana wedding reception."

Sophie said it was time for me to "get out there". It was about a week before Christmas break. We both felt I would be alright over the holidays if I went back home to visit my folks and she did the same with her family. But, for a little practice, it would be good for me to get out and socialize a little before then.

Apparently there was an unofficial "agent's party" taking place at someone's house on the other side of Bloomington that Hurst was unaware of. Sophie drove me there. Before we got out of the car to go inside the house, Sophie took something out of her purse and handed it to me.

"Open your hand." I did as she directed. She put a pack of condoms into my hand.

"There are agents here that work all over the Midwest. You know what we're like, Farley, we all live on the edge. If you get lucky with someone, please wear one of these."

"Oh, no Sophie. I don't need these. This won't be happening."

"Keep them." She forced them back into my hands. "Your power to resist might not be so good. I know for a fact that you haven't even been on a date in over two months."

"If anything happened," I started to defend myself already for any future infraction that the night might afford me, "it would only be because of how long it has been, like you just said."

"I know, Jack." She smiled, "Do you think it has been easy for me since my marriage fell apart? And even when I was married, I did not see Emile sometimes for weeks at a time. We're all human. I am not going to hold it against you for being human. In fact, if all you need is someone for right here and right now, I think tonight is the best opportunity you might be getting for a while."

I was off of the anti-depressants and anti-anxiety pills, so it was OK to drink, finally.

I think Sophie knew exactly what was going to happen. A female agent there looked *remarkably* like Julie, the hot Japanese woman from CIVICS. I ended up talking to her. Her name was Cynthia. She was actually half Japanese. The other half was Austrian. Up close you could see that her Asian features were not as pronounced as Julie's. But, the jet-black shiny straight hair, the olive shaded skin, the smooth-flirty tone in her voice, her body, her legs, and she had on a very provocative dress on top of everything else. Here was my chance to hook up with Julie, but not have to deal with the awkward situation of seeing Julie afterwards – because it wouldn't *be* Julie that I was hooking up with.

We were sitting next to each other at a kitchen table while other partiers were downstairs or in other rooms. I asked her what her last name was. She said, "Vertrauen." I learned later that was not true. But, no one can expect a CIA agent to just give out his or her real last name that easily. I had a feeling though, that she was taking me somewhere with the name, especially in the mysterious way she said it. So, I followed her lead, "Vertrauen, what an interesting name."

"Do you want to know if it has a meaning?"

"Oh, yes." Our eyes were steadily getting closer.

She pulled out a German to English dictionary. *How convenient.* She turned to the word Vertrauen and pointed, and then handed the page to me.

Vertrauen – Trusting.

"Trusting." I said looking back at her.

"Yes," she acknowledged, "trusting."

It wasn't the best of lines or set ups, but it worked for me. We started kissing, and the kissing kept going. She was into it. I was too. It was a great make-out session. She motioned her head towards across the hall where there was an empty bedroom. I was game. I picked her up and swept her over to the room. There was not an actual bed, but a large mattress on the floor. It had all the necessary sheets though, and a comforter, and a couple of pillows. We closed the door and sat down on the bed, still kissing. She was a great kisser – very passionate, very enthusiastic. I pulled her shirt up and over her head and deftly undid her brazier. We kissed a little more. A small little wave of trepidation came over me just a little bit, not enough to ruin the mood. She started to undo my pants. And then, I didn't want it to go further. What had happened up to that point had felt good, but I just didn't want to go any further. I gradually calmed the excitement down and then broke the kiss. Then I actually said, "Could you hold me for a little while." She said somewhat awkwardly, "Sure." Now things *did* feel uncomfortable. I could not figure out why I wanted her to stop. There was no doubt that my *body* wanted more, but a deeper part of me did not. At the exact moment when we started to only hold each other, some idiot opened the door. This guy was really low on the mature scale too: "What? You guys are in here just *cuddling?* Come on! Get with the party!!" He closed the door. I suppose he assumed that after his great words of inspiration we would immediately start humping like rabbits. At the end of the party, I took Cynthia's phone number because of sheer politeness. I did end up calling her a couple of times too, again out of politeness. But, I never saw her again. As Sophie and I got into the car to leave, I didn't say much. Sophie seemed to know what had happened, though. "I heard Clark may have ruined your hook-up. I told him to leave you two guys alone."

"Clark didn't ruin anything. Open your hand, Sophie." She did as directed.

"Here," I placed her un-opened package of condoms back in her hand, "didn't use them, didn't need them."

XXI

Back in the Saddle Again

Sophie and I agreed that even though I might not be ready to be intimate with a woman yet, I was past the dangerous, acute stage of my crises. There was more healing to be done. But I could now "function like a normal person" again.

Christmas break went fine. I saw my family, Sophie saw hers. I had been reliving a lot of the bad parts of my childhood in therapy shortly before this visit, but I managed to put those memories aside during the holidays. I found it ironic that I had at times speculated about Sophia's childhood, concluding that her strange ways in relationships were the result of some kind of traumatic childhood experience. I was now learning that I had plenty of skeletons in my own closet when it came to childhood that fueled my incredibly heightened fear of abandonment; a fear that crippled me when I was forced to face it head on.

As the second semester began, Sophie was finally allowed into *aerodynamics*. I caught up with her and Hurst about some of the more heinous things that CIVICS had been doing in the past few months at our first CIA meeting of that semester.

Two more abortion doctors had been attacked. One was killed, and the other was still in a coma. The authorities were hoping to question the coma patient if she ever regained consciousness. Targeted "liberal entrepreneurs" such as adult bookstores and publishers, risqué clothing shops, and anything else the group determined as dangerous to the Christian and Islamic vision they upheld had been receiving letters filled with ricin. One man had been hospitalized because of this. Mimicking the Unabomber, CIVICS was under suspicion of sending a bomb to the statehouse through a Federal Express package. The bomb was screened and deactivated before it ever had a chance to detonate. There was not enough evidence to charge CIVICS with any of these crimes. CIVICS had only been implicated through grapevine street rumors. That was why we needed someone on the inside like Sophie or me who could get the group on tape while planning one of these attacks. Now that Sophie was on the inside, this information should have been coming soon.

Sophie talked with Hurst and me during our CIA meeting after her induction into aerodynamics the following week. The room where the inner circle met was seemingly impossible to take a hidden microphone into. The door had very high-tech metal detectors and electricity detectors all around it. She had to ditch her mic in a garbage can before entering the room to avoid getting busted. This is what she could share with us, but could not prove yet in a court of law. Her story shocked me and Hurst. "Aerodynamics is all about recruiting pilots." She looked at both of us very seriously. "Some physics' students make good candidates either as pilots or as trainers. But, CIVICS actually likes to target discharged soldiers the most: Air force, Navy, Army, any division that trains pilots. A pilot who is not up to snuff in the air force is a perfect person for CIVICS. The group brainwashes the men to believe that their country has betrayed them, that the pilots who are selected by the armed forces are all chosen politically or as part of a nepotistic endeavor, and basically feeds the poor rejected pilots with as much anger over the rejection as possible to the point of absolute hatred. A lot of these guys are on the down and out anyway. Think about it. The military is often someone's last resort if they did not do well in high school or college or they cannot seem to find a career. If the *military* even rejects you, then a young man often times really does begin to hate the world. The group feeds on these kinds of people. They remind the down and out people of all the hardships they have faced, they blame the government and the status quo for all of those hardships, and then they offer people a way to either have a revolution against such a government or to just 'stick it to the man' in general. It is political activism that feeds upon hatred and vengeance. I just wish the recruits could see what the top level people in aerodynamics are like. They are the most selfish, richest, single-mindedly diabolical people I have ever encountered."

"But why does aerodynamics want pilots, of all people?" I asked. Hurst seemed to already know. Sophie turned to face me and said, "To fly airplanes into buildings."

XXII

One of Many

"This Bloomington group is just one of many. There are a half a dozen others around the Midwest, and dozens of others around the world. Stevens is the head of all of the Midwestern groups. Only here in the U.S. do they use the name CIVICS. In Europe, Asia, and Africa, they all go by Islamic names. You don't find any Christian labels for this group in any of those places."

"Europe, Asia, and Africa," I repeated. I looked over at Hurst, "No South America?"

Sophie answered, "The leaders told me South America is not part of their network."

Still looking at Hurst I said, "And Clinton is searching *South America* for dangerous Evangelist groups?"

"Makes you sick, doesn't it? He probably is searching South America because of all the fine Latin ladies down there," Hurst replied.

"Mmmm. You can say *that* again." I added. Sophie actually gave me a little jab with her elbow.

"Not as fine as *you,* Sophie." Everyone made a little smile. We were acquiring a familiarity with each other. I still didn't like Hurst overall, but I was starting to get him. He was conservative, but he was alright. He reminded me of Ronald Reagan. He was cool about his conservatism.

"I still don't understand the kamikaze thing," I said. "Flying planes into buildings? Really? I understand that it makes a very dramatic effect. But it is a suicide mission. And very likely it will just create a lot of property damage instead of actually killing people."

"That depends on the plane and the building," said Hurst. "A small, single engine plane hitting a huge building will likely create the kind of result you just mentioned – a suicide mission that causes a lot of property damage. But how about a huge 747 hitting a small building? Everyone in the building would likely be smashed and the building destroyed. And even worse, how about a 747 or a DC 10 flying into one of our skyscraper landmarks? Imagine the Empire State Building being hit at the bottom. The crash could destroy the core of the building and the upper levels would all come crashing down. And even though many of the more modern buildings are very strong and reinforced with earthquake resistant pliability, you need to think about the jet fuel. The jet fuel in a large plane is over 1,500 degrees Fahrenheit when it explodes. This would soften the metal framework of almost any building and the fuel tank is almost sure to explode in such a crash. With the metal core softened or perhaps even melted, the building would come crashing down. Everyone in it would surely perish."

"Someone should tell the president about this." I said.

"The president has heard about this from other groups. Unfortunately, he also hears all the rumors of dictators who might be making a nuclear bomb, and countries that might be aiming missiles at us, and groups that might be mailing bombs to us, and hundreds of other kinds of threats. Unless we get these people on *tape*, the president probably is not going to take this threat seriously."

For a little framework in which to consider this situation, remember that it was back in early 1996. No one back then thought of people flying planes into buildings as a huge threat. No one thought anyone would actually do it. Yes, the Japanese had done it in WWII, but that was fifty years ago and they did it to sink battle ships. If only our government, our people, and the clandestine organizations of the United States could have been aware or had the proper direction to pinpoint groups that were working exactly on this kind of attack. But even with the right direction, it is unlikely that anyone could have stopped what was to happen just over five years later in New York City. But one can't help but stop to wonder "what if we had…" Eighteen years later, one can see the security everywhere around our country: security cameras in every store and on every major street corner, people tracking their children's whereabouts with cell phone technology, and most schools having security officers and metal detectors at their doors to protect the children. We got serious about being a secure nation. But it took 9/11 to happen before we finally took a serious look at the issue.

"I have an idea," I said, "I think we can get them on tape, and we can do it now without waiting for them to decide to bring me into the inner circle with Sophie."

XXIII

Gotcha

Later that week before the CIVICS meeting, I saw Ryan Kleinschmidt talking with Armande DeJesus after one of the orchestra rehearsals. I stayed in the rehearsal room marking some things on my bass music. There were always a few musicians who stayed in the rehearsal rooms for five to ten minutes to do things like that. I listened intently to their conversation with my musician's ears.

"Why didn't the air force accept you?" Ryan asked him.

"I don't know. I think it was politics. I flew the simulator test as good as anyone else who I saw or talked to. I could have gotten citizenship too, if they had accepted me and let me serve a full term." "This kind of injustice is prevalent all over the world, Armande. And it is especially prevalent here in the U.S. Do you still want to learn to fly?"

"Oh, yes. But no flying schools here will accept me. And back in Columbia, you need to be very rich to attend flight school."

"I bet you have to be very connected to get into the Columbian Air Force as well."

"Oh, yes."

I almost wanted to shout out to Armande, *"Hey Armande, I thought you were famous in your homeland!!"* He had already suffered enough about that back in Indianapolis, though.

Ryan continued to spin a web around poor Armande, "I know people who could train you for free, Armande. And they also understand the pain and injustice you have had to go through just because you were not born here in America. America, after all, is not such a great place in which to brag about being born."

Ryan was hooking him in. Sophie and I had to work quickly. I did not want to see Armande get all caught up into this trap.

Ryan indeed did bring Armande into the next CIVICS meeting. I sat with the other mid-level leaders and saw the new batch of recruits and listened to Conrad speak to them all. It was pretty much always the same spiel more or less. The wicked peddlers of sin are ruining the country and destroying religion…yada, yada, yada. We must save our country and our souls…. In the back rooms, Sophie was working her magic, partially because of my plan.

When the door to the inner meeting room was first opened, Sophie took out her cell phone as every other top leader had to do if they had one. The cell phone would set off the metal detector and the electronic detector around the door frame if not removed. So, leaders would all put their phones in a little box outside of the room. Sophie drops her phone on the ground, "whoops", and bends down to pick it up. As she moves her foot while bending down, her foot accidentally kicks the phone through the doorway. The alarm naturally goes off. Everyone in the entire meeting room panics. Mid-level leaders who did not see Sophie's mistake take cover behind desks and a few selected mid-levelers even pull out semi-automatic weapons. This was quite a sight for the new recruits, needless to say. They had not had nearly enough indoctrination and brainwashing yet to be prepared to calmly watch people pull out weapons. Top leaders went into the main room to calm everyone down. Other top leaders looked at each other to laugh at Sophie's clumsiness, and only a few people even took notice when Sophie went inside the room to pick up the phone and take it out of the room in order to put it in the phone box. While she picked up her phone, with her other hand behind her back, she planted a wireless microphone under the meeting table. Soon after, the alarm was manually turned off and then turned on again immediately after she put her phone in the box. She had placed the mic under the table just in time.

No plan is perfect, and there was a downside to this plan. What if nothing incriminating was said during the meeting? Very likely, sometime after the meeting was over, the microphone would be found. Sophie could not get away with another 'whoopsie' while trying to get the mic out of the room and consequently setting off the door alarm once again. We realized that. If Sophie's CIA identity was found out because of this, and no incriminating information had been retrieved, then it would be up to me to get something on the group later, and it would likely be twice as hard. I would have to explain that I had no idea she was CIA. I would have to find another way to record the inner circle. Sophie's attempt seemed to be our best chance. And none of us wanted to wait and see another murder take place at the hands of this group. I heard the entirety of the meeting on tape afterwards in Sophie's basement:

Stevens' voice was talking: "We killed the abortion doctors, we scared the state house with the bomb, we sent the ricin through the mail - all these things are good. But we need to start coordinating with the other divisions in Illinois, Wisconsin, Ohio, and Michigan on operation aerodynamics."

He talked about flight training, he talked about pilot recruits, he talked about finding pilots with real zeal and religious commitment, and he talked a little physics in regards to flight trajectory and air speed. But he never mentioned what the pilots would be doing other than flying. The only thing he said they were flying for was Jesus and Allah. He always mentioned Allah first, though. "These kinds of young men will be the best for serving Allah…and Jesus, with their flying skills."

While I was outside in the outer room, I noticed that there were five minutes left in the CIVICS meeting. 'Damn', I thought, 'they didn't get enough for a raid.' Then, I felt Hurst's cell phone vibrate in my pocket. I reached into my pocket to turn it off, 'They are coming,' I said to myself. I reached down to my ankle, there was my .22. I reached behind my dress jacket to my belt, there was Sophie's magnum. In less than a minute, it happened.

I made sure that I was standing on the high risers with the other mid-level leaders. The risers had been added while I was messed up after the Samantha ordeal. It was Stevens' idea to visually position us above the recruits to symbolize us as a goal to 'look up to.' One mid-level seemed to be yearning toward the edge as if to step down with the recruits – I immediately yelled at him, "Don't you go down to their level until the meeting is over! These newbies need to learn respect and earn respect! Don't you just *hand it* to them!"

My harsh words worked. He got back up on the risers. Not even ten seconds later, there were four loud knocks at the outer door, followed by two more. That was my signal. Immediately after the last two knocks, I jumped down to the floor with all the recruits. The CIA SWAT team kicked in the door and shouted to the mid-levels on the risers, "Don't move! Hands in the air and feet spread apart!" Another squad ran to the back rooms. Someone in the mid-levels pulled out a weapon. The SWAT team saw it and mowed down the mid-levels with a barrage of bullets. Twenty CIVICS terrorists were lying down on the risers bleeding; some already showing no signs of life. If the recruits were freaked out before when Sophie sounded the alarm, they were totally traumatized now.

In the back room the SWAT division that ran back there arrived just before the bullets started flying in the main room. They broke down the door to the inner room and held everyone up in the room. They treated Sophie just like she was one of the terrorists. So her identity was kept safe. My identity of course, was not. I was glad for that. This *ensured* that I would finally get my new name and identity. At least that was how I saw it.

XXIV

From Chaos to Happiness

Sophie and I were enjoying our music studies and we both wanted to finish out the year. She even boned up on her foreign languages. I knew she was fluent in German. She took graduate level French, Spanish, and Literary Arabic as well during the second semester. Hurst gave us both a break from CIA work for the rest of the school year. Sophie though, he warned us, would have to begin again at the beginning of next fall. "She is still serving a two-year domestic service sentence for her involvement with Emile Bajaj's activities," he would remind us.

All of the top level leaders in the Bloomington chapter of CIVICS were arrested and taken in for questioning. They were arrested for all of the crimes committed over that past year: the abortion doctor murders, the ricin attacks, and the bomb sent to the state house among other things. I am sure that interrogators were trying to get them to confess to other crimes as well. The link to training pilots to fly planes into buildings was unable to be proven. Even though Sophie had heard it in a previous meeting, it was not on tape. And none of the leaders would admit or confess to it as one of the objectives of the organization. Eight of the twenty mid-level leaders had been killed by the SWAT team's gunfire.

197

The other twelve were being arrested for their involvement in the past year's crimes.

I moved out of the dorm at the end of the school year and then moved in with Sophie as strictly a platonic roommate. We stayed friends for quite a while. Over that summer we both dated other people and even brought those people to the house for a dinner or a video movie. We even double dated once. We later admitted how foolish it was. We never really liked anyone we dated. A few weeks before the new school year, Hurst assured me that I could stay my second year at Bloomington and finish my graduate degree with the CIA's full protection of both my identity and my name. No one outside of CIVICS had really ever linked me to the club, and because I had not gone higher than mid-level leadership, I would explain to the very few people who knew my position in CIVICS that the authorities let me go because I cooperated with them in giving them critical information. That was actually partially true. I had *indeed* helped the CIA to acquire information about the top leaders. I also explained how lost and brainwashed I had become while in the group, and how I was seeking professional help to "deprogram myself". I was still seeing a therapist of course, but for the fear of abandonment issue. Sophie learned what her fate would be for that following school year as well. She could keep her lease at her house, but she would be flown around the world to different places on short two and three-week missions. These missions were to be much safer than what we had done in the past. She would be working the mission control only, coordinating information for other agents who would be the ones risking their necks out in the field. Her language abilities made her very good for this. Her first mission seemed to be somewhere in South America. She would be back for two-week stays in between missions.

When we learned the plans for us that were to come to fruition in just a few weeks, Sophie and I approached each other that evening while at home. Why were we wasting any more time? We immediately embraced each other, I told her I loved her and she said the same to me. At that moment, I knew there was something else I needed to say, "Actually Sophie, let me be clear. I not only love you, I am *in love with you."*

"Oh Jack, and I too am in love with you!" Immediately, my whole body tingled after I heard those words. Sophie and I spent every waking and sleeping minute together over the next three weeks, except for one evening when I insisted that she had to let me go take care of something.

It was now just over a week before Sophie had to leave for her mission. I told Sophie to pack her bags. She asked for how long. I said for the weekend and maybe one or two extra days. She packed, and I drove her to the Indianapolis airport. She found out the plane was going to Las Vegas. She was excited. She had never been there. Neither had I. We arrived and went to the hotel. I told her to pick the most beautiful dress that she had packed and put it on. I put on a tuxedo. She looked at me strangely when I put on my tux, "Are you going to play a gig here, Farley?"

"You'll see."

I took Sophie down to the lobby. There was the hotel restaurant. It was very nice and very elegant with crystal chandeliers and rich velvet-red carpeting. There was a table reserved for us. I ordered Champagne and excused myself to go to the bathroom. I came back to the table quickly after having been to the bathroom. "You *have* to see the bathrooms, Sophie. They are *incredible.*" She was excited, "OK, I'll be right back," she said.

Immediately after she left, I motioned to the waiter to bring the Champagne. He poured two glasses, and I put a little treat inside Sophie's glass.

When Sophie came back, she saw the Champagne and was a little sore, "Awww, why didn't you wait for me so I could see him pour?"

"Sorry love," I said. "How about a toast to us?" I raised my glass.

She went for her glass. "Yes, to us.." and she stopped in mid-sentence. She stared at the glass. Inside, already drunk with Champagne was a ring gingerly lounging at the bottom of the glass.

"Hey," I said, "what's that?"

She took the ring out of the glass. I walked over to her chair. A few people at other tables had begun to notice when I got out of my chair. I kneeled down at her feet and took the ring.

"Sophia Mitchell," I said tenderly while looking into her eyes and placing the ring on her ring finger, "I love you and I never want to lose you. And I want to make a *new promise* with you. That promise is that we will be there for each other *for always.* Sophie, *will you marry me*?"

She was crying, and I was about to as well. I couldn't tell right away whether her cry was a good one or a bad one. "Yes!" She shouted. "Yes, I will!"

"You will?"

"Yes, I will!"

"Are you sure?"

"Oh please Jack, kiss me!"

I kissed her and there was some applause around the room.

When we broke the kiss, I looked at her, "I have one more surprise, but you don't *have* to go along with it." I led her out of the room across a hallway to a small make-shift chapel. In the room were my old friend Steve, and none other than Patrick Hurst.

"We can make it official now if you want to," I said, "otherwise we'll have to do it between your missions sometime. It's up to you, we can wait if you want. Steve is an ordained minister; he just got his license."

"Could we have another bigger ceremony next year when I'm done with the agency? With all the brides maids, and flowers, and everything - maybe with our families there?"

"Yes," I giggled, "I would love that."

"OK," she said. "Let's do it."

Sophie kept her last name. We didn't even know what my last name would be in a year anyway. I missed Sophie while she was gone on missions that year, but I loved the two weeks that we got to spend together about once a month. Hurst congratulated us and complemented us for "no longer living in sin". I tried to explain to Hurst that Sophie and I were only friends for 90% of the time we were living together, but he didn't buy it. It was great to see Steve again, and our friendship seemed to be back on the mend. I truncated my degree when I won an audition at the beginning of spring 1997. It was as a section bass player in New York's Metropolitan Opera. The orchestra played for both the opera and the American Ballet Theater. Sophie and I were thrilled about moving to New York when her domestic service was over. And we both loved opera and the ballet. So all we needed to do was wait for her domestic service sentence to end the following August. What could possibly go wrong before then? Hmmmmmmmm.

PART III
Chasing the Serpents

I

Rock n' Roll

The sweat was inching down my chest and neck. My whole body was pulsing with the tempo. Bodies were sliding against each other, sometimes banging against each other. I watched as if in a dream the scene around me. I was playing my electric bass and singing. We estimated around 1,000 people were there at the height of the party. It was back in 1992, during Spring Break at Purdue University in Lafayette, Indiana. The rich kids on campus had been able to afford the trips to Florida. The students that stayed here on campus were from the working class families, the salt of the earth, what I call real people. It was at a large apartment complex that had the recreation house in the middle of the complex with an adjoining pool and gazebo. The gazebo was packed. My band barely had room for our equipment, and we turned it all up to ten. All I could see was people everywhere. They were packed in the parking lots, around the pool, under the gazebo, and they danced. They danced with wild abandon. It was a moving work of art to watch the crowd. Couples dirty danced with each other; their hips kissing each other with the beat of the music. Girls danced in groups. Some groups were circles with bold individuals occasionally going inside the circle to show the dancing skills that he or she possessed. Boys without partners tried to dance their best either as a group or just by themselves. No one was inhibited. The level of dancing skill did not matter. One of the drunker boys was actually an old friend of mine from high school. He stumbled across the dance floor. At one point, he started to tip to his left. The next two or three seconds played like a slow motion scene in my mind:

'Hey, there's Will. He's dancing awfully close to my amplifier. What the hell is he doing? He's falling over for Christ sake. He is falling right into my amplifier!' "Will, dude! You're going to break the amplifier!!"

Will could not even come close to hearing me; the music was much too loud. I predicted his falling trajectory correctly just in the nick of time to rush over to my amplifier with my bass strapped over my shoulder. My amp was a tall Rickenbacker stack. There was a large bottom speaker with an equally large upper speaker stacked on top of it connected together by a speaker cable. The head was built in to the top speaker of the amplifier. I was lucky that the stack had only two parts and not three. Three parts would have probably been impossible to handle.

After I arrived at my amplifier barely a millisecond before Will collided with it, I supported the opposite side with my back and shoulder and then watched the drunken Will fall into my stack. It still nearly toppled over. I reached my right arm out to support the top speaker as it started to fall to the side. Will continued to fall down to the floor. With the help of a few good-samaritan spectators, I corrected my amplifier over the next five to ten seconds, and then proceeded to go back to my microphone and continued to sing and play. *The show must go on.*

Will was OK - just totally wasted. He kept apologizing to me between songs for the rest of the night. "Jack, I'm so sorry man. Is your amp, OK? Dude, I didn't know I was going to fall." Obviously he didn't know he was going to fall, but anyone watching him through those three to five seconds would have made the same prediction I had made.

There were other interesting things that went on that night. While the music played, some people dove off of their two, three, and sometimes even four-story balcony into the large pool below. I watched in both excitement and fear. *Lord, I hope they make sure no one is in that part of the pool when they jump.* They jumped off like falling meteorites, sometimes two or three in the same five second interval. During one of the music breaks, while the band and I went over to the kegs for some refreshment, another poor drunk soul was having some trouble. And now, let me give a little framework for this party.

This party initially was intended for the population of students at my old high school who were now attending Purdue. This is why I knew many of the people there. I did not attend Purdue. I attended the conservatory an hour south of there in Indianapolis known as the Indianapolis Conservatory. In my high school graduating class, the largest population headed to Purdue. It outnumbered any other destination by over two to one. Of course, other people could come to the party and *many* others were attending. But those that came up and talked with the band and co-mingled with us were predominantly old high school friends and acquaintances. Of the many wild and crazy things I saw that night, the ones that involved my old classmates naturally stayed in my memory the most.

While walking back from the beer kegs, another high school classmate was in a bad situation. He was way too drunk, of course, and being grossly abused by other classmates that I knew. George Rick had barely graduated high school, and now apparently was having a tough time getting through his coursework at Purdue. He had already been kicked off of campus for various academic problems and disciplinary issues. He was trying to walk, but ended up falling down every three or four steps and then took a long breather on his hands and knees while getting up the energy to finally stand up again. Another old classmate ran up to Rick while he was on all fours and gave him a roundhouse sucker punch to the side of his jaw. Rick fell back down. The old classmate was joined by one or two others in waiting for Rick to compose himself, get back on his knees, and then punched him in his face again. Rick instigated them after the first two or three punches when he actually got back up on his feet and slurred, "Come, ohhwn! You want zum ofa me?" He only was able to do that two or three times. The punches continued on poor ole' Rick. The attitude of the abusers was partially that Rick deserved this, and needed this. He needed his ass kicked in order to "get his shit together". The other part of their attitude was that it was fun to beat up a helpless drunk. Their later justification for their actions came from the first theory.

Welts were forming all over Rick's face. Blood was coming from his nose and around the sharp bone structures surrounding his eyes. No one stopped the abusers. I was the musician and didn't want to mess up my hands for the rest of the gig. I also was a little on the small side during that time. I lifted weights a little later and then might have felt tough enough to intervene in a situation like that. There were plenty of big guys around who could have come to Rick's aid, but no one did. I later learned part of the reason why: everyone hated Rick. He crashed parties, never paid his share of the rent, and owed people all kinds of money. Still, I could not help but think that what was happening to Rick was completely unnecessary. Scenes like these were part of the reason I eventually got out of rock n' roll music.

One punch finally knocked Rick out cold. I guess that was the abusers' goal. It took them awhile, though. Probably a good ten to twelve punches were landed before he was out. You had to hand it to Rick, he had a tough jaw. Some people said he stayed conscious so long because he was wired on cocaine.

Oddly enough, my band was not a tough, loud, rebellious, hard-rock band. We could rock out easily enough, but we mostly played originals. Our sound was very unique which came from the variety of tastes the three members had. I had been exposed to more of the classic rock and progressive rock, and of course had had all of the exposure to classical music. The drummer, Azar, had similar tastes to mine without all of the classical exposure. But the guitar player liked a variety of music like the Grateful Dead, Ziggy Marley, different Zydeco artists, and even Jazz. His style was unique too. He played a lot like the Edge from U2. His rhythmic playing greatly contributed to the dance-like sounds that emitted from us while we played. He could do more than rhythm, though. He could play loud and fast when needed; something rock fans never get too much of. His fast playing was different, though. You hear some guitar players that lie on a fast riff and drive it into the ground. This fast riff is usually the same three, four, or five notes in succession over and over again. Maybe it is G-A-G-E, G-A-G-E, G-A-G-E, in succession over and over again. Listen to the *Freebird* guitar solos sometime and you'll hear what I'm talking about. Calvin did not play that way. His fast stuff had variety to it. It had a journey and a direction to it. He would go up and down the scales. Sometimes this little musical risk got him into places where he would play a couple of notes that didn't fit the chord structure, or where he would play a call phrasing and not follow it up with the proper response phrasing, but it made his playing unique nonetheless, and I liked it. He was the first musician to get me tuned into the musical styling of Jerry Garcia, a guitarist whom I regard as one of the most individual and unique players ever to grace the genre of rock n' roll.

Groovin' Hard was my favorite rock-pop band that I ever played with. It was the most original. It wasn't your typical garage band because we were all talented. And our style was perfect for the tastes of the early 90s. A little Jesus Jones-ish, a little U2- ish, a little Dead-ish, a little like the Cars sometimes, a little bit of the Black Crowes – mix those bands together and you can come sort of close to describing our style.

Four years later in the fall of 1996, I was pretty far away from rock n' roll. Groovin' Hard had played together for the last time around 1994. We had graduated college and were headed in different directions. We all had to "get serious" about what we were going to do with our lives. Getting a recording contract with some kind of label had eluded us for the three to four years that we played off and on. It had eluded all of the bands I had played in. You could pay through the nose to get your own studio recording time, of course. But that doesn't make you money. But rock n' roll didn't occupy my mind anymore. I was happy and content – more than I had ever been in my life. I was finishing my second year at the Jordan School of Music in Bloomington Indiana. Sophia and I had busted a terrorist cell that had been recruiting members for domestic terrorism. In the following chronological order Sophie was my schoolmate, and then my obsession, and then my bane, and then my lover, and then my enemy, and then my partner, and then my friend, and then my girlfriend, and now was my wife. My first crush on her developed late in my freshmen year of college. We never officially dated in college but had had a few "friends with benefits" moments that amounted to nothing more than some kissing. After graduating, we came across each other in a popular downtown bar known as Turtle's. Still having unresolved feelings for her, I pursued her when she offered to meet me. We hooked up and I became involved in an international terrorist plot she was already involved in. This caused the death of Jessica, my roommate Steve's fiancée, because the dangerous terrorist group that I had become involved with confused my identity with Steve's. Steve was also my best friend. He was taken hostage by the rogue German terrorist group, and Sophie and I had to risk our lives to save him. Sophie also wanted to get some microfilm that the group was after which she had hidden in the pocket of a jacket coat that belonged to me but was being worn by Steve during the time he had been kidnapped. To make a long story short, I had to trick the group while they were trying to force me into a ménage a trois with them and Sophie. I tricked them into thinking I was picking a fight with their 350 pound henchmen which distracted them while I called the CIA into their house for a bust. So just so you know, Sophie and I had a very rich history and we had gone through a lot together in the past six years, and a hell of a lot in the last year and a half.

The summer of 1996 was the summer where we finally came to terms with our feelings for each other. No more games. I proposed and she said yes. We had a Las Vegas wedding and I promised her a more elaborate ceremony the following summer in 1997. We had to wait until then because Sophie had been sentenced to perform domestic service work with the CIA because of her former connections to a terrorist group, and she was in the last year of that sentence. I was done with the CIA at the end of summer 96, and I would be able to stay at home to finish my Master's Degree. Sophie was going to be flown around the world for special operations. These operations were to be in mission control centers as a communicator with agents. She was not supposed to be out in the field with the bombs and the bullets. The missions usually lasted around two to three weeks, and then she spent the rest of the month at home with me. Those times were beyond wonderful. She had always been my secret desire, even when I had dated other women or had silly crushes on other women. I had thought that Sophie was either uninterested or unavailable during those times. When something doesn't seem to be a realistic option, you forget about it – consciously. Subconsciously though, I had never been able to forget about Sophie. Finally Sophie was both interested and available, and now was even my wife! So you can image what our time together was like especially at the beginning of the school year in the fall of 1996. While Sophie was gone, I concentrated on my studies and playing, and I also concentrated on transforming my body. To risk sounding like a braggart, I turned my body into a finely tuned machine. I was doing over one hundred crunches a day. Along with running and swimming, I was lifting weights and isolating my triceps, biceps, hamstrings, calves, thighs, and my pectorals. I even hooked up a pulley system on my neck to get it tighter and toned. When Sophie came back at the end of the month, she would enjoy looking at me while my shirt was off. She was particularly intrigued by my pectoral muscles – what some people call the male breasts. "Make them shake again," she would ask with her beautiful green eyes coming alive in front of mine. I would alternate flexing the left and right pectoral muscles making a funny looking flip flop motion, a trick I learned from watching the professional wrestler Hulk Hogan. She both laughed and approved at the same time. She would also ask me to flex my thigh muscles. She said my thighs looked like a thoroughbred horse, so my running was paying off. She also appreciated my improved abdominal muscles, the "abs". She would comment that my stronger abs gave me the stamina to do certain things for a much longer period of time. And while she was home we would spend nearly every single minute together. I would caress her beautiful long red wavy hair. When the weather was more hot and humid, a few frizzy curls would appear. Her hair was naturally curlier, but she liked to straighten it in the mornings. It ended up with a large wavy look to it most of the time. We would look into each other's eyes for such long periods of time. 'I love you' was traded quite a lot, but not overused. If I could have dreamed the perfect life with Sophie, it couldn't even have compared with this.

II

Reigning in November

It was now mid-November. I had begun to grow tired and weary of waiting for Sophie to come home each month. After having a horrible break-up in another relationship where distance became a big problem, I did not want the same thing to happen again. Sophie and I talked about it in October. "Jack, I honestly know we love each other. If something were to happen between you and another woman or between me and another man. I don't think it means anything. As long as it only happens once, and it doesn't turn into a long, lingering affair." Sophie may sound quite liberal, and looking back, it *was* a very liberal thing to say. But the 1990s were like that. When President Clinton kept getting caught having affairs with different women, people felt that it was a sign that marriage was too strict. People started to think, *"The reason people stray so much and marriages fall apart is because people are seeking perfection in their marriages. No one can reach perfection. So, if you set up low expectations in the first place, your marriage won't become a total failure or a total disaster."* This concept may be a little exaggerated the way I just expressed it, but the idea of "open marriages" was indeed becoming more acceptable in the 1990s. It is nearly unthinkable in mainstream culture today. Sophie and I agreed on the following ideas: cheating once with just one person ought to be forgiven; anyone could become weak at a particular time, especially when their partner was gone for half of each month or more. If the one-time indiscretion turned into an affair that lasted a short period of time, marriage counseling would be required. If the one-time indiscretion turned into an affair that lasted a long time, specifically more than six months, then marriage counseling would definitely be required and either of us would have an appropriate reason to seek a divorce. The third result would also be available if the indiscretions ever spread to more than one person. Having thoroughly discussed these boundaries, I entered the third month of watching Sophie leave for an assignment wondering how each of us would fare until the last half of the month.

Sophie and I did not need to talk on the phone nightly while she was away. We talked two times a week, and if something was important that week, three times. We were informative and affectionate during our conversations, but we did not engage in any "dirty talk" on the phone. I had done that with my previous girlfriend, and it only seemed to make the loneliness worse. In the second week of November I told Sophie about a musician's party that was going to happen early in the third week. She might not be back by then. She told me it was alright if I went by myself.

The house was on the north side of Bloomington. When I arrived, there were musicians I knew from around Bloomington, and even some I recognized from Indianapolis. Many people were hanging out, smoking and drinking under a front porch awning supported by ornate colonial style pillars. I mingled and talked mostly with other men that I knew from various types of orchestra jobs. I went inside, talked some more, and walked over to a punch bowl. I was aware of someone in my peripheral vision. She had long red hair, and a nice smell. I grabbed my punch glass and walked to the other side of the room where there was a table with pretzels and chips. I grabbed some of the latter. The redheaded woman walked up next to me on my right. I lifted my gaze to hers.

"Jack McFarland?" she asked enthusiastically.

"Laura Wolfowitz?" I responded.

Laura Wolfowitz was a fun, energetic, cute, down to earth girl whom I had known back at the Indianapolis Conservatory. To say she was multi-talented is an understatement. She had a French horn scholarship with the wind ensemble and played that instrument in the orchestra. But she also played flute and violin. By her junior year, she had improved so much on the violin that she had become one of the top four violinists in the orchestra. The conductor would usually put her second chair in the first violin section or first chair in second violins. Laura's status as one of the hot girls in the music school also dramatically improved by her junior year. When she arrived freshmen year she was referred to by the boys as pleasantly plump – pudgy you might say. She was still cute, just a little on the heavy side. After two years she had finished an intense weight loss and exercise campaign and had become one of the hottest looking girls in the music school. I had thought she was hot back then in her junior and senior year, and she definitely looked hot now. I was also impressed by her fortitude, inner drive, and overall work ethic. She had red hair too – which always increased a woman's status in my mind.

"How have you been, Jack?" She smiled at me. She had rich succulent lips like Sophie's. I caught her up on my life in the music field, about my future job, and finally at the end of a one or two minute history session, mentioned my marriage to Sophie.

"Oh, Sophie Mitchell?"

"Yes, that's her."

"Everyone always thought you two looked good together. We thought you guys would eventually get together."

I switched the conversation to her. She was teaching violin and finishing a master's degree back in Indianapolis. She then mentioned a boyfriend and then added a last little tidbit of interesting information.

"He's a trucker though, and I only see him about a week or two each month."

"Wow." I said, "What a coincidence. Sophie has meetings around the country with her work, and she can only make it home about two weeks of each month as well."

"How do you deal with the loneliness Jack?" she had just put her hand on my shoulder. We had had about two drinks each by this time.

"It's hard," I said, "I work out a lot."

"Oh, I *love* to work out."

"Yes, it's great."

"Yes, as long as you work off your calories, you can eat just about whatever you want."

"Yes." I was running out of things to say at the moment.

"What else do you do?"

"What do you mean?"

"You know, about the loneliness."

I looked back at her. Her eyes were starting to speak things to me.

"I think I might need some fresh air." I began.

"Me too," she said, "and there is an ice cream place down the street that is open until late. Let's go get some."

"OK," I couldn't think of a way out of it. So we walked over to a TCBY down the street. It was actually on the fourth floor of a little shopping complex. We took an elevator up to the store. I ended up getting a root beer and a hot dog with fries at a little hot dog place next to the TCBY. They packed up the food for me in a little box. Laura got a large ice cream cone. It could have been a yogurt cone – I wasn't sure yet. As we walked back to the elevator lobby, me holding my boxed food and drink and Laura holding her ice cream cone while taking long slow licks, she struck up the old conversation topic again from the house.

"We'll have to find a way to work off these calories now, won't we?"

"I guess so." I replied still very innocently. The lobby was bare, just the two of us, while we waited for the elevator.

"Mmmmm." She said, "This is soooo good."

She was standing right next to me. I looked over at her and her eyes met mine. Then my eyes unfortunately wandered down to her ice cream cone. She took an extra-long lick. She saw me watching her, and I knew she was aware of my gaze. A little bit of ice cream was dripping from her bottom lip after that last lick.

"Do you want some?" she asked me.

"Sure." I said.

She looked down at her cone for a second, and then leaned down to take another big lick and a large bite. She then looked up towards me and leaned her lips up against mine. She opened her mouth, and I involuntarily did the same. I tasted her ice cream. It was indeed ice cream. It tasted milky and sweet. And when the ice cream flavor subsided, she licked her tongue against mine to make sure that I could then taste her. She had me under her spell.

The elevator suddenly opened. We both broke our kiss and walked inside. It was empty. The elevator closed. We looked at each other. Laura reached to the elevator controls and flipped the emergency stop lever. A not-so-loud buzzing ensued, and Laura leaned back into me again. We kissed. It was good. She broke off and I leaned in wanting more. She put her finger up between our lips to make me stop. "Wait," she said. "Stay still." I did as she requested. She leaned her face in very close to mine. She was lovely. Beautiful eyes, nose, and lips. Her long red hair hung down over her shoulders. She smiled good. She kissed good. And you could see she was in good shape too. Probably in good enough shape to kick a lot of guy's butts. She started to lick my lips. She licked around my upper and bottom lips while I watched her, still keeping still. She did this two or three times. My desire was swelling. Holding back was becoming nearly impossible. My hands were beginning to reach up to her waist. Before my hands reached her, she stopped her tongue and then pinpointed it right in the middle of my upper lip. I was now very clean shaven with short, styled hair. It was the look that Sophie liked the most; kind of the Ken doll look. I found that Sophie liked kissing me a lot when I looked that way. Laura seemed to like it too. Laura put her tongue right in the aforementioned place, and then rapidly moved it side to side on my lip while creasing her eyes in a laser-like provocative gaze into my eyes. My desire was now completely overwhelming. I broke at that point. I shot my mouth to hers and kissed her hungrily. She kissed my neck and ears, I kissed hers. I tried to pull up her shirt, but it wouldn't go up. "It's a one-piece, Jack." *Damn those leotards.* We began to hear voices and shouts from above and below. People were waiting for the elevator. They probably thought something was wrong. We had to release the stop lever. She fixed her clothes a little and I fixed mine. The elevator opened and we were on the bottom floor. There were about eight people waiting there. They looked at us a little funny. As a couple people started to walk in, they suddenly stopped while looking down at the elevator floor and one said, "Ewwww." I looked down. I had dropped my ketchup and mustard-laden hot dog and fries on the elevator floor. The box had been trampled on and the squished food articles and condiments looked pretty gross. "Oh, excuse me." I said, and then tried to clean up the mess the best I could.

III

A Dangerous Rendezvous

"There's another elevator on the other side of the shopping complex," Laura whispered into my ear while I cleaned up my hot dog, "all the stores are closed on that side. No one will need to use it." We rushed to the other side of the building after throwing my food, my root beer, and her ice cream in the trash. We walked inside. The doors shut. We looked at each other. I pulled the stop lever this time. We brought our faces together like last time. "Do it just like last time." I instructed her, "Do your French Horn trill."

In between kisses during that long make-out session, I said to her, "I'll have to make sure that I wash your lip stick off of my shirt collar," I said to her with a twinkle in my eye.

"Yes you will, Farley," she replied.

"Don't ruin it yet!" I said almost tragically.

"OK, Jack! My trucker husband won't mind."

"He's gone, remember?"

"Oh, yeah."

She was very good with her lips. And I enjoyed each and every kiss that we shared in that elevator. After a while, as with everything, the passion finally died down, and we gave our lips a rest. "Thank you," I said.

"You're welcome," she replied.

"And who do you want *me* to be for one day next month?" I asked her.

"I was thinking that trombone player from Chicago who played with you at Lafayette Symphony."

"Ryan Scherwin?"

"Yeah, him." said Sophie.

"Hmmm. I'll have to work on his deep, mysterious voice. I'll have to walk a little taller, too."

"You're about his height," she said, "He has that icy stare, though. Try and copy that."

Sophie was the first woman with whom I had ever felt comfortable enough to do a role-playing scene. We decided last month to start trying it once a month, and this had been our first try. Laura was also a redhead as I had mentioned, so Sophie looked similar to her in that way and in a few other ways as well. Sophie had done a great job imitating Laura Wolfowitz's speech patterns, the way she walked, and had even learned Laura's current relationship status. Laura was indeed married to a trucker at that time who was away for most of each month. We had set it up for me to "meet her" at the Bloomington party. Sophie kept in character almost right up to the very end of that last elevator interaction. It was a lot of fun, and I think role playing did keep us from getting any kind of cheating bug. It was as if we were able to cheat with each other! I would have to start studying Ryan Scherwin now for next month so I could give Sophie a great role playing experience in return.

IV

You Again?

Role playing had been great. We kept our schedule up each month and had great "cheating experiences" through our vicarious play acting. Sophie said I did a great job as Ryan Scherwin. I borrowed a friend's substitute trombone and then glided the instrument up and down her shapely legs. She was quite ticklish, and this "trombone tickle" indeed made her laugh to the point of losing her breath. My next request was for her to play a gorgeous, brilliant, blonde ballerina named Glenda who had graduated from the Indianapolis Conservatory. Sophie actually learned some dance steps for that role. It was now mid-spring semester in 1997. The good news just kept coming. I had won an audition with New York's Metropolitan Opera. I would be playing the last spot in their bass section. I didn't even really need to finish my degree, but I wanted to anyway. My contract was not to begin until September first. Sophie would be done with her CIA service by then, and the two of us could move to New York together! Wow! Living in New York, playing my bass, and being married to Sophie!! Life just couldn't get any better.

Then, on April first, fortune made me its fool.

It was a Monday afternoon. Sophie had left for her April mission that morning. I had finished my afternoon rehearsal and had come back home to check my phone messages. Most people still didn't walk around with their cell phones during this time. I wanted a little bite to eat, too. After checking some messages and writing down some names and numbers of orchestra managers who needed a substitute bass for the weekend, I heated up some *Weight Watchers* in the microwave. I sat down with my snack and a glass of water in a recliner with a coffee table next to it.

Knock, knock, knock. "Just a minute!" I put my snack down on the table in the small kitchen of my rented Bloomington house and then went to the door. There was no need to check the peep hole. I lived in a nice neighborhood. I opened the door.

"Hello Jack." It was Patrick Hurst, the assistant CIA director with whom I had worked for the operations I had been assigned with Sophie. He had also attended our infinitesimally small Las Vegas wedding.

"Mr. Hurst!" I reached out to give him a hearty hand shake. He really wasn't a hugging kind of guy. Most guys weren't back then.

"Jack, you can call me Patrick if you like. But that's not important right now. We need to sit down."

I directed him to a chair and listened intently. His expression was different from anything I had ever seen before from him. He looked scared, concerned, and had trouble speaking. He took off his fedora hat and held it tightly in his hands. Then he looked at me again with that concerned expression, "Jack, Sophie never made it to the airport today."

V

The Snake Reemerges

This was no April fool. I wish it had been.

"Jack, Sophie parked in the airport parking lot. We have footage of that from the lot's cameras. And then two men came up on either side of her. They both grabbed her arms and pulled her into a black van. We followed the black van for a while and then lost them. Sophie has communication abilities with us, but we have not heard anything from her yet. It might not be safe enough for her to try and get in touch with us right now."

My heart dropped. I blocked out the fear, because there was too much to wrap my mind around to have any room for it. "Is there anything, anything at all that the organization was able to learn from the surveillance footage?"

"Just this. And it could be coincidental, Jack. The type of van was a Mercedes Benz. You don't see too many of those on the road, at least not that particular model. There was someone we know who exclusively used that make and model of a van."

"Probably not Emile Bajaj…" I said, knowing that he knew

what I was thinking. My voice trailed off and diminished into nothingness.

"Stephan and Liane rode in a Mercedes Benz limousine when they took you for a ride that one time. And their own mission control people used that make, model, and color of van that we saw in the surveillance."

"Herr Schlangenstein."

"I think so, Jack."

Herr Schlangenstein was the name of the rogue German terrorist group that had taken my roommate hostage over a year ago. The CIA had thought they were very small and weak at the time. The CIA also thought when they apprehended those eight members that it was the entire group. It looked like America's top clandestine organization had misjudged a situation yet again.

VI

Becoming King Arthur

"There was a message electronically sent to our Midwest headquarters in Chicago as well, Jack. It was intended for you. I wrote it down for you." Hurst handed me a quarter sheet of notebook paper. It was not like him to use up a whole sheet of paper on a short message:

Jack McFarland, you are about to embark on a quest.
But to start your quest, you must first pass the test.
What you need to know will propel you forward,
But first you must go to the place in which your sword is.

I was keeping my head clear. I had to. The subconscious panic was definitely there. Sophie had become my world. I linked my entire future to her. Going to New York in the fall meant nothing if she could not be there with me. I thought about the message a few seconds.

"He is referencing King Arthur - that is clear enough."

"They obviously know your past CIA connections," Hurst chimed in.

I didn't respond. In a less serious situation I might have said, "Yes, and you certainly do have an amazing grasp for the obvious, Hurst." Someone knew about my past. I had figured at least a few people around campus who had been recruits with the terrorist group I infiltrated called CIVICS would have suspicions about why I was a mid-level leader in the group and did not have to serve any kind of punishment after the bust. As detailed as my explanations to suspicious people had been about being let go for providing incriminating evidence to the CIA and FBI, I was not that surprised someone pegged me for an agent. But how did Herr Schlangenstein figure it out? Maybe Hurst was wrong about who the kidnappers were. But that wasn't my main concern, getting back Sophie was paramount. "Midwest headquarters are in Chicago. The person who wrote this must know Chicago. It's not like the CIA office has public signs on the highway directing people there. Tell me Hurst, what kind of connection does Chicago have with King Arthur?" It was my turn now to quiz Hurst. I had grown up just outside of Chicago in the suburbs of Northwest Indiana.

"Are you talking about the Renaissance Fair in Gurnee?"

"I think their implication is even more specific. It is not just about the medieval era."

"What are you thinking, Jack?" I had the famous ex-director of the agency guessing.

"There is a well-known club on the North side of Chicago known as Excalibur."

"Excellent," said Hurst. "I will get some agents on it."

"I'm going to be on the team for this one, Hurst. If you say no, I'll follow along anyway."

"I figured you would, Jack. I'm fine with that. Just remember to keep cool. It will be harder than ever to maintain that. I know how much she means to you."

227

"I know," I replied. "And I have a plan for getting in a little more incognito. A bunch of agents together would not work."

"Clubs are not difficult to work, Jack. Just get some young people in their twenties. Most of our team is exactly the right age."

"Well, they may be the right age, but you need a couple people with another quality if you don't want to stick out like a sore thumb."

"What's that?" asked Hurst.

"Gay." I said. Hurst looked back at me slightly confused.

"Excalibur is the largest and probably the most flamboyantly gay club in the entire Midwest. You need at least one person in the group who can work that angle, or we will be way too noticeable."

VII

Finding My Knights

I had an idea and Hurst was game. It was not difficult at all to find gay or bisexual people in the Fine Arts community where I spent most of my time. But, I needed flamboyant party types too, not the quiet reserved homosexuals who often were still in the closet. There was an old friend of mine from Indianapolis who came to mind.

Sydney Spencer was a remarkable flute player. The man was one of the few musicians who voluntarily put on his own recitals every semester. The school only required one recital a year. He played Bach, Debussy, Beethoven, Stravinsky – any composer from any era, brilliantly. He even wrote some of his own compositions. His style was not limited to classical either. He had found his way into a Jethro Tull cover band and could match Ian Anderson's flute solos note for note, harsh screaming tones and all. It was impressive enough when a saxophone player could do the harsh screaming sound that Coltrane came up with and popular players like Clarence Clemens used later as a trademark sound. But, when a *flute* player could make those sounds, it was absolutely mind-boggling. He talked into the flute saying things while playing notes. He screamed from his own voice while playing and then would make the flute itself scream. He could do circular breathing where somehow he inhaled oxygen while playing notes and never needed to break the sound coming forth in order to take a breath. I don't know how players did that. I imagined they breathed in through their nose while they blew out through their mouth, but how is that even *possible*? Sydney loved to party, too. I had been fortunate enough to be invited to a few of his dorm room parties my Junior and Senior year. They were small parties because of the size of the room. But they were *fun.* The incense would always be burning. Psychedelic lava lamps would be projecting a rainbow of light throughout the room. Beanbags littered the floor. Some kind of sixties music would be playing – Sydney loved the sixties. Even the way Sydney looked with his long, wild blonde hair and trendsetting chin-only goatee added to the festive truly bohemian aura of his parties. And of course, the marijuana smoke would be pervasive. He was careful to only invite "cool people" when this was going on. I had also heard that at a few of his parties some Opium was tried and various other psychedelics. I stayed away from those gatherings. But, watching my friends smoke some occasional pot, especially back in the early 90s in college, was pretty entertaining.

Sydney had a close friend, Winona Lerner, who hung out with him back then. No one used the term "fag hag" when referring to her, but she had some of those qualities. She was fun too. She was from the south somewhere around Atlanta, and still had the slightest touch of a southern drawl in her voice. She was a flute player, like Sydney. She too was very good. The symphony conductor would switch off between the two as first chair flute. I think Sydney didn't get the sole spot because he was occasionally unreliable when it came to showing up for rehearsals. Other girls liked to hang out at his parties too. Of course this was primarily because *he* was fun and the parties were so much fun. But, not having to deal with the horny drunk heterosexual guys was probably also nice for the girls. I imagine that was why I wasn't always invited to his parties, even though I never acted like a dog with women when I was at a party. His parties were him, usually Winona, five or six other female friends of his and Winona's, a couple of other guys who were usually "on the fence" sexually or perhaps still in the closet, and then one, and at most two heterosexual artistic males like myself. It was OK to ask Sydney about his sexual orientation. He liked talking about anything and everything, really. If you asked him, he would tell you he was sexual. This actually was a very honest answer. He had had a girlfriend his first two years at college. He broke up with her, and now he was exploring 'the other side' for lack of a better term. He would not do anything openly with men during his parties. He would sometimes make out with a girl at his parties. Understanding the time and the place would help some people with this situation. Our culture was still not ready to accept open expressions of homosexual behavior.

In the 1990s, President Clinton instituted what was then considered a trailblazing policy in the United States Military: Don't Ask Don't Tell. This meant that soldiers could be gay, but not openly gay. In the past there had been a strict policy against homosexuals in the military. People argued that it was too much to ask a heterosexual soldier to room with a homosexual one or to take a shower with one in the public showers. I guess people figured there would be rampant male rape going on or something. Has anyone ever been camping and slept next to someone who happened to be the gender that they sexually preferred? *My God! How did they do it? How could they keep from sexually assaulting the person over and over again? And of course in a public shower, everyone knows that each person does nothing but stare at each other's private parts the entire time!* There were a lot of things back then that did not make much sense at all. I still love the 1990s, but the country, and especially the conservative state of Indiana was still very behind the rest of the world when it came to acknowledging that most homosexuals are decent, thinking, rational people, who do not desire to have romantic relationships with people who are not of their sexual orientation. Even if someone does happen to be the same sexual orientation, believe it or not, they actually want to get to know the person first before having an intimate relationship with him or her. What an amazing concept! These ideas just did not register with most of the country and my home state during that era.

So Clinton made it OK to be gay, as long as you didn't talk about it with anyone. This became the accepted practice not just in the military, but in all of society. It was not OK to hate gays anymore, unless they came out of the closet and said they were gay – *then* it was OK to hate them. I believe homosexuals in the state of Indiana, even twenty years after Sydney's parties, still mostly feel that a majority of people they encounter don't want to hear anything about their sexual preference and the lifestyle that comes with it. And if a person is gay or lesbian or bisexual, they better not talk about it, and especially not talk about it until they have at least graduated college or turned twenty-one.

I called Sydney that night. He was excited to hear from me. He was finishing a Master's at the Indianapolis Conservatory. Winona was doing the same. I asked him if he was busy that night. He was, but not the following night. I wanted to drive up and hang out at his house. He said it was still the same scene – parties just about every night. So I drove up the following evening and reconnected with some old party buddies. It would be hard to truly enjoy myself, but I would find a way to do it. No mention of Sophie's kidnapping would occur. If asked, I would say she was away on work which was usually the case. If I offered to drive up a small group in my van, I was betting on his crowd being very game for a Friday night trip to Chicago's famous Excalibur night club.

VIII

Club Sexy

Hurst reinstated my CIA status and furnished me with the customary gadgets: various listening devices, a watch with a honing device, and three handguns – a concealable magnum, a .38 Ruger revolver, and a Saturday Night Special. I usually took the magnum and the special. I felt my aim was not as good with the .38 and left it at home. "Who knows", I thought, "if I was on the run and had to come back home, I could find my hidden .38 and use it for protection." He also gave me three different miniature wireless cameras. They didn't record that long once activated – only about two hours. They looked like various small bits of costume jewelry –clear, green, blue, red, or yellow stones. Hurst said the best visuals came from either the clear or the blue. Other ones came across with a red, yellow, or green tint to the picture.

I convinced Hurst to let me go it alone with my newly formed "Knights of the Round Table". He of course would be outside the club in a mission control van listening in through my body microphone. The night was memorable to say the least.

While riding in my van. Winona broke out some schnapps.

While I was being the designated driver, everyone else was in back drinking it up. I heard some delightful screams and whoops and hollers and occasionally asked, "Is everything alright back there?" in a teasing way. I guess Sydney could not wait until arriving at the club and was already having a little fun with one of the other partiers. After arriving in the club and being frisked by one of the four incredibly large bouncers at the door, we went inside. My guns were concealed much too well for the bouncers to detect anything. Once inside, my eyes enlarged at the sight before me.

It was nearly all men. I had thought there might be a more substantial population of lesbians, but the women were few and far between. Perhaps one of every seven booths had a female couple in it. The men were wild. They were chasing each other with their shirts off. At the bar there were at least five visible male couples making out. Back in the shadows of the corners of the club you could see the dark silhouettes of two men seeming to be wrestling with each other, but it was doubtful that whatever was going on was wrestling. The bare chested men were in great shape, showing off their bodies to one another. Some were sweating perhaps from vigorous dancing. The dancing was wild and uninhibited. Some danced in groups, others as partners, others as dirty-dancing partners. If I had to give a short phrase to describe the whole scene I would have said it was just one step away from being an orgy. Sydney came alive. He grabbed the two other men who had come with us whose names I didn't know and pulled them into the crowd. They danced, they went to the bar. Within twenty minutes I saw Sydney kissing another new man at the bar as if he had finally found his long lost home. Even for liberal me, this scene had me slightly scared. Winona sensed my fear.

"Jack," she said, "Don't worry if someone hits on you. Just show them your wedding ring." "They'll ask why my wife isn't here with me." I responded.

Winona put her arm around my shoulders and rubbed them a little, "I'll pretend to be your wife, Jack." And she followed the sentence with one of her giggles that said 'Maybe I'm kidding, maybe I'm not. Try me and find out.'

Winona was a tall, very cute blonde, who had sometimes sent me flirtatious signals in the past. I disregarded any importance to her comment and measured any possible action to be taken in the current situation by the paradigm of whether or not it would lead to me getting Sophie back.

I searched the room with my eyes for any kind of sign that I should notice. I didn't see anything. Just a lot of people behaving with a lot of self-indulgence in a lot of different ways. "What could Herr Schlangenstein have meant in that note? This *has* to be this place. What am I supposed to notice?" I thought to myself.

Then the first significant sign emerged. A man walked up behind Sydney after Sydney had finished kissing his latest make-out partner and tapped him on the shoulder. I was pretty sure who it was, but I tuned my musician's ears in on their conversation. "Armande?" asked Sydney. "Sydney, how are you?!?"

Armande DeJesus. He had been an international student from Columbia at the Indianapolis Conservatory and once Sophie's boyfriend during those undergraduate years. Later a jealous stalker when he incorrectly assumed I was dating Sophie during my first semester at the University of Bloomington. And finally, a lost soul that had just been recruited by the terrorist group CIVICS right before learning what the group was about and witnessing its being busted up by the CIA. "Armande is gay?" I asked myself. I could not see it. He had been so devoutly Catholic. Winona now noticed. "Is that Armande DeJesus?" she said astounded.

"It looks like it." I said back to her and thought about how Hurst and the other back-ups were probably looking up information on Armande as we spoke. Armande had left Bloomington at the start of the current school year. No one had any idea whether he had gone to another music school, or had just quit music altogether. Maybe what he had needed was to find himself. If this place was where he belonged, then I could see why he had been so angry and frustrated sometimes in the past.

"Let's go up and talk to them," I said to Winona.

We left our little area of the floor. The three other girls from Indy stayed there in their little group. They did not seem to be melding in too well with the scene.

"Armande?" I asked as Winona and I arrived at the bar.

"Jack, Winona, how are you?" Neither Armande nor I were going to bring up our mutual involvement in CIVICS. He surely wanted to distance himself from that group nearly as badly as I did. "We're great," said Winona, "But Armande," she continued with the most girly, inquisitive voice you could possibly image, "what on earth are *you* doing here? Is there something about you we didn't know?"

"Yes," he replied with a big smile directed towards all of us, "I gave up Catholicism!!"

We all had a big laugh after that one; Armande was a king of understatement. Everyone was drinking. I whispered to the bartender to make my gin and tonics actually with just seltzer water, but to put the colored straw in as if it was an alcoholic drink, and I drank with them – or perhaps I should say *pretended* to drink with them. "Don't worry guys," I said, "I'm just going to have a couple for a little buzz." I was still the designated driver after all, and I wanted to put their minds at ease. I felt something was going to come up, and I wanted to pretend to be under the influence when that something happened.

It did happen. Armande offered us a proposition. "There are some private rooms in back, guys. You can buy one for just $25 an hour. Would you guys like to go back for a little fun?" This suggestion would not seem so weird to you if you saw everything that was going on around us. No one was holding back anything in this club, and Armande was just following suit. Sydney looked at Winona and me and raised his eyebrows as if to say, "What do you think?" Winona was known to try things, even if another girl was involved. I lifted up my wedding ring hand, and pointing to my ring chimed in, "Sorry guys, but I'm afraid I'm out."

Winona looked at me inquiringly, "Will you be OK out here by yourself, Jack?" Then she looked at Armande and Sydney and whispered loudly, "I'm pretending to be his wife." I responded, "I'll be fine. I'll go back and hang out with Sherry and the other girls. They look a little lost, too. Sherry can be my wife if I need one." Sherry was a violin player who was part of our Indy crowd. She liked to party and have fun too, but compared to Sydney and Winona, she was much more reserved.

"OK then." I sensed the excitement in Sydney's voice. He was giving Armande flirtatious looks. "Let's go!"

"Hey, wait one second." I chimed in, "I gotta do one thing before you guys go," I lifted up a hand for a high-five for Sydney. We all felt the excitement and exhilaration for him. There was nowhere in Indiana and perhaps even in the entire Midwest where he could be so much like himself and have so much fun. Sydney lifted his hand. I pretended to be a little tipsy and missed his high-five hand and ended up hitting his hat off of his head. He had been wearing a flamboyant Mardi Gras looking hat that some man had given him earlier and Sydney had refused to part with it since. I apologized profusely: "I'm sorry, Syd! Wait! Let me pick it up for you." I reached down under the bar stools and grabbed his gaudy looking hat with all sorts of fake rubies and diamonds on it. I placed one of Hurt's clear cameras on the hat. It mixed right in with the faux diamonds. There was something strange about Armande. I had a sense that something was going to happen in that room that could be dangerous for my friends. I would get him on camera if anything bad happened.

I put Sydney's hat back on his head, "There you go."

"You *oaf*, Jack!" He laughed and we all laughed. Then Armande said something to one of the bar tenders and handed him some money. The bartender went under the bar and then came back up with a key linked to a rainbow key chain. *What symbolism!* I thought to myself. Then Sydney, Armande, and Winona started to walk to the back of the club. Winona yearned back for me for an instant, "Are you *sure* you don't want to come, Jack?"

Again, I showed her my ring, "I only play with Sophie now. Thanks, though."

IX

Snake in the Room

For me, nothing very eventful happened the rest of the night. After the threesome team left the bar for a back room, I took the opportunity to quickly put in an earpiece receiver in my ear and get in a quick conversation with Hurst in the mission control van outside.

"Hurst, can you hear me?"

"You're all clear Jack, can hear you fine."

"Has the team found anything on Armande?"

"Armande is not enrolled at Bloomington this year, just like you told us. We called his landlord asking about whether the property Armande was renting is vacant. The landlord said the same person who lived there last year is still there. We asked if there were any rules against subletting. The landlord said no tenants are allowed to sublet."

This didn't tell us very much. Maybe Armande still lived in

Bloomington, maybe not. Maybe he was subletting his house without his landlord knowing it, maybe not.

"Anything else? Run-ins with the law? Criminal history check?"

"Nothing on his file since being listed as a new recruit for CIVICS."

I went back to hanging out with Sherry and the other girls. We tried to keep from staring at everything around us, but it was hard. We danced as a group on the dance floor and had a few laughs. Most of the rest of the time seemed to be spent awkwardly trying to talk about something other than the spectacle that was going on around us.

One of the other little hypocrisies of that particular decade was how shock jocks and shock shows began to make it OK for lesbians to publicly display affection for each other. Of course, this pended on one major condition: they had to be hot. Ugly lesbians were not allowed to indulge in such public behavior. I don't see how anyone could come up with any other explanation for why this caveat was added on to the don't-ask-don't-tell rule other than the rather obvious conclusion that heterosexual males enjoyed watching attractive looking women expressing their feelings for each other. Over the next couple of decades the public media fought viciously to be the first to publish any photos of beautiful celebrity women kissing each other passionately. Somehow, the pictures of handsome gay men kissing still don't seem to be acceptable sixteen plus years later.

The freaky threesome returned an hour after leaving with wide-eyed looks on their faces. They would glance at each other and smile and giggle. Our entire group was over the shock of the club at this point. I suggested we get back in the van for a long ride back to Indianapolis. Everyone agreed. I shook hands with Armande. His expression was strange. I tried not to let on that I noticed his insinuating glances that seemed to say, "I know that you know about me. And you know that I know about *you*." The next day in my basement, Hurst hooked up some of the monitors and showed me the footage recorded from inside the private room at Excalibur.

"Excuse me if I don't watch it with you," replied Hurst. "Come get me when you're done. I have already watched the whole scene, and once was enough." He left the room. I soon saw why.

Sydney, Winona, and Armande, were like little kids in a toy store. I cannot mention to you all the things they were doing, but simply put, I could think of very few things that they did not try. They were unscrupulous. At one point, Sydney took off his hat. I became alarmed for a second. If I was to notice some kind of clue or signal on Armande, I wouldn't be able to see it if he put his hat somewhere out of the line of vision. The camera angle from the pretend diamond might end up all wrong. Luckily, Sydney put the hat on a high table that actually ended up giving me an even *better* view of the scene. There was a large black bed in the room and all three of them got on it at one point or another. Armande was saying little phrases from time to time that I considered very corny such as, "Do you take sugar?" to Winona. He also told her and Sydney to call him "Sugarloaf".

At one point, Armande fell off of the bed. I could tell it was an accident. He looked alarmed and quickly got up. It was a laborious task to watch the entire hour worth of what became quite disgusting footage. But I had to make sure there weren't any signs or signals that I was missing. I was getting quite suspicious of Armande. I felt his corny comments were like hidden messages directed towards me. I even got the feeling that he knew I was recording him when he seemed to almost stare in at the camera lens for a brief two seconds.

I later rewound the tape to the place where Armande fell off of the bed. I zoomed in on him. I realized that after he had taken off his shirt, he had always kept the left side of his body away from the camera's eye. When he fell off the bed, his left side became visible for a fraction of a second. I zoomed in further.

241

On his upper shoulder was a tattoo. It was a serpent coiled around a sinister looking dagger. I recognized the shape the snake was coiled in and the face on the snake.

Herr Schlangenstein.

X

Forget the Leppards

I called Hurst back in. When he saw that the TV was still on, he started to go back out again, "Turn that off please before calling me back in the room."

"I've got zoomed in on a still shot, Hurst. All you can see is Armande's left shoulder."

Hurst came in. He looked at the tattoo. He said it was vaguely familiar. I told him what it was. "That German bust from a year and a half ago. Inside the cottage in the wooded area. I don't know if you had as much time to look around the inside of that place as I did, but there was a similar symbol on the wall of the large bedroom area where the final shootout took place. The way the snake was coiled was the same. And the facial expression on the snake was the same." The snake had a sinister smile with a thin forked tongue extending out from the left side of its mouth.

"I think you're right, Jack. With the evidence of the make and model of the kidnappers van, and now this symbol on Armande, I think we can conclude that Herr Schlangenstein is behind the kidnapping."

"And Armande is working with them."

"Yes."

"Why Armande? He seemed to be a good guy last year. He seemed to admire me. I can't figure him out. And then he almost joined CIVICS."

"His being roped into the recruiting meeting at CIVICS shows that Armande is lost and is looking for direction. It is possible that either he put two and two together and determined that you and Sophie were more than just romantic mates after the CIVICS bust. How else could you not have been charged with anything? Or, maybe someone from Schlangenstein who may have had cross knowledge of the CIVICS organization decided to pick up Armande and fill in those details for him. I don't think why or how he became part of that organization is paramount right now. He *is* part of it – that is what we can focus on right now."

I thought aloud for a moment: "Do you take sugar, *Pour Some Sugar on Me*...Sugar Loaf.

"You think Armande was trying to give us a new clue?"

"Yeah."

Hurst thought for a moment and then mentioned, "There is a small mountain in Rio de Janeiro, not all that far from Armande's native country, that is called Sugarloaf Mountain."

"I don't think that's it. He is definitely referring to a rock, but not quite that big."

"What do you think, Jack?"

"Someone out there must know a lot about me. Meat *Loaf* is a rock singer, and Def Leppard is the rock band that sings *Pour Some Sugar on Me*. Not the particular kind of rock band that I was in at this particular time, but I played in a band called Groovin'

Hard which played for a wedding party on Mackinac Island. It was a rich guy with long blonde hair and a beautiful Native American girl. They looked like John Smith and Pocahontas together. Her ancestry was somehow linked to the Native Americans around the Mackinac region. Their ceremony and the reception party right after was held in front of an eighty foot tall mound of rock called Sugarloaf. I think that is what the sugar, rock, and sugarloaf references are alluding to.

"Let's get over there," said Hurst.

I pulled out my van keys, "Let's roll."

XI

Sugarloaf

Manabozho, a great Native American who was known to have magical powers, was said to have retired on Mackinac Island in his old age. He was a medicine man and a messenger of a great spirit. One day ten young braves traveled far up to the island to seek this man and offer him gifts. The offerings were presented in the hopes that the great man would use his powers to grant the braves' wishes. The great man agreed. Nine of the ten braves asked for wishes that were achievable to man and the great man granted them their wishes. The tenth brave then laid down his offering and asked for a supernatural wish. The great man warned him to wish for something more appropriate to man. The brave did not listen and insisted on his supernatural wish. His wish was to never die. "Very well," said the great magical man.

The tenth brave then began to light up, twist and contort, and grow larger and larger. His shadings became that of the color of stone and small bits of foliage and shrubbery appeared attached to his sides as he grew to over one hundred feet in height. He was now Sugarloaf and would live forever as a solid pillar of stone.

Sugarloaf looks somewhat like a big meatloaf that has been

propped up on one of its sides. It has eroded about sixteen inches a year, so in the past couple decades it has dropped from around one hundred feet to seventy five feet tall. From one angle you can see what appears to be the profile of a Native American man's face. This image is probably where the legend of the man morphing into a rock came from.

The next day, I was there at the site with Hurst and an eight member back up team. We came over to the island from the lower peninsula of Michigan the same way everyone else did, by ferryboat. No automobiles are allowed on Mackinac Island, so the back-up team stayed a few hundred feet away under a canopy disguised as a hot dog stand. I didn't see the point in their hiding since Armande and Herr Schlangenstein seemed to understand everything that was going on, but Hurst's team kept to their disguises anyway.

I walked around the monolithic sugarloaf looking for anything. It was not hard to find. Underneath the part of the rock that looked like the Native American man's mouth was a small hole like a miniature cave. I saw something white a few feet inside it. I reached. My reach was just long enough. I pulled out a new message and read it:

> You are perceptive, Jack, and know
> much on the Native American.
> But let's see you now decipher something
> the way in which we think you can.
> Follow the Native path and meet two who
> helped to bring him sorrow.
> You will find your next message Yesterday,
> Today, and Tomorrow.

I was officially getting sick of the silly secret messages. The poetry was somewhat witty, but not exactly W.B. Yeats. The message was easy though. I went over to the stand to eat a hot dog and tell Hurst about it.

XII

The Armpit of Indiana

"This message is easy," I started to tell Hurst.

"Wait, Jack," Hurst whispered through a two-way intercom set up inside the hot dog stand. He was stationed farther away under a different tent. The CIA workers were grilling my dog.

"Don't forget the cheese."

"Don't forget the cheese?" replied Hurst, "What the hell could that mean?

"No. I was talking to the cooks."

"Let's get off of the island and talk at that point. This is not safe."

"Fine, we'll need to get off the island for our next journey anyway."

Driving south down the Michigan Interstate with Hurst's earpiece in my ear, I discussed things with him. "Sophie's captors

248

don't have the name exactly right, but most people who are not from my area make the same mistake. <u>Yesterday & Today for Tomorrow</u> is a landmark right where I grew up, the Calumet Region of Indiana. I lived a few towns away from this particular landmark, but most people from the region know of it. It is comprised of three iron statues, each around twelve feet tall. One is of a Native American, one is a farmer, and the other is an ironworker. The region was famous for blue collar laborers like ironworkers and especially steelworkers from about the beginning of the twentieth century until the late seventies even. We are still pretty big on steel, just not the forerunner anymore like we used to be."

"Believe it or not, Jack, most people are familiar with the fame of the steel mills where you grew up. Working conditions in Northwest Indiana and South Chicago helped to inspire Upton Sinclair's book *The Jungle* which became one of the springboards that inspired America's labor movement in the early part of the century. And of course Michael Jackson was raised right there in Gary Indiana and was the son of a steel worker in one of the mills. So the symbolism of the landmark is very appropriate."

"The word Calumet that the region is named after is also the name of two large rivers that run through the area: the Calumet River and the Little Calumet River. A calumet itself is a peace pipe." I continued talking to Hurst, "My area of Indiana is both respected and abhorred. It is admired and despised. In some areas of Northwest Indiana you will find some of the most extravagant beautiful homes that belong to rich citizens who long to live close to the cosmopolitan area of Chicago, but who do not want to have to pay the high taxes that a wealthy person would have to shell out if he or she lived across the state line in Illinois. It is like a smaller scale version of the rich Connecticut citizens who love to live close to New York City, but do not desire to live in the state of New York. And then in towns sometimes right next to the kind of town I just described, you will find boarded up businesses and homes where no one wants to live, nearly abandoned towns where the only people who stay are the ones who seem to have no means to get out. In the downtown areas of these little cities you'll find the poverty, crime, prostitution, gambling, murders and many other sins and vices that people especially from the middle and southern ends of the state look down on and pigeonhole nearly all people from the Region as being a product of. Indianapolis traditionally has turned up its nose when working with local representatives from our area claiming, 'You get enough revenue from the Chicago citizens who cross the state lines – what do you need state revenue for?' Of course, they don't take much time to see the conditions that some of our poor citizens have to live in. When I came to the Indianapolis Conservatory, I remember reactions from some people when I told them I grew up in the Calumet Region. One fellow student actually asked, 'So where is your switchblade knife? You guys all carry them, don't you?' Chicago has different reactions to Region people. Many of them look at us as if we were Woody from *Cheers*. They think we are innocent and ignorant country bumpkins because we happen to be from the state of Indiana, as if the state of Illinois is all that sophisticated when considered outside the city of Chicago. Chicago people though love to get away each weekend to our Dunes Lakeshore and to enjoy our casinos, and our low sales taxes when filling up their cars at Indiana gas stations. If they went into the inner neighborhoods of Hammond, Gary, or East Chicago, they would see that Indiana people are not all like Woody. We proportionally have just as much seedy, underhanded, corrupt politicians and gangsters as the city of Chicago. We are home to the murder capital of the country a few years back, Gary Indiana. I grew up in one of the few towns in the Calumet Region that seemed to be a happy medium between the ultra-rich small towns and the crime-ridden small cities. My town was middle class, a town consisting of a lot of blue collar and some white collar people who knew what it meant to work for a living. My classmates in high school didn't come from families that inherited all their wealth, but they didn't come from crime families either. They worked and they valued work. I picked one of the hardest musical instruments to play well because I believed in the value of hard work. Just learning *how* to play bass is not all that difficult. But learning how to play it *well* is very challenging and requires many hours of dedication. My working class ethic from growing up in a town like mine has helped me accomplish what I have on the string bass. I am proud of where I am from. Carl Sandburg wrote a poem called *Chicago* that I think is also applicable to the Region. His characters in that poem are described as *brawling, sneering, and laughing.* And they were tough enough to handle all the work that came with being the freight handlers and hog butchers of the nation. I too learned how to brawl, sneer, and laugh. And I learned that whatever it takes to get a job done, you do it. It might take something away from inside you, maybe even from your soul. But that is what you have to do. You do it or you die."

"I suppose it is like learning how to do what needs to be done while someone points a gun at your head." Hurst reminded me.

I then remembered Hurst when he was preparing me for the CIVICs infiltration job. He had said those same words. Those words triggered that tough, dirty, scruffy Region kid in me who learned how to survive while bordering neighborhoods were either killing each other off or living in a rich fantasy dream world. In my town we fought with our fists and bodies, not with guns or lawyers.

A tear came down the side of my face. Hurst to his credit, detected a little bit of alarm in my silence, "How are you holding up over there, Jack? This has got to be tough for you."

"I can't lose her, Hurst. I just can't." A let a couple more tears come down before I shut down the waterworks. That was enough crying.

"We're going to get her back, Jack. I really believe that." Hurst said. I was a little amazed inside that I was actually befriending Hurst. We were becoming close. He was offering me emotional support. I had been without Sophie now for a little over a week. No messages had come in from her. This fact was beginning to wear on me, but I kept it together. And then I asked once again, already knowing the answer:

"Still no transmissions from Sophie, right?"

"Still nothing," said Hurst.

XIII

Yesterday & Today for Tomorrow

I convinced Hurst's team to keep driving into the night until we were in the Calumet Region. They agreed but then insisted that everyone get some rest after searching the <u>Yesterday & Today for Tomorrow</u> landmark. We had driven ten hours to get to Mackinac, and then ten more to get down to Indiana. We needed a rest.

Hurst called a state representative who alerted the local authorities that some men would be searching the landmark with flashlights and not to be alarmed. We arrived in town very late at night and drove to the intersection of the monument, Ridge Road and Columbia Avenue. There were the three statues. They were taller than I remembered, more like fifteen to eighteen feet instead of the twelve to fifteen that I had envisioned. I had never walked all the way up to the statues before and had only seen them from the street. Up close, they were larger. We did need our flashlights because the street lights did not offer enough light to see details.

The three iron statues are made of iron poles and sheet metal that is shaped into round, square, triangular, and cylindrical

252

shapes, whatever that particular statue needs. I looked at the tall Native American statue holding his shield and spear, the iron worker with his protective hat and goggles, and the farmer who is depicted as pushing a two-handed plough. I noticed something in the farmer's right hand. None of us were tall enough to jump up and grab it. Carl, the biggest and tallest one of us who also couldn't reach the white object in the farmer's hand, made a suggestion, "We're going to have to call the fire department and ask for a ladder. We can't get our van into this small space between the statues and the dedication stone. Otherwise, we could have stood on the roof of the van." The dedication stone simply stated that the monument was erected in 1976 by the local Rotary Club in honor of America's Bicentennial.

"Calling the fire department is going to take too long," I retorted, "stay right there Carl, and don't buckle your knees."

I crawled up Carl's back and sat piggy back on his shoulders. I reached up and grabbed the white paper that was protected inside waterproof plastic. "Nice of our terrorists to keep the message dry, eh?" I managed to put in some of my trademark sarcasm. The message didn't make sense to me:

And you probably often sing its violent battle song.

I read it to the guys. They couldn't make sense of it either. "What does the word 'its' refer to?" said Fred the audio specialist. "Maybe America." said someone else in the dark. "What *about* America, though?" I replied. Then someone saw something else.

"In the shield of the Native American, there's another piece of paper!" I got back on Carl's shoulders and reached up to the shield. The shield had little triangular holes and in one of the holes was our message. I pulled it out of the hole and took the paper out of its protective plastic. I read the new message to the group.

Jack, this new destination shows who
your country has wronged.

"OK," I said, "This is obviously the beginning of the message, and the first one we found is the second part of the message."

"Maybe the first one we found is the third part of the message. We haven't checked the iron worker."

"I haven't seen anything on the iron worker," Hurst said. I walked up to the third statue and started scanning it from the bottom up. As my flashlight's beam reached the neck and then the face, I saw something white sitting deep within the iron workers cylindrical goggles. It was in the left goggle. "One more time, Carl." Big Carl stepped up to the statue. This time I had to actually stand on his shoulders and stretch my arm to reach the eye level of the statue. Thank God the iron worker was actually bent over slightly. The heads of the other two statues sat a good three to five feet higher. I pulled out the third message, and performed my public reading:

When you sing that song, what do you face?
Remember what you face and go to the highway of that place.

"We need to put the three messages together. How can we tell which part is second and which part is third?" said one of the sharp shooters.

"The Native American is obviously first. He was in the Region first, and he represents the yesterday part of the monument."

"What would be second, then?" another voice chimed in.

"Probably the farmer. He was the second to come to the Region."

"The farmer represented today, in 1976? But I thought the steel and iron worker industry was already booming by then." Carl added.

"The monument, though erected in 1976, was more about the era when America was founded and when this town was first founded around one hundred years ago. People argued about this too when I was a little boy. Even in 1976, people felt that the future lied in the steel and manufacturing industry. They did not foresee the possibility of the steel industry diminishing the way it has in our recent era of the 1990s. From a founding perspective of this area, Native Americans were the past, farming was the present, and industrialization was the future."

"OK," said Hurst, "let's put the messages together in that order."

Jack, this new destination shows who
your country has wronged,
And you probably still often sing its violent battle song.
When you sing that song, what do you face?
Remember what you face and go to the highway of that place.

"This message was designed for a Region native like me." I said for an instant. "Wait!" I noticed lettering at the bottom of the third message.

CZF

"It was written by a native of the region too, like me. This explains how they know so much about me."

CZF was someone's initials from my past. Calvin Zappa Frank, my guitarist from Groovin' Hard.

XIV

Hunting for Information

"CZF is the initials of a guitar player I played with for a few years in the early 90s. Calvin Zappa Frank."

"I guess his parents liked Frank Zappa." Hurst inquired.

"Yes, hence the middle name. This is really weird though. Calvin is really the last person on the face of the earth that I could imagine wanting to kidnap my wife. He was a neo-hippy for Christ's sake. He was into peace, love, pacifism, the whole new age thing - a true Deadhead."

"You can never truly know some people, Jack," Hurst added, "we will start looking him up as soon as we get back to the van. For right now before we go for some shut-eye tonight, what or where is this message pointing us to?"

"The violent battle song is the Star Spangled Banner. It is the only patriotic song about the end of a battle with phrases like 'bombs bursting in air' and the 'rocket's red glare'. And the thing that you would face while singing is the American Flag."

"But what is 'the highway of that place'?" asked another voice in the dark.

"Just a few miles east of here, on Highway 41, is our next destination. It is called *The Highway of Flags,"* I said.

Everyone soon knew where we were headed. We all slept in our two vans for what was left of that night in the local high school parking lot. I could not sleep at first, and I excused myself to take a walk to a corner twenty-four-hour gas station/convenience store. At the store I bought a long distance calling card with cash so the transaction would not be traceable. I walked outside to a phone booth in the parking lot to use my calling card. I was not going to call home. Hurst was able to listen and trace any incoming calls for me there. I already knew many people were worried about Sophie's disappearance. It had now made the local news in Bloomington. My parents, her parents, friends, acquaintances, close to fifty calls from concerned people had come. I wanted to talk to one particular person who had called: Steve, my old roommate and still best friend.

Though it was late, Steve answered his phone.

"Hello."

"Hello, Steve?"

"Yes, who is this?" I think he could tell it was me, but wanted to hear confirmation first.

"It's Jack."

"My God, Jack. Are you OK? How are you holding up? No one has seen or heard anything from you since Sophie's disappearance."

"I'm holding up. Steve, I can share a couple things with you because I am calling from a pay phone, so I know no one is tracing this."

"Tell me, Jack. I won't tell anything to a soul."

"I know you won't. Steve, this whole disappearance is a kidnapping, even though the police might not be saying that. The group hasn't yet said what their demands are; they just keep sending me little riddles that are messages leading to another riddle message. I've been on a wild goose chase the past week. But Steve, I can tell you one thing we do know about the group. They are people who you are very familiar with."

"Herr Schlangenstein."

"Yes, it's them. They have kidnapped Sophie. Steve, I need you to tell me everything you can remember about them when they held you hostage."

"I can do better than that, Jack. I am coming with you."

"No Steve, I am working with Federal Agents, this is much too dangerous.

"You think I have never had a gun to my face before? I tended a bar for nearly ten years, Jack. Don't think for a minute that no one ever brought a gun into that place. And don't forget those German assholes who held me hostage. They put a gun in my mouth one time. And I also have broken up dozens of bar fights without ever getting one scratch on my face. I can take care of myself just fine, Jack."

"Steve, this has to be done right. I don't want to lose Sophie."

"We will do it right, Jack. I will find a way to help, even if it is just being a look out or an informant or whatever. I don't want you to have to go through what I did when I lost Jessica to those bastards."

My mind drifted back to the day I found Jessica dead at her house, a bullet hole that had entered through the back of her head and exited out the forehead, and then Steve taken hostage. They shot her while interrogating Steve for information that he didn't even have because they thought he was me. And Steve was getting ready to propose to Jessica that very week. Everyone had thought they were the perfect couple. People looked up to their relationship back then the way people looked up to my marriage with Sophie in the present. Herr Schlangenstein had ruined Steve's life. After the ordeal was over, he ended up quitting bartending and going back to school to study business. He also became an ordained minister in the Unitarian Church for a while. He later decided the ministry was not for him, but not before performing a wedding ceremony for Sophie and me in Las Vegas. I always felt partially responsible for what had happened to Jessica. I had apologized and he had forgiven me, but I still felt I owed him.

"And if I can help to either apprehend those sick people or kill them, the retribution will help ease my soul, Jack. It would ease me inside more than you could even imagine."

I was not going to deny him that opportunity. Damn whatever Hurst says.

"OK. Steve. You're on board."

XV

The Highway of Flags

Steve drove up to the region early the next morning and followed our two vans to the Highway of Flags. When his SUV followed us in behind the monument, I quickly got out and stopped Hurst's team from rushing him.

"He's with me guys. Sorry, I should have told you."

"We have to discuss this, Jack." Hurst escorted me inside his van.

Hurst could see in my eyes that Steve was going to have to stay. He too felt sympathy for what Steve went through. Hurst made a phone call to the Central Headquarters in Washington to basically temporarily deputize Steve as a CIA agent. After a relatively short five minute conversation, Hurst hung up the phone.

"He's licensed to kill now." Hurst said.

"Wow, that easy?"

"Yup."

In the late 1960s during the height of some of the Vietnam War protesting that was pervading the U.S., a woman started a monument in the Region and throughout a large U.S. Highway called Highway 41 that consisted of flags. South from Miami Florida and North up to the tip of Michigan you can see these monuments of flags interspersed throughout the states that comprised this distance. She had a son who had served in the Vietnam War. She was appalled at the treatment he received from protesters when he returned home from service and decided to erect these monuments as a way of bringing some patriotism back to our country. In the Calumet Region on the corner of Ridge Road and Highway 41, you can see the monument. It has a large cement foundation painted white that is about eight feet high, four feet deep, and over forty feet wide that supports seven tall flag poles. The middle flag pole holds the American flag highest and the surrounding six flag poles hold the flags of the six states that surround the great lakes area.

We walked up behind the monument and very easily saw a large handkerchief tied around the lowest portion of the American flag pole. Its black, red, and gold striping clearly did not fit in with American colors. Carl reached up and untied it. It was a handkerchief-sized German flag with another message folded inside of it. This message didn't bother with the tedious riddling.

Jack, you have done an excellent job following our path. But of course, if you had had trouble, we would have politely found a way to direct you in the right course. We do indeed have Sophia. Perhaps you are aware, or perhaps not, but Sophia helped your country to take $500,000 worth of products from us. We either want the products back, or the money back. So, tell whomever you are working with that you need to be at the symbol of the fall of our wall when the sun sets on the evening of April 15, 1997 with either product or cash and we will release Sophia back to you. We can meet you directly under the gate as the sun sets. And please, don't insult us by claiming not to know where to go. If you found all these American places, surely you can find one German place.

Oh, and one last thing. When you bring what we want at the designated time, you must be ALONE. Any non-compliance with any of our requests will result in Sophia's immediate death on the morning of April 16, 1997.

I finished the reading. I was a little embarrassed to admit I did not know the exact location, and looked at Hurst, "The Berlin Wall, right?"

"Yes," said Hurst, "specifically, at the Brandenburg Gate."

"You know where that is?"

"Yes."

It was the evening of April 13.We had to move.

XVI

Deutschland

Germany is a beautiful country. I had the opportunity to vacation there as a young boy with my family. My father had been stationed in Germany for a year and a half during the U.S. occupation after the Second World War. When my family went, it was as a reward from his insurance company for being one of the top salesmen in the state. The German countryside is a lush green and every village seemed to have beautiful little houses with colorful flowers planted under the windows. The streets are small as in most European countries and you also must drive on the left. My sister and I liked the trip, but we did not have the proper appreciation for all of the rich history that the country had. The huge beautiful castles and churches were astonishing when we toured the first three of them. And of course, when I went, the Berlin wall was still in use. This was not the only wall, there were others dividing some villages and of course the walls that sometimes protected the castles. So after seeing about the eighth combination of church, castle, and wall in a particular region, my sister and I came up with a refrain:

Churches and Castles and Walls
Churches and Castles and Walls

What do you find in Germany? That's all.
Churches and Castles and Walls

Of course, this child's refrain was hyperbolic. There *were* other things that we saw. But still, for children, all of the boring history about how long a particular castle had been standing and why the wall was there and who built a particular church just did not thrill us after a while.

Our special unit arrived in Germany a day before the rendezvous. Hurst gave me a briefcase that was handcuffed to my arm with the money in it. It had a tracking device inside it too. I was assured the tracking device was utterly undetectable by anyone accept us. I had the key to the handcuffs. I was not going to unlock the handcuffs unless we had Sophie. This *did* seem odd, I imagine, but it was actually my idea. I would get to be with her one way or the other, even if the other was death. That last part, I did not tell Hurst. Hurst was sure that they would not kill Sophie. He was concerned that they would snatch the money, keep Sophie, and run off to ask for more money later. The sharp shooters would be stationed far away at the edges of the public area in which the Brandenburg Gate lied. Any closer would be too dangerous. I had my one earpiece in my ear in order to communicate with Hurst. The only other gadget I had was some special large steel tipped boots that looked like the German style, but had a secret holding area in the soles for a .22. You sort of swiveled the soles and there would be the gun. I had a gun in each sole.

The history of the Brandenburg Gate is rich. I was familiar with the term Brandenburg, a region of Germany, from playing Bach's Brandenburg Concerto in many different orchestras. The Gate, however, has much significance to the fall of the Berlin Wall in 1989. After the wall finally came down, the Gate was then opened for East Berliners and West Berliners to pass freely as they pleased. No more was the capitalist western part of the city separated from the communist eastern part of the city. When communism began to fall in 1989 and then continued to disappear from other Eastern Bloc countries, the Brandenburg Gate became a symbol for the new unity that had come. Celebrations still take place there every November ninth. A great song that expresses the joy in people that came with the fall of communism throughout these countries is called *Wind of Change* by the rock group The Scorpions. In Germany, I believe it is the number one selling single of all time.

The Gate itself is huge. Standing approximately one hundred feet tall and supported by six ornate stone sheets that resemble Roman pillars, on top you can see a statue of a man riding a four-horse chariot with a powerful looking bird flying just above him. It may have been an eagle, but I could not see the details so far up.

I stood under the gate. It was a large open walkway area that I was facing. On the other side of the gate were rows of linden trees. On the large walkway there were many tourists walking along taking pictures. Some people were hailing taxis far away at the edge of the street. I did not notice much else about the huge brick walking area other than a small three-foot tall soldier figure in the middle of the square. Some people stopped to look at it. I heard from passing conversations that the little soldier was new. The gate used to be protected by soldiers during the Berlin Wall years, so the little figure seemed appropriate. Then people around it let out a cry of shocking delight.

The soldier had come to life, so to speak. As if it had just been wound up, it started to walk. It walked in the awkward stepping motions of a wind up soldier toward the Gate. As it walked ten, twenty, and thirty feet, it became apparent that the soldier was walking towards *me.*

"Hurst, there is a small mechanical soldier, about three feet tall. He is walking towards me."

"The sharp shooters have him in their sights, Jack. We can take him out."

"Take him out? He's a machine!"

"Take it easy, Jack. I don't think this is a booby trap. They want their money. This organization can't be dumb or crazy enough to set off a bomb at the Brandenburg Gate."

"You don't *think* it's a bomb? That's just great."

The soldier walked closer, twenty feet away, ten feet away. "I'm taking out one of my guns, Hurst." I swiveled out my right sole and grabbed my .22. I aimed it right at the soldier's head.

The solider stopped four feet in front of me. Some kind of spring clicked and a tongue shot forward from his mouth. There was something attached to his tongue. It was white.

I reached out and grabbed the white object. It was a piece of paper wrapped around the tongue with a rubber band. "It's another goddamn message, Hurst." I said not too loud. People around me were staring. I put my gun back in my boot. "Polizei!" I shouted the word for police and showed the crowd the fake badge that the CIA had furnished me, "Polizei! Polizei!" Then, softly to Hurst, I read the message.

Do you like our little man, Jack? Then
come and see some more.
We had to make a change of plans. I hope you aren't too sore.
To see a few more little men, both with and without hats -
Five O'clock tomorrow to the Glockenspiel in the Marienplatz.

"I think I have been there before Hurst, but I can't remember which city it is."

"It's in Munich," he replied, "And we better get to the high-speed train right now."

XVII

Riding and Dreaming

On the train, Hurst was not surprised that Schlangenstein wanted a change of venue, "The Brandenburg Gate has to be one of the most guarded and protected places in all of Germany. I'm actually surprised that no one searched that little soldier. Odds are someone placed it there only minutes before we arrived. Making an extortion trade-off there is a little like making a drug trade in front of city hall. The Marienplatz is probably less guarded. Still, they would do better not to pick such well-known tourist spots. Maybe they are hoping to blend in with all the other people."

I nodded. Hurst could tell I was tired, and he let me nap. I still remember the dream. It was about the not-so-distant past.

Sophie and I had married in Las Vegas. We spent one night in the hotel, and then decided to spend her last work-free week with me driving up the California Coast on Highway One. We rented a red convertible and plotted a course to L.A. where we would stay a night and then up to San Francisco where we would spend a couple more nights, turn in our car, and catch a plane back to Indianapolis. Our car went through the desert, through the mountains with the green pine trees, and into the tropical area of L.A. with its palm trees. And then we drove up the coast, the beautiful coast on Highway One where you can see the Pacific crashing against the rocks below. In some spots the road is at sea level and at other spots you look down a three hundred foot cliff at the sea rocks that gladly accept the splash and spray of the oceans waters, the white water cascading down the cliffs after each spray. You could feel the mist when the car was close to sea level. There were wineries along the way too, especially closer to San Francisco. We would stop the convertible whenever we saw something we liked, a nice view or a winery with free wine samples. When the road was straight and predictable, I had opportunities to look over at Sophie. She smiled to me. Her eyes beckoned to me. She would hold my hand on top while I shifted gears in the stick shift. When I could stay in fifth gear, I would interlock my fingers in hers. She would caress the inside of my palm with her thumb. I would do the same back to her. A very thin layer of moisture caressed our two palms, lubricating them and enabling them to slide back and forth across each other. No other woman I have ever met could excite me so much just by holding my hand. The wind blew her lustrous red hair back, no more resembling the snakes that I had imagined over a year ago. Those snakes were gone. The real snakes were our enemies who were trying to hurt us and our country. Sophie's hair blew like the beautiful waves of the Pacific. The wind rippled her hair back and she often had to shake her head back and forth to keep her hair out of her face. The wind also blew into her thin tank top that she wore with no brazier sometimes. The top had spaghetti straps, and she had told me that she didn't like the way her bra straps would show under the spaghetti straps. The almost sheer fabric of her tank top now clung to her firm breasts and tight stomach, the outline of her nipples faintly showing though. Sophie didn't always show off her upper body, but she definitely could when she wanted to. Her green eyes had that glowing quality, too. I was the luckiest man in the world who was driving through heaven with an angel at his side. The image of her during that road trip was one I would never forget and could never forget for as long as I lived.

A bell rang. "Munchen!" The conductor called out over the intercom.

We were in Munich now. I got up and gathered my luggage for another car ride to another hotel and another meeting and plan about how to deal with the newest dangerous development.

I just wanted to go back to my dream.

XVIII

The Glockenspiel

    I had remembered the Glockenspiel as a boy because it was not one of the "churches and castles and walls" that my sister and I had witnessed so incessantly while in Germany. The Glockenspiel has a magical quality to it like a Disney movie. It feels as if you might see Pinocchio walking up to you and saying hello.

    It sits about three stories up on the side of a large building in a large town square in Munich called Marienplatz. The Germans call it the Rathaus in Marienplatz. Each day at 11 AM and noon the Glockenspiel gives its little automated performance that lasts about twelve to fifteen minutes with over thirty automated mechanical life-sized figures. With music-box style music playing, the top level shows figures celebrating the wedding of a beloved duke. At the end of the performance, two jousters on horses combat each other, with the jouster for the duke's country winning. After this, the bottom level shows dance figures dancing through the streets during a horrible plague that infested the area. The actual dancers during those tough times had shown positivity and loyalty to the German government. It is said these dancers were the only thing to smile about during that horrible event. After the figures finish their cuckoo-clock like fifteen minute demonstration, a mechanical golden bird resembling a cock crows out three times on top of the display informing spectators that the show is over.

From March to October, the Glockenspiel also makes a demonstration at 5:00 PM. This was the designated time for the rendezvous. I arrived with pretty much the exact same arrangement as before: the briefcase with the handcuffs, the shoes with the guns, an earpiece so I could talk to Hurst. The square was *very* full this time. People really loved to watch the Glockenspiel. One very distressing fact was how many *children* were in the square. We put rubber bullets into the sharp shooters rifles because of this fact.

I stood directly under the figures. Five o'clock came and the show started. A man squeezed up next to me. "Hello Jack," his Latin accent very clear.

"Armande." I said nothing else.

"Follow me to the back of the square," he directed.

I did as instructed and walked back with him to the curb. I couldn't resist a question or two. "What got you into this organization? Was lying your way through life not working anymore, so you decided to look to bigger sins?"

"So judgmental and self-righteous aren't you, Jack? Anything that goes against the United States must be wrong, correct? Tell me, what makes someone who is *born* in your country so much better than anyone who hasn't been born there?"

"Armande, you could have been a citizen if you were patient enough."

"Hah, that shows what *you* know. When you are at the top of your game in terms of playing, looks, abilities, fresh out of training at one of the best music schools in the country, would you wait twelve more years while a country decides whether you are allowed to live there?"

"What about the temporary visas?"

"Those run out, Jack!"

"Tell me then, how accepting is your wonderful homeland of *Columbia* when it comes to illegal immigration?"

"I'd like to see you last three days in my country with your American braggart ways."

"You hate us all, yet you want to be one of us, Armande? What gives?"

"I don't want or need to be one of you anymore. I had better skills than half of those white-bred boys that they accepted into the air force. I could have served and then had my citizenship. But no, in the land of opportunity they forget to tell people seeking admission that you still need to be connected. You still have to have the right name and be friends with the right people. You still have to belong to the correct fraternities. Do you know who is getting ready to run for your next president, Jack? George Bush."

"George Bush was already president six years ago."

"Actually five. No Jack, it's his son. He goes by George W. Bush and he is the governor of Texas right now. How many terms was a man named Roosevelt your president, six? And how far back do you know your history, Jack? John Adams and John Quincy Adams, remember them? And now you will have George Bush and George W. Bush as president. Nepotism Jack, pure Nepotism. There is *no* opportunity here. It is all a big dog and pony show."

"Bush hasn't won yet, if he does even run. And all those other men you mentioned were elected in free democratic elections."

"That just shows how naïve you are. You really think those elections were honest? Have you looked into the Kennedy election? Right next to your hometown, the Chicago vote was totally rigged. And the only reason his brother Bobby wasn't elected was because of his assassination. Then we could have added Kennedy and Kennedy to your leaders of nepotism."

"It is funny you criticize Kennedy. He was our first Catholic president, someone of your faith." "I am no longer Catholic. And he is nothing like me. He is a European Caucasian like all of the rest of them. Tell me Jack, when is your country ever going to have a man of color as a president, a Hispanic like me, or someone African American? Or -"

"Or a woman?" I chimed in, "How about that? Does your crusade for equality extend to women? Or how about homosexuals? Are they included?"

Armande laughed, "Oh my Jack. You defend your country's faults only by directing attacks against me. I am not the one in charge. I do not have the power. Before you can institute change, you must first utterly destroy the current system. When Herr Schlangenstein gets just a little more power and influence over the next few years, we will finally be in position to topple one of your corrupt democracies and begin a true new world order that will bring true equality to all people, including all those groups that you just mentioned."

I just stared at him. He was completely lost, completely brainwashed. That last bit about "instituting change and breaking down the current system" did not sound like the old Armande from Indianapolis Conservatory at all. I had one last question, though.

"What about Calvin? How did *he* get into this group?" My old guitarist from Groovin' Hard, his signature had been on one of the messages from Schlangenstein.

"Calvin? Who's Calvin?" Armande looked at me like I was a silly boy. Then he had a small epiphany and started to laugh, "Oh yes, *Calvin*. Ah, Jack. I tell you what. If you make it through this and get to see Sophie again, *she* will tell you about Calvin."

Armande took a two-way radio out of his jacket and called for a car. In less than thirty seconds, I saw a medium sized black sedan approach the curb. It was medium sized by American standards. In Germany it was huge. It had tinted windows, so I could not see inside.

"Roll down a window so I can see Sophie." I instructed.

Armande picked up his radio, "You heard him."

The rear window facing me electronically lowered. There was Sophie's face. She looked tired and weary. Her eyes looked worried and sleepless. My heart fell to my feet and emotions swelled within me. I swallowed and got control of myself again. 'Imagine there is a gun to your head' went through my mind, which was pretty much true at the moment in terms of my marriage and my happiness. I heard her very haggardly say, "Jack," and then the window went back up.

"Give me the money now, Jack," instructed Armande with his arm extended.

"I'm going to unlock these handcuffs. When I unlock them, I want Sophie's door opened."

"That's fine," he said, "I'm leaving my radio on, so they can hear your instructions."

I unlocked the cuffs, and Sophie's door opened. I kept my eyes on Armande, and could sense Sophie in my peripheral vision. Sophie took what seemed to be one step out of the car. When she tried to take a second step, someone reached out from the car and held her in her current position.

"Hand me the money," said Armande sternly. I extended the briefcase towards him and he placed his hand on the handle next to my hand. I did not release my grip from the handle yet.

"Tell them to let her go." I said.

"Open it down here first," said Armande, pointing to the ground. I thought that was odd. But I did it. I flashed it open quickly so only he could see the rows of one-hundred dollar bills that were inside. Armande then took some kind of metal-detecting device out of his coat and flashed it over the briefcase. Hurst was correct. The tracking device inside could not be detected.

I picked up the brief case again, "Why don't we count to three?" I suggested, "On three you release Sophie and I release the briefcase."

"Jack," *Oh shit, it's Hurst.* Hurst was communicating to me through my hidden earpiece, "Jack don't make a move or respond to my voice in anyway. Steve is not following the plan. He is dangerously close to the situation. He is dangerously close to Armande."

I didn't have much time to think. I had faith in Steve. I knew Hurst didn't, but I did. I had to start the count immediately. If Steve got too close before the count, the people in the car might notice him and make a break. Steve looked like a very ordinary muscular man in his twenties, very non-spyish for lack of a better term. He was of German heritage too, so he fit right in with most of the other people in the square.

I began quickly, "One, Two...Three!"

"Wait!" The driver had just noticed Steve closing in behind Armande, but he was too late. I had already called three and Sophie was free. But Armande had been given just enough notice to swing the briefcase around and nail Steve in the head. Steve fell to the ground temporarily stunned, but not unconscious. Blood already trickled down from next to his eye. I lurched for Sophie and took her by the arm, and we ran towards the designated corner where there was back up and a car waiting. Armande turned around to run to the sedan, but Steve shot a leg out while he was on the ground and tripped up Armande who fell face first into the ground. Someone reached out from the car and grabbed the brief case. The case was pulled into the car and the vehicle sped off, leaving Armande stranded there. Steve got up and started to make short work of Armande. He was on top of him and had him pinned. Armande had his full guard up which protected him from blows, but he had nowhere to go. Steve could just lie on him there until back-ups quickly arrived.

I ran with Sophie to the car. We got in. We were with a sharp shooter specialist and a sniper/driver specialist. I still had Hurst on my earpiece.

"We're going to get that car, right Hurst?"

"That's right. Go after them," Hurst's voice now came through loud and clear over the car's CB radio.

We all wanted to bust these people. Letting them get away just opened us up to more attacks, kidnappings, and extortion. We had to smoke these snakes out of their snake holes and cut them off at the head.

XIX

Slaying the Serpent

The hidden tracking device in the briefcase was not working. Hurst did not mention that over the CB when he told us to go after their car. The reality he was hiding from us was that we *had to follow the Germans and catch them right then.* Failure to do so could result in losing them forever, and then having to be subjected to future attacks and extortion attempts. Whatever the outcome that may have resulted in this chase, it was better to go into it with a feeling of enthusiasm instead of a feeling of desperate fear. I imagine that was Hurst's rationale for not telling us the full situation.

So we were on the chase. The driver stayed on the left side of the road like the European laws required. The streets were small and narrow. The culprits did not take care or heed of any pedestrians. One man was hit by their car. We quickly stopped and one of the sharpshooters tended to the man while the rest of us continued our chase. Hurst's car had come up behind us by this time. We almost lost the culprit car after stopping to help the man. Hurst's voice came on the radio, "Guys, from now on, just radio me if you see someone get hurt and I will call the German medics to help them. Don't stop anymore for Christ's sake."

From the back, Sophie and I held on to the front seats. Our driver now talked to us. "Which of you is a better shot?"

I looked at Sophie. If she felt healthy enough, there was no doubt that she was better with a gun than I was. "I am," she told the driver.

"Climb up and over to the front passenger seat then. You will be sitting shotgun."

I now understood why people called that seat the shotgun seat.

There was a semi-automatic rifle available on the seat. Sophie picked it up, leaned out the window and took aim. She seemed to be aiming for the tires.

"CAPOWW!! CAPOWW, CAPOWW!!" Bullet holes began to litter the rear right fender of the black sedan. Someone in the rear right seat of the sedan leaned out of his window and returned fire.

"CAPOWW-CRACK!!" Our windshield had been hit but did not shatter. The bullet sat there stuck inside the glass with about a three inch diameter spider-web shaped crack around it.

"It's shatter proof," said the driver, "but it can only withstand about six shots."

Sophie shot two more rounds. The sedan fired three back. One hit somewhere in our engine, one seemed to miss, but the third one hit the other side of the windshield from the first hit.

We took a harsh corner – our car nearly spun around, but the driver maintained control. The sedan had not gotten too far ahead and we closed the gap quickly. Sophie continued to fire, and more bullet holes littered the back of the sedan.

"Do we have another clip?" She asked.

"In the glove compartment," shouted back the driver.

I wished there was something I could do, and then I remembered my .22. "I have a small pistol, why don't I shoot from the other side of the car?"

"Use my .45 magnum. It's in between the two front seats in the console," the driver replied.

I opened the console. *Jesus, it looks like Dirty Harry's gun.* It was a huge magnum.

"It's got a hell of a recoil. Don't shoot it immediately in front of your face!" the driver instructed.

I did as instructed and started to take shots from the left side of our car. Apparently, the sedan only had the driver and the shooter in it. That made sense since they had to take into consideration whether Armande would have to leave the scene with Sophie if the transaction didn' t go down as planned. So two empty seats needed to be available in their four-seat sedan.

After I started shooting, the shooter moved to the left side of his car and began shooting back. He never shot out his back window because the back window turned out to be a bullet proof Kevlar plate. The sedan would have been able to get much better shots back at us if their shooter didn't have to lean out the side windows to take a shot. After we had the shooter distracted on me, Sophie was freer to aim for the tires.

CAPOWW... PSSST! "I got it!" Sophie shouted. The tire had exploded and the sedan started fishtailing. Their driver didn't seem to know what to do and was just hitting the gas harder and harder. The black sedan spun into a crowded brew house. People were running everywhere. The car violently crashed into a limestone pillar and stopped there while we witnessed a body propel out through the windshield and into the pillar. The man's back gruesomely cracked in two like a brittle stick as he hit the pillar. When we cautiously approached the car, the driver's side window was thoroughly cracked and dark red blood was streaming down from the inside. The three of us surrounded the door with our guns and quickly forced it open. There was a blonde haired young woman with blood all over her face. She was unconscious. I looked at the face for a while and then I mouthed, "Liane"?

XX

Epilogue

The German police were on the scene in minutes. An ambulance arrived. When I saw Hurst, I approached him with my discovery.

"Hurst, I could swear that was Liane driving that car: the blonde hair, the features like a German doll."

"Yes, I see the resemblance, too. But it's not possible. She was killed in that bust from two years ago. This girl's still alive, and we will find out who she is when she comes to."

"How about Armande and Steve?"

"Steve did a great job, Jack. He sat there on Armande and Armande basically couldn't get up. Steve's size is a big asset. Armande is in custody and he will be rigorously questioned."

"I hope we got all the snakes this time," I said worriedly.

"We always hope that, Jack. But, new ones always seem to slither into the light. Sometimes they use the same names as the old ones, and sometimes they go by brand new names. But their purpose is never all that different: terror, destruction, chaos, and evil. We won this round, thank God. But the war is not over. It's never totally over."

"I know it is early to request this," I said pleadingly, "but how soon can Sophie and I leave and go back home?"

"We have a hotel for you to stay at here in Munich. I will assign double guard duty to your room. That's four total guards just outside your room door. In three days, we should have all we need and then you can return to Bloomington. We will contact you again from there if that's where you plan on staying."

I whispered something to Sophie. She whispered something back to me. "OK," I responded to her. And then I said to Hurst, "We want to get packed and move out early to New York as soon as we return to Bloomington. We are ready to get a new identity, too. Would you please let Sophie out of her domestic duty for the remaining four months? She has contributed quite a bit to our country already, I think."

"I think we can do that," Hurst put one hand on each of our shoulders, "I can't *guarantee* that, but I think we can do it. Would you consider this? We put off those last four months for a year or so, and then she makes them up later, say, two months at a time over two years."

I couldn't believe him. Why couldn't he give us a break? I looked over at Sophie. She shrugged her shoulders and nodded.

"If that's the best you can do," I said a little sadly, "I guess we'll take it. But we definitely need those new identities."

"Oh, you'll definitely have those Jack. You will *definitely* get those."

During the first night and following day in our Munich hotel, Sophie needed some rest and recuperation. She wanted us to sleep together, and I flat out told her no; she needed to rest. Some doctors came in to give her a physical, and outside of a lack of sleep and being slightly dehydrated, Sophie was OK physically and was given a clean bill of health. I asked her how she was treated and she said fine. I asked for details. She told me they kept her in a hotel room. She didn't know exactly where. She knows that they kept her in the states for the first week, and then flew her out to Germany sometime during the second week. What bothered her most she told me was how they kept interrogating her with questions about me like where I grew up, my past history with music, and any other details. She knew they were going to use that information to 'mess with my mind'. This explained how Schlangenstein knew so much about my past. And Sophie had to tell them; otherwise, they said they had nothing to use to 'clue me in on what to do next'. Schlangenstein wanted to give me riddles that only I would know the answer to. Later, they decided to test my knowledge with some of the German area riddles. Otherwise, almost every riddle was centered on an allusion to my life.

And this explained Calvin's initials at the end of one of the messages: CZP. The CIA had finished looking into Calvin after the car chase and found that he was still living in the Calumet Region. He had no ties to any terrorist groups whatsoever. I still was a little baffled on that, though. I had not remembered telling Sophie about Calvin.

"You mentioned him during one of your drinking binge blackouts after Samantha dumped you," Sophie told me the second day in our hotel room. "You talked about how much you missed playing in that group, and how you wished groups today sounded more like Groovin' Hard. You laughed about how his parents gave him the middle name Zappa after Frank Zappa."

Everything seemed to fall into place. Our second night, again, Sophie wanted to make love. I was still scared. I didn't want her straining her body or her mind if she was still under Post Traumatic Stress Disorder. She didn't seem to be, but I told her if she still seemed fine the third day – nothing would stop us on that third night.

On the third day, Hurst came to visit us. I found out about Liane.

"It was Liane's sister, Jack. She is three years younger than Liane and her name is Leona."

My mind flashed back to the two previous years with all of the confusing similar names: Samantha and Sandy, Diane and Dyena, and now there were sisters named Liane and Leona.

"Why can't people use names that sound different from each other, for Christ sake?!"

"You're starting to sound like *me*, Jack," Hurst said and the three of us had to laugh.

Hurst continued, "Leona had a vendetta against you two. Somehow, somewhere, Liane had mentioned both of your names to her sister Leona. Leona figured out that the two of you were the ones who operated the sting on her sister that led to her death. She has been on a crusade the past two years to revitalize her sister's terrorist organization and find you guys in order to get retribution. She did indeed intend to keep harassing you two and extorting you in order to get money to make the group stronger. Eventually, she would have killed both of you."

I sat there dumbfounded. Sophie and I just looked at each other.

"Thank God we stopped her," I said.

"Thank God," said Sophie, and took my hand in hers.

"And as far as your requests, Jack," Hurst began. Sophie and I perked up our heads. We listened intently. He continued, "You may indeed move to New York, but you must decide on a new last name before the move. I suggest you stick with another Irish name that suits your heritage. You would look odd with a name like Kareem Abdul Jabar."

"We'll think of something within the next two days," responded Sophie smiling.

"And as far as your duty, Sophie," Hurst started up again. Sophie and I were on pins and needles, "It has officially been suspended indefinitely, pending when you turn thirty, because we would not require you to do anything after you turn thirty. Since you're twenty six now, if you're not called up in the next three and a half years, you're in the clear."

Sophie and I breathed a sigh of relief. I decided to venture another question. "What do you think are the chances that she might get called up to serve those last four months?"

"With *this* president? Very small. He has slashed and cut funding for the FBI and the CIA like you wouldn't believe. We have downsized so much, there is nothing for us to do, and we hardly have the capability to do what there is to do."

I was a little confused by his response, but I got the gist of it. I still had a little worry, "But if funding is low, wouldn't it save dollars to use a free agent like Sophie?" Sophie gave me a mean look after that one. I responded to her, "*Hurst* doesn't make the call on that Sophie."

Hurst gave his old conservative smile. "With fewer operations, we need to reserve spots for the *new* people who we apprehend. It's a little like prison. When the prison is overcrowded and underfunded, we let the small criminals go free. We just apprehended a very serious terrorist a few days ago, and we need to give her a chance to get some time in to serve just one part of her very serious sentence."

It made sense to me then.

Hurst got up from the chair he was sitting in and reached for his hat and his jacket. He put on his fedora and turned to us. "Enjoy your last night in Munich's finest hotel. We will protect you guys now and until your move to New York where you'll have new identities." He walked to the door and opened it and turned around to tip his hat to us, "I shall not forget the two of you. I hope you never forget each other. I have a feeling you won't."

"Thank you for everything, Patrick." I responded.

"Yes, thank you," said Sophie.

"You're welcome," he said, "And for *your* sakes, I hope that if we ever meet again, it is just to say hello. Good bye my friends. *Stay cool, Jack!*"

Hurst walked out into the hallway and shut the door.

XXI

Moving Forward

That third night, Sophie and I did indeed make love. I don't need to tell you what it was like. Wonderful is a good enough word. It did not need to go on all night. It was sweet, it was romantic, we told each other how much we loved the other one, and I finally had my gorgeous wife back. After our love making ended, before we fell asleep, Sophie did say an odd thing.

"I hope we're OK," she said.

"What do you mean?" I asked.

"Oh… nothing."

I did not want to put her through a Dr. Phil psychology session, so I left it alone. I discovered what she was worried about a couple of months later.

Four months after that night was our big family wedding ceremony on August 20th. My parents were there. Her parents were there. Steve was there. We invited Hurst, but he couldn't make it. To us, it was big, but in actuality, probably less than fifty people were there altogether. We couldn't invite a lot of the CIA types we had been working with, and we had just moved to New York barely four months prior to the occasion, so we didn't have a huge list of new friends just yet.

Oh, we decided on a last name. It was Morrison. It was the last name of one of my favorite rock singers, Jim Morrison and it was definitely Irish. It had three syllables like McFarland but was different enough without the Mc at the beginning. Sophie agreed to that last name as long as I agreed that if ever we had a child and it was a girl, that the name of the child be Nadia. Sophie had loved gymnastics as a little girl and as a result, her childhood hero was Nadia Comaneci. Comaneci had won three Olympic gold medals in the 1976 Summer Olympics in Montreal, and two more gold medals in the 1980 Summer Olympics in Moscow. She was also the first female gymnast to receive the score of a perfect ten in the Olympics. I am not aware of whether a male gymnast has ever even accomplished that feat.

So while people arrived at the wedding ceremony, everyone commented about Sophie's dress and usually gave each other an awkward look. What they weren't sure of was whether Sophie had gained about fifteen pounds, or whether she was pregnant. The latter was true. So everyone learned at the ceremony that Sophie was expecting. I assured the older crowd that we were *already married* a year ago in Las Vegas and that we were having this ceremony so the families could be involved. So, there were no questions about whether we became pregnant before marriage. It turned out that what Sophie had been worried about during our third night at the Munich Hotel was whether or not she had taken too long to take her next month's dose of birth control. Her pills had been left back in the states before the terrorist ordeal which resulted in making her about two weeks late in taking that dose. The Germans would not let her contact anyone; otherwise, she could have asked me to send her pills to her. Sure enough, we had conceived a child that very night.

We were both very happy about the baby. The flipside of the baby situation when it came to Sophie's involvement with the CIA was that now there really was no way they could use her for an assignment. She was a pregnant woman now, and then would be a young mother of a very small child for the next two years. They *couldn't* expect her to serve under those conditions, at least that was what *we* felt.

So the wedding was fun, and the reception was fun with dancing and a big band playing the 1920s songs that we loved to dance to. We did some Charleston and some good dips. Everyone had a blast.

New York was perfect for both of us. The CIA changed our school records to Julliard instead of the Indiana Schools, and all public files listed us as being born in the state of New York and having always resided there. We were Mr. and Mrs. Jack Morrison. Jonathon and Sophia Morrison. It had a nice ring to it. I loved playing in the Metropolitan Opera, and Sophie continued to prepare for her delivery.

On January twentieth, 1998, after over thirty-six hours of labor – I know because I was there the whole time – Sophie delivered. It was a girl. She was beautiful. She had a teeny, tiny lock of auburn brown hair at the bottom of the back of her otherwise bald head. She might possibly grow hair that was brown with red highlights.

"It's a girl," the doctor called out to us. And then after I held her in my arms I called to Sophie, "She has some red in her hair, babe. And her name is Nadia, right?"

"Yes," Sophie said exhausted, "her name is Nadia."

"Welcome to the world, little girl," I smiled to my little one. And then I sang to my daughter her first lullaby:

> *You are my sunshine, my only sunshine*
> *You make me happy…*

The End

Printed in the United States
By Bookmasters